LOVE SEES NO COLOR – Racism Kills

The novel portrays the story of two teenage lovers who face obstacles and threats after they both have fallen in love with each other but find that no one wants to see them together due to their differences in color, background and ethnicity,

The book is written purposely to draw readers' attention to the negative effects of racism and discrimination – the idea of depriving one of what he or she wants. Racism can be lethal even in the absence of killing devices such as guns.

LOVE SEES NO COLOR, novel – globally available at both online and Brick and Mortar bookstores, and on iPhone and Sony Reader - as EBook

First printing…
Library of Congress Cataloging in Publication Data

Library of Congress
Cataloging in Publication Division
101 Independence Ave., SE
Washington, DC 20540-4320
Includes bibliographies
Library of Congress Control Number (LCCN): 2007907473

ISBN: 978-1-64316-074-0

I. Love Sees No Color. I. Title.

PUBLISHED BY:
WORLD WIDE VISIONARY ENTERTAINMENT PUBLISHING

A DIVISION OF WORLD WIDE VISIONARY ENTERTAINMENT INC
P. O. BOX 8624
CHATTANOOGA, TN 37414 (USA).

DIRECT ORDER/PURCHASE ALWAYS AVAILABLE AT:
Amazon, Apple, Target, Barnes and Nobles, Best Buy, Wal-Mart, and the likes.

Editing credit goes to Dr. Jean-Marie Dauplaise

Photograph Cover by Langston Photography, Chattanooga, Tennessee.
http://www.langstonphotography.com

Printed in the United States of America

Cast of Characters

Bolaji is a young Nigerian-American man blessed at birth with good looks, good fortune and love. Bolaji's mother is **Ronke**, a young black Nigerian woman and his father, **Jamal**, a handsome young African-American man. They were married for four years prior to the birth of Bolaji. Ronke came from Nigeria at the age of nineteen after graduating from one of the top Nigerian Universities with first-class upper standing; she won prestigious scholarships to pursue her graduate schooling in the United States of America. She met Jamal when both were attending graduate school. They dated for two years and when both had reached top placement, became engaged for a year and then married. They loved each other deeply and sincerely, as the story will explain. Jamal traveled with Ronke to Nigeria. The thought of knowing her family, culture and other things worthy of learning appealed to him. *Sans* regret, they returned to the US after thirty days of visiting West African Nigeria. He loved being over there and he wanted to go again and again; he told his work mates that Africa was not as poor as they made it seem to be on The Discovery Channel and reported that one would hardly notice that he was no longer in America in some parts of Nigeria. Jamal's mother was **Malinda**, a sweetheart of a grandmother to **Anita**, Bolaji's older sister.

Malinda was a good mother of her era and she made sure she educated her son with words of advice and at the same time ensured that he had a quality education. She hustled solely to pay for her son's school expenses until he graduated. Jamal, however paid his own way through graduate school because he had by then begun making money for himself. Malinda had had Anita, who was a year older than Bolaji, upon the tragic ending of her parents' lives. Malinda developed severe medical problems following the death of her son and her daughter in-law; she passed away at last herself as the result of a heart-attack. Bolaji never had the opportunity to meet her; he was too young. Only Anita could recall and remember them vividly as real pictures in her mind's memory.

Anita was the first child of Ronke and Jamal, Bolaji's older sister. She was three years older than him. She was the one who took control of their parents' properties after their untimely deaths, which were very sad and inexplicable. Indeed, she missed her brother for almost seventeen years before he returned from Nigeria. From elementary school until college she had many friends, boys and girls. She was told not to date boys until she entered college, which is precisely what she did, following her grandmother's wise counsel.

Tasha was Anita's high school friend and after graduation, they remained friends and went off to college together at the University of Tennessee at Chattanooga. Tasha and Anita had other friends together: Lamanika, Tamika and Jessica. Tasha was originally from Memphis, Tennessee; she was only attending the University of Tennessee at Chattanooga because she and Anita had met when the latter went to Memphis to attend high school. They both agreed to attend the same university together. Tasha knew a great deal about Anita's brother, Bolaji, and had always been eager to meet him. She asked Anita why he was living in Africa and Anita said their mother took him there. Anita would keep quiet sometimes when Tasha began asking too many questions that she felt she could never answer.

Lamanika was a Texas chocolate girl with very fancy attitude who inspired boys to yearn for her; she hated being a young girl and had been impatient to develop. She claimed she came from a wealthy family and believed that none of her friends deserved an explanation for why she didn't own her own car or even sometimes borrowed friends' clothing. Surprisingly, her ruse of belonging to a rich family never struck others as untrue, since she looked fresh and shiny as a new penny every single day. She shone.

Tamika was Lamanika's roommate; she came from Nashville, Tennessee and was a year older than her friends, Tasha, Lamanika and Jessica. She was very athletic. However, she refused to join any campus team or group. She earned average grades in mathematics, particularly in comparison to some of her brilliant peers in the same class. Despite being mixed into a class in which the male gender tended to outperform the young women, Tamika was the best at math amongst her group of close friends. She told her friends she had stupidly lost her virginity at the young age of fourteen. Although she found the subject embarrassing, in secret, she held a special place for her partner in both her heart and mind.

Jessica, whose name sounds a bit like "Jessy," or "Jersey," was indeed a Jersey girl who came all the way from a sensible home to her, taking up residence in Tennessee in order to avail herself of the opportunity to further her education. Jessica loved to wear dresses with the words: "Jersey Girls" boldly printed on them. She owned a remarkable number of such dresses and t-shirts and always proudly presented herself as a Jersey girl wherever she went or appeared. Boys loved her in her dresses and some of her moderately sexy but reveal-nothing jeans. During her spare time, she loved to share with her friends and roommates stories about Maryland and New Jersey; they all loved listening to her. It was no great surprise that she majored in Communications.

These girls, Anita, Tasha, Lamanika and Tamika, were the campus queens, attractive young women who inherently drew young men to themselves; they were smart, beautiful, sexy, and popular.

Karl was Anita's boyfriend. I surmised that both his intelligence and his tall and masculine build won Anita's heart because she shunned dozens of other young men at school who had tried but failed to woo her; if they wanted to try again, they'd have to wait until they were reincarnated in another lifetime. Karl hailed from Louisville, Kentucky, the same hometown as the famous heavy-weight champion and the best boxer of all time, Muhammad Ali. He was his parents' third child. Karl was very handsome, six feet tall with a well built body that drew the opposite sex like honey draws flies; many girls loved not only to see him, but longed to touch him as well. He matriculated at the University of Tennessee in Chattanooga in order to study Mechanical-Engineering, although he later changed his mind. After spending only one semester as Engineering major, he changed his major to Art and Theater. His dream was to one day become a successful actor.

Adam was a sexy Brazilian guy who had lived in America for more than a decade. He lived in many well known places in the United States including Los Angeles, New York and Detroit to name but a few. He later settled to live and attend school in Chattanooga, Tennessee where he met Bolaji a week into his studies at the University of Tennessee in Chattanooga, also known by the acronym "UTC." They loved each other as friends despite their different ethnicities and colors. Their friendship ran deeper than merely that of classmates. They ate together, drove together, hung out together and even regularly visited one another's apartments. Adam was very smart, intelligent and motivated. He sometimes came across as being arrogant, but he was actually quite humble and never overly proud. Sometimes he and Bolaji fooled around, even to the point of taking pranks on some of their professors, especially Dr. Duane, who was the head of their department. They mocked him and his pronunciation of words, his dialect being overtly Southern. Like many students, Adam and Bolaji called their professors names behind their backs. "Isn't that rude of us?" Adam once asked aloud, hoping to gain the heart of Beauty's friend, Tracy.

Dr. Duane was one of the best professors at UTC; he was absolutely brilliant. He graduated from college at the young age of sixteen and then finished his graduate certificate when he was only eighteen. He was a rare genius. He always told his students to make hay while the sun shines because it might become more difficult for them when the earth's surface turns dark and wet. It may be hard for some to believe, but most of the professors who taught at the University of Tennessee - Chattanooga were all well-qualified and that many were even brighter than some of the world's best-known professors.

Bolaji, as I revealed earlier, was taken to Nigeria in West Africa at the age of one. As a teenager, he learned that no matter how dark or light one's skin color appeared to be, whether black, white, brown or albino, in the state and country he lived in, people didn't discriminate against one another when it came to friendship, courtship, employment and so on. Ergo, he learned to love everyone just as his grandmother had taught him to do. She told him human beings were all the same no matter how tall or short, how dark or light, how intelligent or dull any one particular individual seemed to be. She taught him that God designed us as we were intended to be – in his image. According to Bolaji's grandmother, "We are all created from the same raw materials, very raw, that God shaped into precisely the image of our Maker's own design." This was what Bolaji had in his mind and heart ever since that time, and when he came to the United States of America, he stuck by his upbringing and knowledge, never judging, always loving towards anyone whom he met. Neither black nor white were seen as being any better or worse than the other. He met Beauty, a lovely young white girl from Atlanta, Georgia; they fell in love with one another, but as an inter-racial couple, they encountered problems and obstacles in their life together.

Rebecca became a single mother after she lost her man to a tragic murder at an all-black nightclub. She took care of their two children from the time that they were born until the time that each had grown to make his or her own way in the world. She warned them both to stay away from black folks after what she had experienced; however, one man's poison is another man's cure. Frank followed Rebecca's teaching, but Beauty didn't really see or notice anything wrong with going out with people of different colors or races. Rebecca regretfully suffered the loss of her beautiful daughter and felt that only God knew what happened to her afterwards. She had Rachel and Mandy as friends, along with Rebecca, Mandi, Sara and Nicole.

Beauty was the second golden child of her parents' children; she looked two years younger than her actual age, appearing to be only sixteen when she was eighteen, for example. She was brilliant and well-known in her high school and after graduating, wasted not a second of time before furthering her education beyond high school. Beauty was so enchanting that everyone wondered how her mother could have known she would be so lovely. When she came of age and lived up to her name, Beauty, everyone exclaimed that her name could not possibly have been more perfect. She was like a glowing rose, the most beautiful and colorful of all other flowers. She had never lived around people of color as they would call blacks or African Americans. Not even a million words would be enough to articulate her feelings from the first moment she saw Bolaji. He appeared to her as a scarce star, one that could be seen only once in a lifetime. She thought hard about how to draw Bolaji's attention and her device worked. Bolaji perceived her as being both a beautiful and a romantic girl. She had a brother named Frank. Their mother thought it would be good for both of them to attend the same college so that each could look out for the other. Beauty had many friends at school, but she considered Tracy, Trish, Mickey and Cindy, aka "Faith," as her best friends.

Mickey wanted to become a model and was always very jealous of Tracy, who did modeling for some local companies. At school, Mickey studied for a degree in Physical Fitness with a minor in Communications. She hailed from Savannah, Georgia, which lay only a few hours southeast of Atlanta, which is where both Beauty and Faith were born and raised. She attended many different modeling and acting auditions, but good fortune never smiled upon her. She simply didn't have that certain something that frequently booked models apparently possessed. Saddened, she was unable to discern quite what it was that she was missing.

Cindy, when she was finally born thirteen months after her conception, was named after her grandmother. Her mother had given up the faith before Cindy finally said hello to the world, which is why she nick-named her Faith despite the name on her birth certificate reading, "Cindy." Faith explained the aforementioned reason to her friends; amongst her friends, she was a simple girl – both outgoing and down to earth. She loved to party a lot and the same time was scared to be around people of color, which is why she turned down any hip-hop invitations that came her way. She hated the idea that Beauty was going out with a black man; she knew, however, that her own opinion certainly wouldn't stop Beauty from being with Bolaji.

Tracy was a Kentucky girl; her grandmother lived in Chattanooga. Tracy's mother encouraged Tracy to stay with her grandmother while attending college at the University of TN-Chattanooga. She started modeling at the age of four with some local companies and television stations in Kentucky. Although she intended to stop modeling while attending college, she could not help sometimes being roped into a shoot, so nonetheless did a few local modeling jobs. She was apt for any type of modeling. She had no reason to tell anyone she was a model; her wardrobe gave her away. She was more well-known than any of her other friends and thus sometimes encountered both jealousy and envy.

Trish was a fabulous ghetto girl; she was hardcore, but no mere sex symbol. She was heavily tattooed and sported multiple piercings. She had three piercings in each ear, and her mouth had two labret hoops – with round rings on both her upper and lower lips. To some, she looked scary indeed. She was heavily into hard rock and claimed that she would become a rock star one day after finishing her education. Her rugged voice made her friends discount her hopes because they felt certain she would never make it as a singer. She was really interested in dating Beauty's brother, Frank, and had many times tried to persuade Beauty to help her get his attention, but Beauty told her that she wasn't be able to guarantee anything.

Frank was a handsome white boy who any college girl would love to be seen with; he had gorgeous blue eyes and a chiseled, well-defined face. He seemed to be gentle, but could kill a snake with his bare hands. He was mean to Bolaji when it came to his sister; he detested the idea of his sister dating a black man. He argued with his sister and fought with Bolaji. He later hired four black gang members to try to scare Bolaji away from Beauty. The attempt failed, however. Frank realized that it was virtually impossible for anyone to intervene in the love shared between Bolaji and his sister, Beauty. He never stopped scheming, however, to try to find a way to drive a wedge between Beauty and Bolaji.

Cobra was a thug who originally hailed from New York, but he claimed he was raised in Tennessee. He had attended college for only a few months before dropping out and focusing on the riches that gang-banging and drug dealing brought his way. He figured why bother getting a degree in anything when he could make more money in just one night than some people did working full time for an entire month at a straight job. Cobra's real name was Anthony Thomas; he earned the nickname Cobra early on when he was jumped into a Tennessee-based gang. He dealt with many undergraduates at UTC as well as some professors. He was skinny and looked unhealthy, but his appearance was deceptive. He could easily smoke up a bag of weed faster than a cheetah could run and overcome an antelope. His gang affiliations extended to connections all across the state of Tennessee. He was a thug's thug and many aspired to reach the level of gangster success that Cobra had established. His closest homies were known as Jug, Saint and Leo.

Samuel Edie, "Saint" was originally from Tennessee. He was smart, brilliant and very handsome. He didn't appear to be the type to be involved in thug life. He hung around with his high school friend, Leo, who easily led him astray. His parents had no idea their son was involved in gang life. Saint also won the heart of a beautiful young ebony woman during his first year dealing drugs at TCU.

Leo Martin didn't use a thug name, although Anthony, aka "Cobra" called him "Khadafi" sometimes. He was born in Chattanooga and lived there for his entire life. He was afraid of heights as some people are, never daring to fly in a plane. Leo was a vagrant. He lived and hustled on the streets and was notoriously considered loco and dangerous.

Justin Milan aka "Jug" was from South Carolina originally. His parents relocated to Crossville, Tennessee. They enrolled him at the University of TN at Chattanooga, but he was lured into thug life by a group of gang members who came to watch him perform in a school production. The thugs had all applauded and insisted on meeting him. It wasn't long before Jug dropped out and, like the others, devoted himself to the thug life in Chattanooga.

Introduction

Bolaji is a word and of course a noun, coined from the Yoruba language, a cultural name from his mother, Ronke's side of the family. The name has multiple meanings. One such meaning is that of a golden child, a child born with a silver spoon in its mouth, born into a wealthy world. A *bolajical* child means having qualities of Bolaji; Beauty is a noun that emphasizes elegance, magnificence, completion, highness and the like.

The two names are just halves of one another. The first is not complete in the absence of the second and vice-versa. Bolaji would not have been beautifully enjoying a beautiful life if not with the help of Beauty, and Beauty, on the other hand, might not have been *bolajically* elegant if not for the presence of Bolaji in her life. It is noted here that they are each meant to be with the other.

History made Ronke, Bolaji's mother, hateful about white people even though Jamal, her husband, tried to correct and convince her to let go of her worst memories. On the other hand, circumstances and the loss of her husband forced Rebecca, Beauty's mother, to withdraw her love and association from black people.

The untimely death of Bolaji's parents and the belief that they were both murdered by white men made Malinda warn Anita to stay away from white people in general. Rebecca did the same by telling Frank at an early age to stay away from black friends because she believed her husband, Lambda, would not have died if not for the black friends he hung around. Bolaji grew up in Nigeria, West Africa. He had no clue about how death took his parents and even if he knew, he would accept it as kismet. Beauty was so young when she lost her Father that she did not know how or when it happened. As was the case with her boyfriend, Bolaji, she was not going to be judgmental about the whole case even if she had known exactly what happened.

These two innocent young lovers, the orphan boy and the singly raised girl, were actually already in love with each other before they even met. It started through dreams and later happened in real life. They met for the first time ever at the University of Tennessee at Chattanooga and instantly they fell for each other and agreed to be each other as future partners. They didn't come to realize they had come to the wrong world because people were not always open to love *qua* love, but instead insisted upon categorizing others by color, race, religion or ethnicity. They faced threats, obstacles, hatred and various circumstances that you will learn only if you continue to read this tale.

PART ONE: LOVE SEES NO COLOR

One –The birth of Bolaji…Chattanooga, TN

The clock struck one and the sky was very dull, threatening rain, as if warning everyone to remain indoors. Given these conditions and for the sake of security, no one would dare wander about so late past darkest midnight. I knew beyond doubt that it would be very difficult, if not impossible for a smart dog to see a demon walking around the neighborhood as if the stony clouds in the sky would switch on the lights they were given millions of years ago. It was inky black up there. Had the angels in heaven taken leaves of absence, or was it possible that they were merely away on vacation? At 1:05 am, the entire neighborhood experienced an absolute blackout. What was happening? A very unfriendly storm struck the scared and housebound people over and over again; their fears multiplied then increased exponentially. "Oh God," I thought, "this is too scary."

It was then revealed that none of those angels were on vacation; it was about to rain again. A few minutes later, another storm swept down along with still heavier rainfall. There was icy hail falling from the sky that seemed colder than any cube of ice from a home freezer. The icy hail that day, combined with the horrid wind was strong enough to bloody a man's face. Luckily, it was later reported that no one was hurt. No ordinary African or spiritual vigilante would dare to pass through the storm on that terrifying evening. The storm then halted as quickly as it had begun and the world returned to itself almost as if nothing had happened at all.

Ronke was in deep pain and moaned impatiently. She prided herself on having the nerve to fight the pains and keep them to herself, but, she wondered, would these pains let her live long enough to awaken the next day? I, for one, doubted it. She kept fighting on her own and she felt her own pain along with her husband's heavy, asthmatic breathing and snoring. His asthma had been nagging at him for weeks and she found the noises it caused her husband to make truly irritating. She also tried very hard to ignore his heavy snoring and hoping to fight on and remain strong until morning. He would have noticed that something was not right with her if not for the asthma that deprived him of hearing her moans. She was so disheartened and thirsty that she felt she could easily swallow a gallon of fresh water in the blink of an eye. Could this be possible? After the storm the dim light of a half-full moon lit the bed chamber through the windows. It was now three o'clock in the morning. Indeed, she had been strong enough to make it through two more hours. She wondered to herself how her husband could possibly have slept soundly through everything she'd heard and experienced that night – especially the dreadful storm, the blackout and the stony maelstrom of hail that had fallen from the sky like an avalanche of ice. She wondered whether or not she should wake him up. His snoring was really annoying her. Should she just lay awake until the sun rose and smiled upon the earth, she wondered. She turned her thoughts then to her swollen belly, curved and wide, nestling a living soul eager to greet the world, ready to witness the rumors of human earth that it discerned.

Ronke tried to communicate with this small being within her. She felt like talking aloud so it could hear her, but at the same time she hated to wake her husband, so she willed the fetus to be patient and wait for the rooster to crow. She learned for the first time in her life the precise length of time that lay between the twilight of sunset and the first moment of the breaking dawn. She pondered the premonition that this second child would be her last as she lay in pain and she wondered why this second of her two babies was so strong and aggressive.

Jamal rolled over twice to change his position on the bed and accidentally bumped Ronke's swollen abdomen. She amused herself with thoughts of striking him or biting him, but instead yelled out, "my belly!" He forced himself awake and tried to engage his mind in the present moment. What had he just done? Coming to his senses, he got up out of bed, afraid he'd hurt his wife and unborn child. He feared he had done something wrong.

"Is it the baby?" he asked.

"Why didn't you wake me up? Oh, honey I am so sorry. How is it...?" He paused for a while, then ran into the bathroom and then back out into their bedroom. He had no idea what to do. At 3:45 a.m., he knelt down beside her and leaned into the mattress, regarding her face with sympathy. He embraced her as she spoke.

"What are you doing, Jamal? You need to call the ambulance! Something's not right! Hurry," she shouted. Shaking himself awake, he finally called for help

In no time it seemed, the EMT's had arrived and were motoring her to the hospital. Jamal followed the ambulance in his own car. Ronke's pains were now stronger and more excruciating than they'd ever been before. By four-thirty in the early morning, the EMT's transferred their patient to a wheeled hospital gurney. She stared at her husband and they exchanged a meaningful look, he mentally conveying his sorrow for having caused her this pain. Her thoughts swam and she felt slightly crazed, thinking that her husband had done this to her. Trying to calm her, Jamal moved closer to her. He caressed her face with his hands trying to ease her tension and silently praying for her to have a safe delivery of their baby. Ronke was then wheeled into a delivery room, where as quick as lightning, the doctors and nurses swung into action. Two hours had passed and still the baby hadn't left the birth canal.

"Excuse me!" Jamal interrupted. He pulled aside the hospital mask that covered his lower face and faced one of the doctors working on his wife. The doctor told Jamal to relax, that his tension was making things harder for Ronke. Finally, before another hour passed, the baby made ready to escape from the womb, its head crowning. A nurse yelled out, "Here it comes!"

"Keep pushing, ma'am. Don't stop now," another nurse added. The baby finally arrived. The doctor cut the cord. Ronke passed the afterbirth easily as a nurse washed her new baby clean and placed him in his mother's arms. She was delighted. If it was possible, however, Jamal may have been even happier than she was at the moment; he was thrilled that both mother and baby had survived and secondly because she had given birth to a baby boy. He told his wife he owed her many thanks and smiled with great pride when she handed him the bundle of baby and blanket.

"Congratulations! Congratulations!! Congratulations!!! You did a great job! You have a healthy baby boy!" Ronke was then transferred to a private room and the baby boy taken to the nursery so that both mother and child could rest. Jamal sat awake near Ronke's bed as she slumbered lightly. Only a short time had gone by before Malinda entered the door, which shut behind her. She came in with a three year-old girl, Anita, carrying a teddy bear with her; she was Jamal's and Ronke's first child and she had been living with Jamal's mother since she was a year and a half old.

Malinda rushed to her daughter in-law with joy and embraced her as her eyes fluttered awake. She was thrilled for both of them and ecstatic about the baby's safe delivery. She congratulated them both and, holding her son's hands together with her own, told her son what a fine man he had become as the father now of two children. His heart swelled with love and pride.

"How did you know so soon, mother?" Anita asked Malinda. Malinda replied to Anita that Jamal had phoned her. Malinda then rushed Jamal off to contact Ronke's parents overseas. He replied that he'd intended to and that it would be the first thing he would do when he arrived home the next day.

"Have you thought of a name?" Malinda asked.

"Ronke and I discussed that two weeks ago. We planned to give him a traditional *Yoruba* name. I think we should wait to hear a reply from her parents."

"...waiting for replies? Don't you know they will not permit you to take the baby out? You have to give him a name otherwise your wife will remain in the hospital for however long it takes for you to get a name."

"Oh, I've never heard of such a thing. What should we do, honey?" Jamal asked his wife.

Knowing that Malinda wasn't serious about the hospital rule regarding discharging newborns and their mothers, Ronke answered right away.

"I'm thinking maybe *Bolaji* or *Yemi*… we have thousands of names to choose from. Which of those do you prefer, honey?" Ronke asked.

"I think the first one has the sweetest sound and is very cute. How did you say it, Bola...?"

"*Bolaji*, is that what you like better? Cool. We'll choose that." She smiled happily as she changed her position on the bed. The name was registered on the birth certificate and Jamal had the certificate. He impatiently demanded to take his wife home right away, arguing that his mother would complete the remaining tasks on his wife. The hospital wasn't quite ready to release Ronke, yet, however. Jamal held his daughter's hands and congratulated her for having a younger brother. She smiled in return, then moved close to her mother and asked her if she was doing alright. She wanted to hold her newborn brother, but she was told that was too early to do, that she would have to wait. She did not comprehend totally the reasons for that, but she agreed. A nurse entered the room before their departure and delivered some pills to Ronke. The nurse gave Ronke specific instructions on how to take the medication, then with a quick, "Good luck," the nurse left the family alone. Malinda told the couple she brought her car and there was no need to call a cabby. She and Jamal helped Ronke to the car and they were all set to be heading home.

"I will go to Target tomorrow for the baby's needs. You don't have to bother yourself," Malinda told Ronke while driving. She was driving at about five mph above the speed limit. Jamal noticed and pointed this out to her, but Malinda ignored him. She claimed that one could drive even ten miles above the speed limit and still not get pulled over. This became the subject of heated debate until they were about halfway towards their home destination. She applied the car's brakes at the four way intersection; the traffic lights were red. The light changed a moment later and she hit the gas pedal. The road was narrow and seemed endless.

"You followed the longest way, mother," Jamal told her. "What? You know another way to your home? Why didn't you tell me?" she asked in return. She argued again that she had been living in the city twenty seven years before she had even give birth to Jamal and that she certainly knew her way around town. He told her that there was no need to fight on this mere matter and she should continue driving on so they could get home sooner. She finally stopped the argument and drove in silence for another ten minutes.

"Oh my God…!" Malinda yelled out as if frightened and acted out convincingly. Ronke and Jamal were afraid and even Anita wanted to know what had happened. They all stared at Malinda at once. Only the tiny baby remained unperturbed. They all thought she had hit someone or something. She acted as if she was trying to recover from a shock. Even the color of her eyes seemed to change. She was definitely a good actress.

"I missed the road. God!" she said, deceiving them all. "What should I do now?" she asked, her face seeming perplexed.

"Missed the road!? I told you, didn't I? You should've listened to me," Jamal yelled madly.

"Gotcha…!" She smirked because she'd just used slang.

"Oh, you are funny. That's a good one any way. You got me" he admitted and in less than five minutes Malinda made a right turn at one corner and they reached home safely without a single speeding ticket. She pulled towards the front steps to make it easier for Ronke to step out of the car. Just as they'd helped her into the car, they now helped her out. Malinda carried the baby into the house and laid him down in the crib where he continued to slumber. Anita helped her grandmother unload other things from the car. Meanwhile, Jamal found a pen and a sheet of paper to write with, scribed a quick note and then took out an envelope upon which he wrote an address in Nigeria, West Africa. Jamal then entered the bathroom where

his mother and wife were and he immediately stepped back, realizing was not welcome there; he told them he would be heading to the nearby post office, and then closed the bathroom door. He asked his daughter to join him on the trip to run this errand and the two left together. While they were gone, Jamal's mother cooked rice, beans and fried plantains with hot pepper soup, all of which was ready when Jamal and Anita returned. Jamal thanked her heartily for preparing the meal.
Jamal sat at the dining table facing his mother and his daughter sat on a chair next to him; he rushed through his meal without giving any explanation. His mother curiously demanded some explanation for his haste. He told her he had to be at work. As she was setting a glass of water onto the table, Malinda asked, "Why do you have to be at work?" He was, after all, the General Manager. He told her he knew that perfectly well, but had to go anyway, because, he added, when he was gone he couldn't trust most of his employees to be working diligently.

Instead, he assumed that they'd all be goofing off in his absence and that he wanted to surprise them by showing up unexpectedly. Malinda told him she would be leaving for her home as soon as she and Anita emptied their plates. He waved good bye as he took three steps in between them and the door. The door swung shut behind him. Anita asked her grandmother when her Daddy would be back and she replied that she had no clue. She told her they should get going and let her mother rest for a while with the promise that they would both come to see her again the following day. They had cleaned the dining room and set everything in order before they departed, leaving just Ronke and her new baby boy alone.

It was very hard to explain the sun's vague face, every inch of its rays coming down to earth was shining but the air felt cold; luckily, he had a sweater in his car. It was a surreptitious sunny day, as bitter cold as winter time. Why was everything in such a nondescript state? The natural air blew nothing but body-soreness, no discourser could come out and speak clearly about the unexplainable humidity even if he could claim to be a weather expert; throngs of people were caught off guard by the uncommon chill and many were admitted to the hospital for the flu, a fact covered on the evening news.

"Was it due to the godless rainfall that had happened hours ago? Who knew? The whole road would be wet and vehicles would find it impossible to maintain their friction against the tarred roads. Insurance companies would be always happy or sometimes unhappy when they knew it would snow some days. This one was a two-inch snow. God, there would be vehicles' smacked-down everywhere. Sometimes I felt like I should smash my beautiful car against a tree or something. It's not worth paying for something without getting reimbursed. Maybe I should speed up and destroy this car. What if I hurt myself? It might be pretty ugly. If I die today, who is going to take good care of my family? Who? Perchance my lovely mother would, but my wife, she would miss me a lot. She would want to commit suicide if I were to disappear never to be found. Jamal had all of these thoughts while driving and he drove past his place of work while over-thinking and so had to back up his car again.

As Jamal suspected, his employees were doing exactly what he had predicted. Some were singing, some were listening to music, some were eating and some were just idly busy with something unproductive; they were all acting as if there was not a single brain cell left amongst the lot of them. Perhaps, he wondered, he should have them each take a drug test. They had the heaters working and hence they didn't feel any cold at all. It seemed they'd hardly even noticed that it had snowed outdoors, which was too bad. Each of them carried on doing whatever he or she pleased.

Jamal had dressed hastily and looked horribly disheveled. He was shivering severely, and all of his employees burst into laughter. Some of them were even acting out a burlesque of him shivering. He was an ice-berg at the moment; he asked what was so funny and none of them could explain what was really funny. A female employee who had always been enraptured with him schemed to seduce him. She dressed like any girl would dress to try to get a man's attention. Her revealing and sleazy looking pants and tops made for a very unprofessional impression. She was asked to go home immediately and to return dressed professionally. He looked around and was disappointed with all the indelible shame his employees would have caused him should any external visitor or inspector have visited the premises. He was astonished to see an employee who'd placed food on his lap. Jamal had to change his face not to reveal his furiousness. He felt like he should lay all of them off right away, but he never would.

"What a downpour of disgrace this is. Are you having breakfast or lunch? I am very sure that neither such meal is suitable at this time. Perhaps it's a brunch that you're having. I need some explanations, Johnny," Jamal said, angrily demanding an answer. Johnny stood up, quaking, and actually wet himself surreptitiously.

"Sir, yes sir... I am..." He was yet having cold feet.

"Don't you sir me a wit. Why are you stammering now? That's not fair. Speak up and don't babble. I can't understand when someone is babbling. Go on. Explain yourself." Jamal stood waiting for Johnny to speak.

"Sir, it ain't what you think. I woke up late this morning, you know..." He then paused.

"No, I don't know. How could I possibly know that you woke up late today? Maybe you came in late, too. What I do know is that it's not okay.

"Sir, I did not come late. You can ask anybody around here," Johnny suggested.

"Oh yeah? What if they say you came late? Now you keep quiet." Jamal was checking out some papers while talking to Johnny. He turned unannounced and caught James mocking him, but he ignored him as if he hadn't noticed a thing. He continued checking the documents. He thought to himself that he would never fire anyone even if it was deserved. He felt fortunate to head up a company owned by a white man during that period. Jamal's qualifications were exceptional. He was a well lettered black American compared to many other African Americans; he graduated from graduate school at the top of both the dean's and the provost's lists with a G.P.A. of 3.9. He worked for his family and told Ronke, his wife, not to be stressed. She stayed at home even when she was not pregnant. She was a lucky lady.

Jamal was at his office when his assistant came in with a letter in his right hand. As he was giving it to him, he accidentally knocked a full cup of tea off of the table because he'd left the edge of his right sleeve unbuttoned. "I am sorry, sir." He cared. He then rushed out to find some napkins to wipe and dry the table top. He came back in with some paper towels and yet the sleeve was not buttoned up. He was wiping the table and at the same time eye-balling his General Manager with his left eye; perhaps he thought he would be angry and say something aggressive. Jamal thus spoke as he thought, "Why are you eye-balling me, sir?"

"Are you aware that you caused that mess?" he continued, now working on his computer.

"I know, sir. Forgive me." Johnny sought for his forgiveness.

"I forgave you already, but you haven't fixed the problem, have you, Johnny?"

"I am working on it and it will soon dry out," he replied.

"You don't have any idea what the heck I am talking about. Do you?"

"Are you talking about the table, the tea or the entire mess?" He asked with confusion.

"The cause, Johnny… I am talking about the cause." He was pointing to the sleeve of his right hand.

"The cause..." Johnny repeated with surprise.

"Mmmmmmhmmm," Jamal nodded.

"What cause, sir?" He looked about fretfully and continued wiping the table.

"Well. I guess I should tell you. Your sleeve's button was not fastened. Perhaps you left it on purpose. Look at how you dressed up for God's sake. You knew it. Please work on it," he begged.

"Oh, pardon me, sir." He apologized and was buttoning the sleeve. He picked up the napkins after being used for wiping the table and he was taking them out to dispose of them in a trash bin.

The sun started to wave adieu to the earth's surface as the day grew long. Jamal was ready to go home; he stepped into the general room and an employee, a black man, confronted him with his words. He already acted as if he had swollen his stomach with six bottles of Hennessey, or seemed as if he had chip on his shoulder, but he didn't. He seemed to be drunk, as if he'd just downed a bottle of whiskey or cold 45.

"Congratulations, sir. I heard your wife gave you a baby; oh that's a good lady. I ain't hating. That's why I came, hailing.

Sir, show me the love, not the cuff. Hug me, don't punch me. What's wrong? You've got to be strong. You look bored, late to the board? Again congratulations with the situation. What? You wanted to send me away? What did I say? I..." Derek kept playing on those rhymes until Jamal interrupted him.

"Quit it, Derek", Jamal commanded. He asked," What, are you a rapper? Why are you acting like a drunken man?" He then turned around, as if searching for something. Derek was a loquacious man. Jamal thanked him later for congratulating him about the baby. Other employees did the same and Jamal loved the compliments. He then felt relieved and he was very pleased with himself now. Nonetheless, he still suspected that Derek might well be really drunk.

"I know you won't pass it," Jamal said to Derek.

"Pass what exactly, boss?"

"A drug test. Do you want to take it?" He asked confidently.

"Nope! That's not necessary." He replied in a quandary and got himself settled on a chair. Jamal stared at him for some minutes. He decided to leave at thirty minutes prior to closing time and left with a quick, "Good-bye." He stopped at Wal-Mart to pick up some flowers and a couple of lovingly composed greeting cards for his wife. He met his old friend, Tony, at the store and they discussed past subjects.

Hours later, Ronke had got up from bed and she was spooning some rice into her mouth and the same time forking some plantains with it, the food was delicious and she felt like she had never had such a fine meal. She ate hungrily, having woken that way.

Jamal entered after he had used keys to open the front door and he bounced back for a moment, however, thinking he might have just entered the wrong house. He then froze and took his time checking out the half-naked glamorous-looking lady sitting on a chair facing directly towards him. He assessed her further. "Wow," he uttered. She glowed like many carats of diamonds and sat there smiling with her perfect cheeks. No man would ever want to lose her as his wife, even if she were going to live her life until well into her hundreds. He felt like he should drop everything he had in his hands and take her straight into the bedroom. He handed the flowers and the cards to her and yet he was baffled by her beautiful face. He breathed heavily and rushed into the refrigerator to cool his mind with iced-water. He was absolutely captivated with her buxom beauty and also feeling qualms about a day old boy, Bolaji.

"How I wish you had delivered a year ago," he thought to himself. He sat down on the couch, wishing she would disrobe entirely. He asked her to join him, and she did. She made a bee-line for her man. She rested herself on his thighs and was trying to enjoy the natural sensation of his manhood; she felt relaxed like never before and started intoxicating herself with the sleep that she'd been denied through the vigil she kept last night. He managed his lust, powered past his lascivious needs and tried to focus on massaging her face from chin to forehead. She enjoyed every inch of the massage and she wished covertly that he would not stop. He continued rubbing her entirely with excitement; he was afraid to look at her face because she was so beautiful and he then began to run his fingers through her hair, caressing it. Soon, she was fast asleep with sensation. He couldn't wake her up, so he let her continue resting on his legs and they fell asleep.

***

One week after the birth of the baby, cars were parked all along both sides of the road. It was only for a day and that's not too bad. Neighborhood friends, college friends, work friends and relatives from hometowns and out of town were already there sitting under the set up tents; it was hot and sunny. It was not uncomfortable at all to sit outdoors. Sumptuous meals with soporific drinks were prepared by special cooks they hired. Everyone got his own groove on at that moment. There were numbers of invitees who showed up but who had not initially been invited. Friends of friends, siblings of friends and relatives of others all paid their respects to the couple through their presence. It was now the toast time. Jamal was expected to drink to the health of all of the souls participating there; everyone held a cup full of soda and raised it up into air. They were waiting for Jamal's words. He stood up with his own glass being raised up as well as others' and standing beside him was the lovely and beautiful lady, Ronke. She wore a dress of shining lace material from Nigeria. She was the cynosure of all eyes. She was dressed fabulously with some scarce golden rings and necklaces. She had indeed earned them all. It had been a week already since Bolaji was welcomed to the world of happiness. He was already seven days old and he would have loved the day should he have grown old enough to be aware of it. His sister could use some portion of the excitement, which she did.

"First of all, I thank you all for coming out today. I appreciate your time and the love. I would like to make a toast to my beautiful wife and for the wonderful love she has for me, as well as for the lovely new baby she brought into this world a week ago. I love you, baby." He proceeded to drink by hitting his glass but carefully against his wife's. He then gave her a simple kiss on her lips and she accepted his lips with a smile. Everybody then cheered. Anita was the luckiest one with gifts from her parents' friends; she couldn't understand completely the reasons for those gifts, but she did to some extent. For the sake of kids and religion, no liquor was consumed that day. Miss Malinda rose up from her seat and gave words of thanks to all the participants; she loved the day. Here came Derek, Mr. Rhyme. He dressed in baggy jeans and an extra large shirt that were too big to fit his size and he acted like he didn't really give a hoot about people staring at him. He walked towards his boss, shook his hand and started his words.

"Boss, I bowed with the bowl. For your post, I am supposed. We are all here for the beer. We ain't mad though for the soda. Why shoulda? I can't dispute that's why I salute. Man, you are the man. Give me some dollars for the colas. Even if you keep me late, I'll be straight. You know what boss, I can rhyme and mime. I can sing and wing."

He stopped with laughter and was waiting for Jamal's comments.

"I applaud you even though your words are not clear to my mind. Perhaps you should quit and pursue your dreams. You got some flows. I ain't lying. What did you think?" Jamal asked.

"I don't wanna be any rapper. I enjoy rhyming, that's all. What makes you think I would quit my job? I love my job, boss. Did you hear me? I love my job." Derek claimed.

"I thought that you wanted to be a rapper. I am sorry if I've offended you."

"Offended me? Not in this world. You, offended me? No way. You are straight with me."

"Okay, we're cool then."

“Did I tell you that you were the best boss I have ever met in this world?”

“No, you didn't say that, not yet, anyway.”

“Now, I just did, didn't I?"

“Yes, you did. I guess,” he joked. “Any way you are a good man yourself,” he added. He joined others and began dancing happily with his wife. After thirteen hours of grooving, the party was rounded up. They were ready to depart.

“Hold up! You almost hit the cars behind you. Back off a little bit.” Jamal was watching for a driver who was trying to move his car away from the drive way. “Is it good now?” the driver asked. Jamal was then demonstrating with his hands, “Turn...yes. Turn the steering wheel to the left. Yeah to the left! No, not to the right. You are going to harvest my mailbox,” Jamal said. The driver finally got it right and thanked him.

“I appreciate it,” the driver said.

“You’re welcome, bro. Take it easy,” Jamal responded.

His mother left with Anita. Everyone had vacated the place, leaving the couple behind and alone. By the time that Jamal cleaned up all of the mess, it was twelve forty-five in the morning. He was definitely a little tired and they both went to bed.

“Good night, honey.”

“Good night, honey.”

“I love you."

"I love you, too.” They exchanged some kisses in bed and then blacked out temporarily until they woke the next day in their bedroom.

***

When November arrived, the postman delivered their mail to the box and then rang the doorbell for oversize boxes that he couldn't fit into the mail box. Ronke opened the door and showed her teeth. “What a cute smile,” the postman thought, although he kept that impression to himself. He greeted the lady of the house and delivered the boxes instead and he left, with lust, immediately. She placed those letters on the table waiting for her man's arrival. It was only ten minutes before he’d be home; provided there was no emergency, he’d be home soon. Oh, here he came. She clung to him as he entered and they shared some wet kisses. She then untangled herself from him.

"We have some letters and boxes from Nigeria," she said with pride.

“I hope it’s good news.”

“What’s in them?”

“I don't know yet. I waited for your arrival.”

“Oh, what a lovely wife you are. That's so sweet of you.”

“Open them and let's see what’s in each.”

“Okay, this one first,” she said, opening one with a brown envelope.

“What does it say?”

The letter greeted the couple and informed them that Ronke's mother wanted her to visit Nigeria with her family. Perhaps she wanted Bolaji to stay in Nigeria for some years before returning back to America. They thought the idea was just like skating on thin ice. Jamal developed cold feet, but Ronke pretended as if she was going to have the nerve to let him go; she was trying to be brave and she decided that he could go there.

“He is only seven months old. Why would he have to go there alone?” Jamal argued.

"Maybe I should stay with him. What did you think, Jamal?" She placed her hands on his chest. She then raised her forehead up to look into his eyes as he was talking. She kept smiling as his lips moved.

"What did I think? I don't think anything. The answer is heck no."

"Heck no? Why are you getting angry? Anita is living with your mother. What do you have to say about that?"

"That's different. And she is in America, not far away from us."

"You know what . . ."

"What?"

"We will take him there next year. He will be a year old by then."

"Suit yourself, young lady."

"Sure, I will young man."

They avoid crossing swords with each other and were ready to fill their stomachs with some food. At the dining table, she expected her man to feed himself. He complimented her on the meal; they exchanged and shared some romantic feeding. They presumed Bolaji was too young to understand such acts if he were to witness them. Jamal tuned into a local TV station after the romantic dinner; the subject on television was a historical documentary on black folks.

"I never want my kids to be with white people," Ronke claimed, detesting the white race fully.

"Why, because of this program? What is it?"

"You know, a lot of things have something to do with it."

"A lot of things like..." He was waiting for her to complete her thoughts.

"History, Jamal... slavery, hatred, torture, lynching, Jim Crow laws, discrimination and more . . ."

"That was in the past, honey."

"They are still hating on us. They have never stopped. I don't think they will."

"That's not true. Not all of them."

"Yeah right…"

"You know it's the law of nature, even if the whole world was nothing but the same color. I learnt that there were histories as you claimed, but it was all over the world. Blacks even hate on other Blacks; whites did the same. They hate one another sometimes. That's just the nature of the world. Ignorant people seem to hate anything or anyone that's different from them."

"No, they don't."

"I know they wouldn't have done what they did in the past should they realize it's not godly and fair. You know the same white men fought for us afterwards. Our fathers have been free since Emancipation."

"What about discrimination? Has that stopped yet?"

"It has been diminishing, Ronke. It hasn't stopped completely."

"So what's the point?"

"My point is that you are discriminating now. Not all white men revere that happened many years ago, although some may yet harbor fears about black men. We need to work together to attain peace and harmony. Segregation because of color differences is wrong and of course I don't endorse it. Remember my job, though. The company that I head is owned by a white man, remember?"

"You earned and deserved the position. You got that job because of your qualifications, Jamal."

"Let me tell you something. There were numbers of qualified persons for the position. He loved me, and that was why he hired me. So forget about worrying if someone hates you; God loves everybody and He never discriminates against any one. And you know what else that does not discriminate, baby?"

"What, honey?"

"Love. Love doesn't discriminate against anyone. It sees no color. It catches you no matter what your color, religion, race or any other group that you might belong to. It chooses between anybody and anyone it wants. Let me ask you a question, Ronke?"

"What is it, baby?"

"If Bolaji or Anita grows up and falls in love with someone other than a member of the black race, what would you do? Would you tell him or her not to be with whomever he or she wants?"

"I'd kill either one of them."

"Kill them, your children?"

"You know what I mean. I won't let it happen. Not in my presence."

"Why are you so hateful about white men?"

"…because they already hated us."

"You are only acting on history. You haven't witnessed it, have you?"

"Well, I don't have to, Mr. nice man."

"Well, we will see."

"Hell yeah, we shall see."

She stood up angrily and left him alone. He called her many times and she ignored him. He went to her and tried to cool her mind with words. He begged her for almost an hour before she finally claimed she was not angry with him. They decided to go out and spend the rest of the day enjoying fresh air and seeing some places, so they went to a movie theater.

The whole theater was filled up. All of the seats were taken save for one; they paid for two tickets, but there was only one seat left unoccupied. Everyone in the theater stared as they forced their way shyly through the crowd. They had to walk through thousand of legs, all the way to the front lines before they could reach the lone seat. They apologized for the inconvenience as they made their way through the room, bumping into others' seats. Reaching the empty seat, Jamal asked his wife to sit on his lap so that they could enjoy the show. It was only seven seconds away from the beginning of the movie. The bright lights dimmed. Music began to play and on the screen, a very huge and super scary shadow of a giant demon was cast across a palm tree. There were three poor innocent men sitting under the tree; they were all playing cards and were buried in it with every inch of their minds and brains. Then it was revealed inch by inch, but no hand was made visible yet to show the holder of the mortal axe which had a very keen blade; it was new and had never been used before. Later, in about another seven seconds, the hands of this evil spirit were made overt to the entire audience as if the demon were before the screen rather than projected onto it. Everyone in the audience was very tense.

The demon stepped across the ground, intent on wetting his mouth with human blood. The more closely he approached the three men, the less they cared and noticed. Only one of the three men heard the suspicious noise coming in their direction. "Run!!!" the audience cried out. The men on screen wished they could run, but had been caught unawares. One of these three men stood up with pride to pronounce his victory over the others and he heard the scary foot steps behind him. "Oh dear!

Holy Molly," the man uttered. The demon raised his axe up into the air and set those three heads on the ground in just a minute and he was then happily satisfying his thirst with the men's blood. The demon was still hungry for more. Ronke's eyes were closed utterly; she couldn't watch the men be murdered by the demon.

"Open your eyes. He's left the scene already. Ronke, open your eyes. You are going to miss it all," he whispered into her ears.

"Ok, I will," she said.

The movie continued until the credits rolled.

"Why did the movie did start with a demon and why did he kill those men?" The unresolved questions consumed the audience members. There had been ninety minutes of disaster, mystery, and confusion. Once the movie had ended, everyone searched for the doors. Ronke was wiping her face when Jamal yelled her name; he asked her to let them go and she listened. It wasn't until they exited that Jamal noticed that his wife had been crying during the movie. Poor thing, he thought to himself. He leaned towards her and she rested her head on his chest. He tried to convince her that it was just a movie and not the real world. She claimed that she knew that perfectly well, but that she'd been emotionally touched. They entered their car and drove off. They got home a few minutes later and they went to bed without wasting any further time.

Ronke woke up the next morning and her husband had become gold; she closed her eyes and thought she was dreaming. She opened her eyes one after the other and yet the man had gone. What? She jumped off the bed and rushed into the living room, but couldn't find Jamal. Where could he have gone to? Different thoughts forced themselves into her mind. She fought these and she claimed that she trusted him with everything of her life. It was Saturday, a weekend, not a week day. She called his phone and it had been switched off. What was happening? She broke into tears without explanation, and then walked into the bedroom again. She lifted up her son, took him to the shower bath and bathed him thoroughly and then breast-fed him to lull him to sleep. She took her own shower and got ready to cook some food for her man. She cooked with less satisfaction than usual, but she refused to eat and kept waiting for his return.

She promised her soul that she would wait for him even if he didn't return until the following day; she was a rare wife. Her stomach was overwhelmed with hunger pains. Her tummy ached. Two hours passed and still he didn't return. She kneeled and prayed to the Lord for His guidance and to protect him, wherever he might be. She waited another hour then two more; she grew annoyed, but then fell asleep.

Jamal peeped into the key-hole, and then snuck into the house like a gentleman of the road. He sat on the same couch that she slept on, but he didn't wake her up, he stared and kept watching her body as if it were the first time. Her navel, very sensitive, was moving up and down with the command of her heavy breathing. He was gentle with excitement and he enjoyed watching her exposed body through the mini-top and skirt she wore. The extreme but flat belly she had at the moment helped him sense that she had been starving all day long. His cerebral hemispheres communicated with the help of concentrated bundles of axons, called commissures, and both his thalamus and hypo-thalamus awakened keenly and he sensibly wrapped up his viewing and woke her up. She had slept for hours and yet she thought she only had the shortest sleep ever. For both the first and the last time, she hissed as she woke up. She removed his hands off her repeatedly. She thought she had earned an apology and an explanation, but he kept smiling as she got angrier.

"I am so sorry, honey." He mouthed the words out romantically. She acted like she didn't care for any romantic words at the time and walked up to the kitchen where the food had become colder than an earthworm's skin. She only acted this way once in a blue moon. He felt his patience being taxed. He couldn't get angry whenever his wife was.

"You're acting like the king of a monarchy," she said as she was microwaving the food to reheat it. She had heated her body with anger and the vessels dilated and an increased the volume of blood flowing through her skin. The heat dissipated and her body became flushed; she was sweating profusely and walked up to the air conditioner to reset her body temperature. She placed the food on the dining table and planned to be taciturn. They remained silent for almost five minutes and Jamal couldn't take it any longer. He therefore he broke his silence after four minutes and asked, "Why are you so angry with me?"

"Who told you that?" she asked in reply.

"I feel like you're mad at me", he answered, stirring the rice on his plate. She handed salt to him should he need it and then spoke.

"No, I'm not," she lied and cried.

"Honey, what's all this?"

"What!?"

"Why are you crying?"

" . . . because I had to, Jamal. I needed it"

"Did you really need to cry? For what…?"

"For exactly what you did to me."

"What did I do? How did I hurt your feelings?"

“Ain’t it the same bed we shared? We slept on the same bed last night, didn't we? Why must you go out this morning without even telling me where you were going? I called your cell phone, but you had it switched it off. And you then spent twelve hours outside before you returned. Now you are asking me a baloney question.”

“Are you alright, girl?” He was touching her neck to detect whether or not she was doing okay.

“I’m fine. There is nothing wrong with me.” She took his hands off of herself.

“First of all, what I asked you was not baloney.”

“Yes, it is. How a man could do such thing to his wife?”

“Would you please let me speak?”

“Like I’m not listening? I can hear you.”

“Thanks. I got a call this morning around three o'clock. It was an extreme emergency, from the C.E.O.”

“And you couldn't leave me a note? I'd understand if you left a note, baby.”

“I did, honey.”

“No, you didn't”

“Yes, I did. It was under your pillow with the lovely poem I always write every morning.”

“You are lying.”

“No, I am not. Did you read your poem today?”

“See, when I opened my eyes . . .” She was interrupted.

“Did you or didn’t you?”

“I didn't. My brain was overwhelmed when I couldn't find you. That's why I forgot to read them.”

She then stood up quickly. She rushed into the bedroom; she looked and found beneath her pillow the explanatory note and a lovely and well composed poem that he wrote. She kissed the paper several times and walked up to him at the dining table.

He was hungry, but he seemed to be fully satisfied already. She had changed her dress and wore only panties and hadn't covered her breasts. "The taste of food was not as romantic as the odors he perceived from her body, and the aroma was one that he needed every day. She apologized for her behavior, which he kindly accepted.

Their kisses were gently shared and exchanged; they ignored the meal on the table and began nourishing each other's bodies. They exchanged some sensual words as they moved along with the foreplay that neither of them wanted to ever end. They were too eager to go to their bedroom despite the many years that they'd been married. They feared that going to bed might diminish the strongest emotions they were experiencing as they became entangled with one another in the dining room, and then moving to the nearby living room where they landed on their longest couch. They continued to exchange saliva, still flirting like two love birds. Her breasts felt like two mangos and he took his time and exploring his talents while playing with those two juicy fruits with his mouth stuck to them while his tongue licked the tips of each one by one exactly like a greedy snake with a freshly scented flower; she enjoyed every bit of his movement and shut her eyes for the whole time. When they finally finished with their sensational excitement, they were both hungry. Ronke reheated the food again and they fed one another lovingly and then held hands as they went up to bed to sleep.

"I love you, babe."

"And I love you more, baby." After uttering these words, each of them slipped into a captivating slumber.

***

Two days ahead of Christmas day, the couple visited Jamal's place of work. It was the first time ever that Ronke had ever seen the place. They were greeted with honors by his employees. He shook hands with each of one of them and he later told them that he would be going on a trip with his wife to Nigeria. They were pleased with his announcement, particularly since they knew they'd all have to chance to do as they pleased on his days off. He then warned each one of them to be a progressive but not an aggressive worker. Then Derek stood up and began his usage of slang and street language.

"Why must you be so talkative, D?" Jamal asked.
"Sir, you have got it twisted. You know I am talk-active not a talkative. There is a difference." He joked with those words and was walking backward to his seat. "I knew you were always trying to be funny," he pointed out. "I spent sixteen years of my life in sin city, Vegas that's..."
"Speak English Derek," Jamal commanded. He told his wife to come with him outside and they left the place. She suggested that they go to either K-Mart or Wal-Mart to buy gifts for her mother, siblings, cousins, and some old friends abroad. Her father had passed away since she was fifteen should you think she didn't like her father. Yes, she did.

Inside K-Mart, Ronke stood in the clothes section asking her husband to join her so that they could find some quality items. He agreed and helped her to pick out some gifts which she liked a lot. They proceeded to the next line, which was the shoe line. The shoes she chose were too many, and yet she had an uncanny thought that there weren't enough. They carted the items to the scanning center. The employee who was about to scan their things was astonished and asked, “Are you going to do some give away on Christmas day?”

“Oh, nope...” Jamal replied.

“I'm sorry; I’m not trying to be nosy.” The employee smiled.

“It’s alright”, he told her.

Ronke eyed an album as the scanning was in progress; it was a debut album of Whitney, a local singer who had recently released a duet on the radio a week ago. She was dying to have it and she got it at last; the album was titled "You and Me." They emptied their things into the car after being carried with the cart. She put in the brand new album that they’d just bought into the car’s CD slot and she began dancing and miming the words of the song. She told her husband she loved the track that was playing as soon as it was debuted on the radio last week and she continued dancing until they reached home. They called Jamal's mother afterwards to inform her of their trip to Nigeria. She was scared about their journey, but she wished them good luck on the plane.

After seven days of preparation and on the first day of the New Year, they began packing their baggage. They had four suitcases filled up, but there was still more to pack and no room left. She agreed they should leave them behind. She finally realized how much they’d bought. She opened the door and stepped out to see what was happening out there. It was so hard to see a bird flying in the sky. The whole street had dried out like crops suffering from a lack of irrigation for years. They should be celebrating the new day and the New Year. Her husband told her the whole neighborhood might have gone to worship their Lord at church.

She suggested they should pray inside, too, lovingly and carefully, which they did. Afterwards, they needed to take their goods to the car. Ronke wasn't the only one carrying those bags to their vehicle and was only carrying the lightest of them. She drank a great deal of water, but still wasn't comfortable. Jamal stopped her from toting anything further. A man of both words and action, he took all the left-over bags to the car and uttered not a word about his back hurting.

Now their flight was just hours away and Ronke decided to take a bath. Oh Lord!

Jamal called for his patience to stick around because he didn't want to lose it, it being his mind. She promised to be as fast as she could. They were running out of time prior to take-off. Thirty five minutes had been lavished and she was now applying make-up. She was making sure her whole face was glowing and attractive.

"Are we going to a modeling contest? I don't understand the meaning of all this, woman!" He was shaking his legs with let's-go attention.

"Come on, Jamal. I'll be right out," she pleaded while glancing at the mirror. Her beauty deserved words of praise to God, even if it was only conveyed with a single word: "Wow!" He was so intent on catching the plane that recognizing his wife's beauty would make them late. He urged her to get into the car and they drove off. Names had been called and the coordinator had passed over theirs. They arrived some minutes later and they were fined for their tardiness. Thanks to God, the plane was still on the ground. They nearly missed their flight, and now there was another obstacle. Each passenger was only allowed to travel with just one piece of luggage. The couple had four suitcases. They made their pleas and argued, finally paying extra money for the extra bags. Ronke's make up was nearly messed up, but she managed her emotions to save herself the mess. All of the passengers, including the couple, were finally seated an hour later.

The flight started gently on the tarmac, moving like a Saturn sedan on a smooth road. Its wheels became less visible as it began airing upwards, then fear emerged in each heart as it started quaking before it could air up farther. Everyone said his or her own prayers and there was silence. Shortly thereafter, a flight attendant arrived with her service of food and drinks. The plane was now cruising at about a thousand and half feet above sea level. Jamal peeped through the side window hoping to see people or something. He told his wife to look down. Perhaps she could see something. She looked and it was hard for her to see anything. Everything appeared just like a pin in the darkest room. He had looked ahead of her before he could sense the beauty of the lady seated beside him, his lovely wife. She didn't appreciate his comments at first because to her it seemed to have taken him far too long to notice her glowing and irresistible beauty. He always knew he was a lucky man with such a beautiful girl. She would look nice and pretty even without a makeup. She glanced at the flight attendant's buttocks as she passed by them and told her husband to look at them. He laughed with her silliness and wrapped his hands around her. She felt warm inside and enjoyed joking with her man.

"Do you like that?" She teased him.

"Like what, hers?"

"Mmmmmhmmm. Hers"

"Come on, don't be ridiculous. You know I only like you and everything in you."

"I know. I am just kidding."

"Ok, drop it."

The earth's surface was covered with blue-black clouds. Then, after some hours had passed, daylight vanished and the moon shone on its light on the world. The stars were bright and seemed to be dancing a lively and colorful waltz. It paved the smoothest flight for the pilot; he journeyed for sixteen hours without getting bored. Over the PA system, the pilot announced the first and the only stopover to all passengers; they landed at one airport and everyone sought for drinks and food inside. The plane aired up into the sky again after two hours of refreshment; it spent another four more hours and yet the destination was not reached. Some passenger's bodies were sore from the long journey and others slept. Jamal was wondered how far the flight from the USA to Nigeria was. He was curious, but didn't want to ask. After two to three hours of sleep, some finally woke up and they were not happy when they noticed that they were still a bird in the sky rather than a duck on the ground. Then the pilot announced that they were now only one hour away from Nigeria's Lagos Airport. This was good news and every one settled after checking their belongings to make sure they were safe. The plane shook, which frightened some passengers during the landing. The entire flight had taken twenty four hours and fifteen minutes.

After the baggage arrival, each headed to the screening room for identification and registration. They were made to pay some fees that Jamal had difficulty understanding. He suspected they were bribes, but they were not. Ronke tendered both her Nigerian and American passports for identification and she told them that Jamal was her husband and that they came together to visit family. The officials addressed the couple in Yoruba, but only Ronke could respond; Jamal didn't understand a single word of it, which didn't bother him a bit at first. After this, they stepped out to find a taxi. The driver charged the couple some naira equivalent to thirty five dollars US. They tipped him with an extra five dollars and he finally drove them to their initial destination. They changed vehicles three times before they arrived home at last. Bolaji had slept through it all as if seemingly indifferent.

Just like the hungriest eagle would be cheering and flapping both of her wings up in the sky when she spied a chicken down on the ground, Ronke's family cheered for the couple's arrival. They were treated like royalty. The noise woke up most of nosy neighbors who crowded to show their curious faces even though they had not been formally invited. The couple was amazed by the love and kindness showered on them and Jamal had a thought that another excursion would not be bad at all the following year. He enjoyed the people, the love and the whole environment; he was embarrassed though, because was unable to speak the native language. He sat there watching their mouths dancing up and down with different words that he regarded as gibberish; he asked his wife to translate some of the words and he would laugh when some of those words were funny to him. He aimed to learn some of the native language before they were scheduled to leave. Although Ronke's brothers and sisters spoke English, their accents were difficult for Jamal to understand. Ronke's mother could not speak a word of the English language. Jamal noted that Ronke strongly resembled her mother and he was impressed with God's work. Although of course she looked older than Ronke, which was good, because if not, Jamal might have mistaken his mother in-law for his wife. You know what they say: like mother, like daughter. Jamal felt lucky that his wife had inherited such beauty.

Bolaji got the most love. Ronke's sisters and relatives were competing over who was going to carry him first; they fought with one another, but of course, not physically. Ronke's mother held him last and she placed him on her back by wrapping a piece of glossy silken cloth around him. He fell asleep again almost immediately thereafter.

Jamal watched as a hot yam soup was prepared using a traditional black cooking pot; peeled yams and peppers blended with mortars by the cooks caused them to sweat profusely. Jamal felt as if he were watching an interesting movie on a big screen. He was learning a lot from this trip. The attractive scent of the soup's aroma permeated the entire house. Jamal felt his greedy mouth water. "God, I can't wait to taste this delicious meal," he thought to himself. Ronke smiled at him to ensure that he was comfortable with the surroundings. He let her know that nothing was as comfortable as where they were now. He was eager to have the meal, to have soup dance upon his tongue.

The dinner, served at a late hour, sated every appetite. One soul, however, was suffering. Jamal stopped eating suddenly. What had just happened? Everyone was clueless save his wife, Ronke, who sensed instantly that the soup might be too hot for him. She rushed to the cold pot to get some water; he drank the water but it simply exacerbated his condition. Hot peppers…? They could have told him not to drink water! He was suffering severely from the heat of the soup. Jumping up and down without any instructor, it seemed he lost some pounds from this exercise. Ronke told her family that the soup was too hot for him; they all laughed and were so surprised to hear that complaint. He was lucky afterwards to get a sweet candy which, luckily, helped him gain relief. Finally he asked, curious to know what kind of pepper they used for the soup. He claimed he had tasted many of his wife's soups, but that he'd never before had soup so hot. After the meal, the group rapped till dawn, then each fell asleep without saying good night. The sky changed its color as rapidly as a chameleon; it became dull and dark.

After just an hour of sleep, when the golden teeth of the sun were being set to bling the face of the earth, a happy rooster crowed and made a cock-a-doodle -doo to wake those lazy boys that might still be in bed snoring like a little Bolaji at that hour. The members of the family roused up and began heading to the bathroom where they each took turns brushing their teeth and performing their ablutions before congregating together to observe the morning prayer. They told Jamal his name was a Muslim noun. He told them he'd learned that when he was twenty years old when he had studied the Qur'an, seeking knowledge about Islam. He joined the family and they prayed together; he later learned that Muslims must observe Salat (daily prayer) five times a day.

He sat outside to enjoy the environment. The fresh air kept battling his naked legs, which were exposed by the shorts he wore. He had the thought of seeing some wild animals running around the neighborhood, but he couldn't see even a monkey. He wanted to ask one of his brother in-laws, but couldn't because he wouldn't understand his English language inquiry. The accents were totally different from one another. While Jamal thought they were too fast for him, they thought he was the one who talked very fast and were very difficult to understand. One problem was they didn't pronounce English words the long way as Americans do. They would shorten their word pronunciation, instead, pronouncing "off" as "of" and "cart" as "cat," "heard" as "hard," and so on. It made it difficult for Jamal to comprehend the words they were saying. The conversation would be just like that between the dog and the cat, very difficult. He was so glad to see his wife appear and he asked her the animals he'd expected to see were hiding. She nearly wet her underwear with laughter when she heard his inquiries. She told him that not all African people lived in the jungle, and that he should go to a zoo if he really wanted to see those animals. Thus, he agreed readily with Ronke that they should do just that the next morning.

At the zoo were widely fenced yards with over a thousand species of animals. Many people visited the zoo that very day. It was very fun and amazing to Jamal; he fed some of the monkeys with bananas and he got a chance to see leopards, deer, lions and elephants with his naked eyes for the first time. He had seen those wild animals before but only on the screen. The zoo indeed gave him a chance of life time; he was very pleased. The couple toured the entire zoo for almost two hours; they began with the terrestrial animals, and then moved to the aquatic zone where they met alligators, crocodiles and different types of snakes and other reptiles. Jamal acted like he never wanted to leave. He wasted more time than necessary, Ronke thought, though she didn't complain.

A week prior to their returning back to the United States, there was a marriage celebration scheduled to take place. Jamal and Ronke had spent three weeks in Nigeria already and they needed to wait for the last week, even though Jamal had been worried about his job and the employees. After the usual prayers and the meal in the morning, the whole house was rowdily populated with other members of the extended family; these people brought clothes, grains, vegetable oils and gifts of different kinds that could be best described as valuables, especially for a bride. Jamal kept asking himself what and how different things might be used for and Ronke helped him learn before the marriage ceremony.

Early in the day, the women began cooking using very huge pots; these pots were set atop firewood enclosed within three-stone set-ups. All the foods were strange to Jamal; some of the foods were wrapped with plastic bags. As the day grew longer, things grew interesting with the marriage ceremony. Drums were used to communicate some meaningful words that were very poetically translated. After the meal, Jamal was amazed to hear people, teenagers and adults, miming those words that each of the drums were saying. Jamal wondered why it wasn't difficult for each man that was beating each drum to carry and beat the drums for such long hours. People, especially women, danced to the drums impressively as if there were competing with one another for something of value. Some showered the women with naira, appreciating the dance; Jamal took this as an invitation. He stood up and did the same thing by showering those beautiful ladies with dollars. Then another group of women gathered to sing around the neighborhood; they sang without drums and the song was melodious. They, too, got money out of Jamal's pocket.

More and more groups came performing and astonishing Jamal. These were rampant until four o'clock p.m. At five-thirty, there was a congregation of young and very beautiful high school aged girls; they were beating something the Yoruba called "*Kengbe*." Each song featured a chorus and they seemed happier every time one of them initiated a new chorus. The words were very much sexual and mature, though not at all obscene, merely amusing. It was controversial nonetheless because the words referred to men's private parts, although they were joking. Men paid these girls even though they commented on their body parts. It was regarded as part of their culture and it didn't bother them at all.

Later that day, they proclaimed the loss of bride. As if it were a movie, Jamal was very disturbed and felt this was an inauspicious ending. He called to his wife and gathered the entire family together and told them that they needed to call the police right away, but they mocked his idea. He kept wondering why they didn't take his words seriously, but then later that night the bride appeared and he was curious to know who had kidnapped her. His wife revealed to him that it was all planned and it was part of a cultural game. She explained that the bride groom and his friends or family would have to pay before the girls on the bride's side of the family would release the bride and this had been the tradition for years. She further told him that he would have experienced the same thing should their marriage have take place in Nigeria. The obsession faded away in his mind and he felt newly in love with his wife's culture. It reminded him of hip-hop.

Three days later, women paid their visits to Ronke's mother. She was the appointed neighborhood advisory mogul whom all other women in her street turned to for counsel about everything. She then started introducing many people that Ronke had missed while she was away. Jamal loved it even though he couldn't understand a word of the language; all he could do was watch the movement of their lips and their reaction towards any statement or conversation. They all sat on the mat, and circled facing one another. Ronke's mother pointed at one lady and said: "This is 'Morenikeji.' " She was introducing the lady to her daughter, "...she debuted her first son last month," and she told the news. Ronke then faced the lady and said," *E barika o!* which translates to "congratulations." Jamal imitated his wife and mimed those words to the new mother; they laughed at his accent and the way those words were mouthed out; he wasn't embarrassed at all; he joined them instead and they all laughed it out together.

Ronke's mother and her entire family looked disturbed; they didn't want Ronke and her husband to depart. They were very pleased with their company for four weeks and felt they needed more time. The couple couldn't stay; they had to go.

Luggage was packed with new African acquisitions, ranging from clothes to food. Ronke's family helped the movement and they called on a taxi driver to take them to the nearby station to join a vehicle that would take them to Lagos state where they would finally join their flight. Luckily, there was room for both Jamal and Ronke on the bus. Ronke and her mother painfully exchanged tears and finally said good bye to each other. God, it was hard for Ronke to leave her son, Bolaji, behind; her mother promised her that he would be going with her to the United States next year when she came back home and she agreed. Jamal didn't weep; he acted like a bold man and gave his family in-law some money to manage with for a short time. They arrived at Lagos state bus station after four hours of traveling and they joined another vehicle to take them to the airport.

Following the path to the departure area, they were screened and then moved in to find their seats. The journey was smooth, even though they exchanged flights three times before getting to their destination. They detoured to Amsterdam for two hours, and then later stopped at Memphis before heading finally to the Chattanooga Airport. It didn't take them long at all to get out of the airport; they were American citizens although Ronke obtained her citizenship by naturalization. It was easy for her to get her citizenship after being married to an American citizen for three years. The taxi driver took them to their house, received a one hundred dollar bill and was happy. Lights were turned on and bags were unloaded without wasting any time. Their bodies were temporarily feeble and very sore; they managed to clean their bodies before going to bed afterwards. It had been a very tiresome twenty four hours plus journey by air. Early in the morning, a week later, Ronke stepped out and noticed that a newly moved-in white couple now occupied the house next to their own. She was happy and eager to meet them.

She was watering the garden flowers when the man next door came out from his house; their eyes met and he frowned. She wanted to greet him, but he seemed angry and unreceptive.

“What the heck are you looking at?” he said as seemed to be searching the area around his car. She thought perhaps he was joking and so she smiled innocently.

"You think this is joke? I don't come here to be friends with any Negros or whatever names they are calling you. Don't talk to me, not even to my wife. You got it?" he asked her.

"Slow down, sir. We don’t even know each other,” Ronke said. “I can't even understand why you are so upset with me. I haven’t even spoken to you yet," she explained.

“So don't,” he said, and then stormed into his house. She was upset and felt blue about the situation. As soon as Jamal arrived home from work she told him about the incident. He believed the story because he trusted his wife, but he was confused about the whole situation.

“Did you greet him?” Jamal asked from his seat on the couch.

“I was trying to, but he didn't let me,” she explained. Jamal then turned the TV on and tuned into CNN.

“I am trying to figure it out. Sometime it’s too hard to follow women's comments," Jamal said, opinionated.

“So you don't believe me?” she asked, very clearly upset.

“Not that I didn't believe everything you said, I do. I would suggest that you should leave them alone if that is what they want. They sound like racists to me. You know I don't want any trouble. Let's continue enjoying our peaceful lives. Love you, baby,” he said, then kissed her.

“You know what honey? I heard a bad rumor today,” he said, sounding depressed.

"What is it, baby?" She set the loaf of bread she held onto the table and was ready to hear him out.

"Derek revealed that some men summoned a meeting behind my back when I was away. They were trying to take over my post. Good thing the CEO was mad at them and laid them off." He breathed heavily as he began applying butter to a slice of the bread.

"Thanks be to God Almighty. How could they be so cruel? Why are men were so hateful and godless? Let me guess; they were all white, weren't they?" she asked eagerly.

"How did you know? We have black employees, too, though not many of them, compared to whites," Jamal declared.

"How did I know, Jamal? I told you they were so hateful from the beginning. They should be held in prison, too, perhaps for the rest of their lives. God…!" She uttered those words with excitement.

"You know I feel bad for them and at the same time I am so scared." He laid the words down cowardly.

"Scared of what? Them…? Don't be ridiculous. And don't even feel sorry for any one of them. Don't you know they would have killed you if they could? And you were sad because they got fired. Poor thing; you should be celebrating!" She hissed angrily.

"I am scared they might want to come after me and my family. You know. I can't let that ... let that happen. If something were to happen, I would not be able to forgive myself..." he explained further. He put a slice of bread into his mouth and continued listening to her.

"Nothing is going to happen, Jamal. Be a man, not a mouse," she joked and lovingly clung unto him, and then they both managed to finish their bread.

Everything was going smoothly and peacefully; there was no news of murder, theft, kidnapping or any disaster until the Saturday morning that marked the end to Jamal's and his wife's lives; it was totally untoward kismet for the couple.

Eyes were watching their movements but, they were so essentially clueless. Jamal and Ronke were inside their home, enjoying each other romantically. They then felt like exercising around the neighborhood. They dressed up to go out running and they began their exercise, passing one house then moving to the next until they reached the road's dead end, where they stopped. As they were headed back home, a group of men pulled up in a red vehicle and parked against the curb. There were five occupants in the car witnesses later confirmed. There were two in front and three in the back seats; all five wore masks. A barrage of bullets discharged from the red car, fatally dispatching five bullets into both Jamal and Ronke's bodies. The gang drove off well before the police and the ambulance arrived on the scene where the dead bodies lay. The police interviewed witnesses. Some claimed the killers were white and others said they were black, or dressed up in black and wearing black masks.

God knows and sees everything for He is the ubiquitous; the killers had perpetrated a motiveless crime. News of the killings aired around the nation and there were no particular suspects to put before the law, although the man who had recently moved in next door claimed to deal with couple after a fight between them two weeks before the incident, but making it clear that he did not mean any harm other than argumentative spoken words. The news spread quickly both through media and mouth-to-mouth. Malinda was hospitalized for emotional shock and spent an entire month in the hospital. A friend of hers cared for Anita.

By the time Malinda was discharged from the hospital, she knew that from then on, life would never be the same for her no matter how hard she tried not to remember it. The memory was etched indelibly in her mind. The mystery of Jamal and Ronke's deaths remained unsolved. The case went cold.

Malinda had her suspicions, though, believing everything that Derek told her about his co-workers who may have had something to do with it. There was, however, absolutely no evidence to prove it. Malinda wrote a letter of condolence to Ronke's family abroad and it was terrible for them all, although they had no choice but to let it go. That was how Bolaji got to stay in Nigeria for almost seventeen years before he could return back to the United States of America and started living a new life with his sister.

Anita, on the other hand, knew something was wrong, but her knowledge was inexact. All she realized was she never saw nor heard from them again. She entertained hopeful fantasies of the reunion they might have someday, always secretly hoping to see them, but resigning herself finally to the likelihood that she would not see them again in this world.

Two – Two and a half years later ...Atlanta, GA

It was blowing like balloons in the air, slamming things against the motionless poles and trees and at the same time splashing water on those cars left outside many garages.

Rebecca was searching for her daughter, Beauty, who had secretly crawled outside their house and was playing with moistened soil. Rebecca took her away from the blowing wind and locked the door to block her escape. Beauty sat helplessly and she was crying and feeling deprived. Frank had just got back from school and was waiting for his mother to finish cooking dinner. He sat on a chair pretending to do his homework, but his mind was really on the food. He wanted to ask if he could play with his younger sister, but he couldn't. He was supposed to be doing homework, so he said nothing. Rebecca left the food on the stove and was trying to hush her daughter with a lullaby; she tried hard with different songs and couldn't decide which noise was loudest, her crying baby or the rainstorm outside. She kept trying until the food got burnt on the stove.

The smoke alarm went off noisily, which furthered her irritation. If the alarm had been a real man, she would have wanted to slap his face into silence. There was smoke all over the living room and they were finding their way to other rooms in the house. She was mad at the stove, the food and the noise-making fire alarm. She had no other food left to cook. She told her son that there was no other choice than to rip off the burnt parts out of the potatoes. He agreed because he was truly famished.

"You stressed yourself at school; that's why you were so hungry," his mother claimed as she cut away the blackened spots from the potatoes, crying softly as she did so. She stared at the picture on the wall; it was of her husband, Lambda, who had just died some months ago. He was a very successful business man and a good husband for seven years before he met Keith Smith, a black friend. Rebecca would hate any of her family to associate him or herself with black people again, though she did not hate them as human beings she attested.

Frank asked her why she was crying; she told him he was too young to understand now, but that he would in time. She did though tell him to stay away from black friends. He told her he didn't really like them anyway, so he accepted the advice without question. Beauty was the only soul in the house who had no clue of this yet; she sat there on the floor, playing with her many toys and babbling in babyish gibberish.

Then a knock came at the door. It was one of Rebecca's old friends from Kansas City. Rebecca was so surprised to see her and at the same time wondered how she knew where she was living. Rachel met Mandy unexpectedly last week when she came to Atlanta for a week of fun and vacation; it had been some years since their departures from high school. Rebecca then asked her how she knew her house and Rachel told her she had met Mandy, another friend of hers who stayed in the same city with Rebecca. She had given her the directions to her place. Rebecca was overjoyed to see her. Rachel smelled the smoke and she couldn't keep it to herself, so she asked what had just happened in there. Rebecca explained. As she explained, Rebecca, frustrated, began watering her pretty face like a little girl who had lost her toys. Rachel was just trying to know all about her and her man provided she had gotten married to someone. Rebecca explained that she had been married to Rick Lambda for seven years, but that he had died some months ago. "Died?" Rachel yelled. "Yes, as in dead ...gone, forever... He will never come back to this life again," Rebecca said, still crying.

"Girl, I didn't even know you got married. What happened? Was he sick?" She wanted more explanation. She took a seat and asked Rebecca to do the same. Rebecca offered her something to drink, which she accepted gratefully. She was ready to hear the story from start to finish. Rebecca introduced

Frank to her, and she explained that she and her husband had Frank after three years of marriage and then they'd had Beauty not too long ago. She then asked Frank to go and play outside. He obeyed – glad to leave the ladies alone. He leapt up and headed for the door without hesitating.

"How is everything else, Rachel?" She smiled unhappily.

"You know. I am managing things," she replied.

"Tell me what happened to your husband," Rachel asked again.

"He got shot in a fight. There were six bullets; he had died almost instantly, though, the doctors had told her. It was too much for him to survive." She shed more tears.

"Stop crying, my friend" Rachel said, her voice rich with care.

"It was an all black club," Rebecca shared, revealing both disdain and discomfort.

"A black club, is that what you just said? Why did he go there?"

"I told him not to, but he didn't listen. He had a black friend named Keith Smith. I called him K.S."

She was then ready to tell the whole story to her friend. She stood up and lowered the volume of the television that Frank had left untouched before going outside. She sat back and continued. "Rick was very handsome man. Take a look at the photograph, there," she said, gesturing to his picture.

"He and I met ten years ago. We began dating a week after we met at a friend's birthday party. We seemed to be perfect for each other and we dated for three years before we finally tied the knot. He was very brilliant, very smart. He graduated with a degree in Business Administration. He got a job and he was lifted to the highest post before he later started his own business. Everything was under control. The business was thriving. He had many customers, both male and female. He was doing great with his family, me, our kids. Then there came this stupid man, Keith Smith, the black psycho who needed to go back to the wildest desert of animals or wherever it was he'd come from. Knowing Keith changed everything for Rick. God, I hate him. I swear if it takes me hundred years to meet him again, I will kill him. I promise. He has ruined everything for me, my joy, my life, my family..." Rebecca stammered as she continued to cry.

"Oh, I am so sorry; please stop crying," Rachel begged.

"It wasn't your fault. Why are you begging me?" she asked.

"You know, I felt like I brought back the sad memories."

"I wish I could kill him now. That's the only way I'd be happy. Rick started drinking immediately after he met him. I was so mad and confused the first day I knew. My husband didn't listen to my words. Had he known it would end this way, he would have followed my advice. Then he started gambling with his business money until everything was gone. He stayed out late at night. I remember so vividly. I was so frustrated that I jumped in front of him. I leaned against the door trying to block him from opening it. He shouted at me and even slapped my face when I didn't move away from the door," she confessed, sobbing. She poured another drink and quenched her thirst as she paused.

"He slapped you? Did you call the police?" Rachel asked angrily.

"No, I didn't."

"Why didn't you?" She accidently tipped over her glass.

Rebecca started mopping up the mess, confessing to Rachel that she couldn't call the police because she loved him so dearly.

"I knew if I called the police that he would go to jail," she explained.

"That would have been better than what happened, though," Rachel suggested.

"I know. It could saved his life, too, but I didn't know it then. He left angrily that day and that's the last time I got a chance to see his handsome face. The next day the police came to my door knocking and I let them in. They showed the pictures and I thought he got arrested because he was drunk the other night. They told me the horrible news, though and I couldn't believe it. I cried no, no, it couldn't be and I was led there. I witnessed his dead body at the morgue. I reached out to hold him, but they wouldn't allow it. I was speechless, knowing all the while that that idiot K.S. was behind everything, but the police said they'd been unable to locate him! The witnesses at the club said they were all playing friendly games till one of the black men started talking trash to the other guys. Rick was only trying to calm him down, but things got out of control. Keith pulled out a gun and started shooting. Others pulled theirs out, too. Rick was the only one who was unarmed – and he was shot six times by more than one weapon. The investigation is ongoing. She sobbed against her friend's shoulder. Rachel offered her tissues to dry her eyes.

"It is okay, my friend."

"Thank you. Thank you for listening. Oh, God! Sometimes I feel like I will go absolutely mad, so please, let's talk about you now. How have you been all these years?"

"You know, same old stuff. Nothing much has changed, not yet, anyway."

“What in the world, girl friend? Why are you talking like that?” Rebecca asked surprised.

“...talking like what?” She asked in return.

“Have you been hanging around black people, Rachel?”

“Oh yeah… I have four black friends. They are all down to earth, my friend. You just don’t know what you are missing.”

“Four black friends? What happened to white people?” Rebecca asked curiously.

“Nothing, I have both black and white friends at my place of residence.” She smiled as she jokingly pushed her shoulder. Rebecca then stood up and walked into the kitchen to get some paper towels.

"Well, you have learned something today from the story I shared with you. So think about it before it's too late". Rachel didn't care but she kept laughing instead. Rebecca told her that she would be heading to the bathroom to clean up and that afterwards they could both go to their old friend's house. Rachel then tuned into a music video. She was watching the channel along with Beauty, even though she had no clue of what the pictures were all about. Thirty minutes later and when Rebecca had finished with her bath, she then came into the general living room; she was not happy with the channel her friend was watching and then asked her if she was ready to go. Rachel offered to carry Beauty and Rebecca agreed with her, holding Frank by his hand and walking towards Rachel’s car. They all got in and drove off. Beauty was in the back seat, playing with her toys.

Rachel suggested taking the highway to Mandy's house. She should have listened to Rebecca and follow the main road instead of the highway; she got lost on the way.

“Look at the freaking map you have printed out," Rebecca said.

“She said four traffic lights and make a left turn at Georgia Avenue, then go three or four blocks and make a right turn onto Cardi street . . .” Rachel said, double checking the MapQuest route she’d printed out.

Rebecca was rolling her eyes and asked, “why did you follow highway when she had told you not to . . .?

“I thought it'd be faster! I am so sorry.” Rachel apologized.

"It's alright. We don't have anywhere to go today anyway, do we Frank?” asked Rebecca.

“Take your time,” Frank piped up, sounding more mature than his years.

Eventually, Rachel realized that they were now on their way to Savannah, Georgia. She turned around and it took them thirty-five minutes to get back on track towards Mandy’s.

"I just don't understand this state of yours; mine ain't like this. You take a highway; you get to where you are going faster. Here you take highway, and you get lost," she exclaimed.

“You got lost because you didn't know the way. It's simple,” Rebecca declared.

Later they laughed it off and in less than ten minutes they were set to meet up with Mandy. They pulled into her driveway and then walked up and knocked on her door. Mandy answered the door and invited them in.

“We were this close to calling 911,” she joked. "What took you so long?” Mandy showed them in and introduced them to four of her friends that neither Rebecca nor Rachel had ever met before. She brought out more bottled drinks and glasses to the table as she introduced Mandi, Rebecca, Sara and Nicole.

"Rachel, Rebecca, this is Sara. We met three weeks ago and she's become a good friend," Mandy explained as she was poured drinks into glass cups.

"Nice to meet you," Rachel said, stretching her right hand to shake Sara's.

"Pleasure meeting you both," said Sara to Rachel and Rebecca.

Rebecca had Beauty hoisted up on her left hip and called Frank over.

"What do you say to these ladies?" Rebecca asked her son.

"Nice to meet you all," Frank responded by rote.

"What a little gentleman," the ladies chimed.

"There's a swing set and a sandbox in the back yard if you'd like to go outside and play, Frank," Mandy offered as she strolled into the kitchen to prepare some snacks. Rebecca nodded that it was okay and Frank was off and out the back door like a shot.

"Rachel, I know you ain't talking to me. Are you?" Mandy asked.

"No Ma'am," Rachel replied jokingly.

"That's what I thought."

"Let me finish up our introductions," which Mandy did with swift efficiency.

"I hope that Mandy's told you all good things about the two of us," said Rebecca as she referred also to Rachel.

"Quit having qualms about yourself, Rebecca." Mandy said. As the sun moved across the sky towards the western horizon, the temperature dropped and a cool breeze blew in from the parlor windows.

Rebecca stepped outside to check on Frank who was playing assiduously with a bastion of dump trucks cars and other toys. Frank waved at his mother to indicate that he was fine and Rebecca was glad the back yard was fenced in and seemed safe. Beauty had drifted off to sleep and had been left to rest in the guest room.

Mandy finished the meal preparation and she set everything on the dining table. Everyone took a seat and prepared to enjoy the meal. They asked Rachel to lead them in prayer.

"Bless us oh Lord and these thy gifts, which we have received from thy glorious bounty. Amen."

A round of "Amens" sounded around the table as the ladies beheld the feast Mandy had prepared.

"Mmmmm. I knew this would be delicious, Mandy, but you've outdone yourself," Rebecca declared. Everyone agreed and ate voraciously and agreed with Rebecca.

A sleepy Beauty toddled into the room and Mandy quickly pulled up a chair with a booster seat for her.

"Are you hungry, little one?" Mandy asked.

As if prompted, Rebecca leapt to her feet and called Frank in to join them, which he did reluctantly – and who could blame him. He was the only boy in a house full of women.

After being joined by the children, Rachel and the others continued to eat. Beauty seemed especially enchanted with a lovely fruit salad made with miniature marshmallows. Rebecca made a mental note to get the recipe so that she could make it herself.

"You see. Beauty loves the salad, Rebecca." Rachel then continued eating. They meal concluded, all of the ladies helped to clear the table and put away the few leftovers. While they were discussing going to watch a newly released movie; Mandi asked Rebecca about Beauty's father. Rebecca tearfully shared her tale and the others commiserated.

***

Two weeks later, and around 7:00 am in the morning, Rebecca rushed Beauty to the hospital. She was running a fever. The medical center's architecture confused her. She finally located the pediatric block and hurried into the already full lobby. There were no seats left, so Rebecca had to stand, holding Beauty in her arms. She paced a bit, but didn’t want to lose her place in line. The queue wasn’t moving and Rebecca grew increasingly fretful. She started a conversation with another woman in line.

“Are you here for yourself, or for your little angel?” the woman asked.

“I came here for her,” Rebecca answered, gesturing to Beauty.

“Oh, what happened to her?” the woman inquired further.

“I don't even know what to call it yet. She’s running a very high temperature and also has diarrhea or something else. I just can't wait to get a doctor. This line..." She was interrupted.

“I know the freaking line ain't moving at all. I’ve been here for over an hour already,” she explained.

“Are you from here?” Rebecca asked the woman.

“Do I look like a Mexican or a Russian to you?” the woman replied.

“I’m sorry. I don't mean any offense. I mean here . . . in Atlanta,” Rebecca explained, smiling.

“Oh, you could have said that in the first place. No, I am not from Atlanta. I was born and raised in Baltimore,

Maryland and then moved to Detroit, Michigan. I just came here about three weeks ago," the woman said, smiling in return.

"I kind of noticed an accent, but couldn't place it, which is why I asked," Rebecca clarified.

As Rebecca continued to wait in line to see a doctor, she looked further ahead to see how many people were left before she could get a chance for Beauty to be seen. At that moment, however, a badly injured man was rushed in on a gurney. The man's head was a bloody, gory mess and Rebecca pulled a blanket up over Beauty's face to shield her from seeing the spectacle.

Everyone else was craning to see the injured man. The whole room fell silent. He was rushed into the emergency theater and rumors started to circulate. Some whispered that the man was a stunt double for a film that was being shot on location in Atlanta. Shortly thereafter, three separate gurneys were rushed past the line; there had been a terrible motor vehicle accident. Someone in line thought that they recognized one of the bodies as being a Mexican drug kingpin, but who knew? The queue was jostled and energized by the emergency arrivals, but hadn't budged an inch.

"I hate coming to hospital," shared the woman with whom Rebecca had been chatting.

"Absolutely – especially with the dire emergencies like the ones just rushed past us," Rebecca agreed.

"Well, this is the 'Emergency Room'," said the woman who finally introduced herself as Donna.

Rebecca sighed with resignation and Beauty squirmed in her arms, her fevered body uncomfortable.

"Look at her sharara," Donna whispered, nodding towards a nurse. "Why isn't she wearing a uniform?"

"Her?" Rebecca asked, pointing to a nurse in an informal dress.

"Yes. That's the one," she said.

They continued waiting for the line to move. Finally, there was a doctor ready to see Beauty. She was dehydrated and required a saline I.V. as well as several injections to bring her fever down. It took an additional three hours before Beauty was finally discharged. The doctor recommended that Rebecca should breast feed her regularly for at least three consecutive months to regain some of her system's lost nutrients. Rebecca waved goodbye to Donna as she passed her in the hallway on her way out of the treatment room.

***

Just when she thought things had been settled with Beauty and she'd put the baby to bed, Frank approached her and she was shocked to see her son's face was cut. Frank had gotten into a fight with two of his classmates. His injury was obvious, but not too serious, thankfully. Rebecca cleaned the wound with hydrogen peroxide, then added some antibacterial ointment before covering the cut with a band aid.

Rebecca wanted to take Frank back to school to make sure everything was settled with the misbehaving students. She drove to the school, parked and then headed to principal's office to resolve the matter. Her footsteps were audible and distinctive as she purposefully made her way to the principal's office. The principal heard her coming his way from down the hall and she met him in the doorway.

"Are you the principal?" Rebecca asked, her voice sharp.

"Yes, ma'am, I am. Ma'am I am the principal of this school, Mr. Peters." He smiled.

"It seems you're having some trouble doing your job," Rebecca said, miffed.

"Madam, what exactly is your point?" Peters was hurt, but managed to conceal it.

"Where were you when this happened to my son?

Answer me!" she demanded stridently.

"I can't. I just want to know." Her whole body was shaking.

"What is his name? I mean your son?" The principal asked her.

"Frank. Frank Lambda." She replied arrogantly.

"Okay ma'am. Lambda, Frank." He repeated the names as he was recording them.

"Please make sure you talk to Frank's teacher. You know it would be difficult for him if I went to court to file a lawsuit against him already. I am only trying to be nice, which is why I came here to let you know. And for the record, I am not mad at you. I am just reacting to the condition of my son. You know every parent would do that for a child. I don't want you to think maybe I am taking it out on you. Please talk to him." She had finally regained the patience that she'd previously lost.

"I understand. And I am glad that you decided not to go to court. I'd do the same thing you did for my kids. See I've got everything down on my file and it's going to be the first subject we are going to talk about on Monday morning. I'll talk not only to his homeroom teacher, but to all of the school's teachers. They need to know how to handle their students better," he said to her.

"I'm glad that he's not here right now. This whole thing could've gotten uglier. Look at his face for God's sake. How could a teacher let another student do that?" Her eyes were red again as she was looking at her son's face. The principal kept his patience and wisely recorded her complaint. He promised her, with his own words, that he would talk to the teacher involved. She left the school with Frank and they stopped at a grocery store on the way home. She'd been so upset that she felt ill for the rest of the day.

Time passed and Beauty reached the age old enough to attend kindergarten, so Rebecca enrolled her at one of the nearby schools. She took her to and from the school each day. One weekday she was coming back alone after accompanying Beauty to school, when a man, a jogger, actually, approached her from behind and started up a conversation with her. He jogged in place while he talked. He said he had never seen such a beautiful woman before seeing Rebecca. He added that he'd never seen her before, because surely he would remember. She didn't say a word, but just smiled.

"Did you just move here?" the man asked.

"Ten years ago, actually," she replied.

"Ten years! You are very funny. Ain't that long enough?" He smiled.

"Maybe or maybe not. It depends on what you think. Where are you running to now?" Rebecca asked.

"No place in particular. I just wanted to run through the neighborhood. I'm on sort of a zigzag route. Would you like to join me," he asked, teasingly.

"No way am I fixing to join you. I don't need to lose any pounds around my waist. Why do I need to run? I do exercise some, though, but only when I feel like it," she explained as she was parting away from him towards her place.

“Okay. Could I see you tomorrow or something? What's your number?” He continued jogging.

She stood, speechless.

“See you tomorrow!” He waved at her with great excitement.

Two weeks later, Rebecca was coming from a nearby store; she was footing it all the way home because it was a short walk. As she strolled, a vehicle approached from behind her. The driver honked the horn and she jumped off the road like a mad woman and was trying to recover from the shock. The driver rushed out of the car at once when he realized he had made a huge mistake by trying to surprise the poor lady. She stared madly when she saw him coming out of the car; she was then finding her feet. He was very embarrassed about the whole situation, and he apologized profusely.

“You…!” Rebecca uttered.

“I didn't mean to scare you, miss,” he pleaded.

“So what are we going to do now? I dropped half of my groceries when you startled me!”

“Can I foot the bill for the loss, perhaps?” he asked jovially.

“I don't know. You tell me.” She frowned.

“You know I am just playing. I'll pay for it.” He smiled.

“Really? You almost killed me!”

“I am so sorry, but do you mind if I ask why you’re hoofing it all the way home? Did something happen to your car? Come on. Get in the car,” he offered and she did so comfortably.

“My car is fine. I decided to foot it to the store because I felt like it. What do you care? Why are you so . . . .? She was interrupted.

“...trying to be nice?” He said, completing the statement.

“That’s not what I was going to say,” she lied.

"So you are trying to lose some pounds now?" He laughed out loud.

"No. Don't be silly."

"Are you in hurry?" he asked.

"Why do you ask?" She wanted to know what he had in his mind.

"I just think maybe a couple cups of coffee would be nice to share. What do you think?"

"First of all, I don't drink coffee at all. Second, if I were going to, it wouldn't be during lunchtime. I hope you know what time it is," she declared.

"Alright, let's go for lunch then. After that we can replace the groceries you lost. What do you say?" He was expecting and hoping for yes.

"Wait a minute. Is this a proposition? Because you men..." she paused.

"Men can be pigs. Yes. I admit it, but that doesn't mean that every act of kindness is a disguise for an effort to get into your panties," he said.

"Ain't that what you're doing it for? You're all the same," she claimed.

"Maybe you're right. We're different though, in everything." He explained.

"Let's keep things straight first. Do I know you or do you know me?" she asked meaningfully.

"Yeah, you know me. And I do know you. Remember? We met two weeks ago," he joked.

"We met two weeks ago? That doesn't mean you know me. I mean, do you know me? Do you know what kind of woman I am? What pisses me off? What makes me happy or sad? And I don't know anything about you either," she told him.

"That's alright. As time goes by, we will learn those things from each other. What's your name any way?" he asked.

"Too late... What's yours?" she asked in return.

"Hudson. Hudson Simon..." he said.

"Cute." She loved the name.

"Excuse me; did I hear the word, 'cute?'" He was happy to hear that.

"I meant what kind of name that is," she fibbed, jokingly. They reached the grocery store and purchased the items Rebecca had lost. She told him she needed to also pick Frank and Beauty up from school and he agreed. They picked Beauty up first and then did the same for Frank. The two kids sat in the back seat of the car behind Rebecca in the passenger seat and Hudson in the driver's seat up front.

"Mummy, who is your new friend?" Frank asked.

"My name is Hudson, Frank," he replied.

"Quit being smart, Frank…" Rebecca warned.

"Hi, Hudson. I'm Beauty," she said demurely.

"Nice to meet you, Beauty..." Hudson said to her.

Together, they all went out to a well-known barbecue restaurant and ate until they were full. There was no rush, but once they were finished, it was time to head back home. Hudson pulled into the drive way and helped the kids to get out the car safely. He spoke softly to Rebecca and they exchanged their digits. Hudson's smile nearly knocked her off her feet. She entered her house and got ready to prepare a bedtime snack for her kids. Minutes later she got everything ready. They said their prayers first and then began eating although they were still full from their dinner earlier.

"Mummy, where is daddy?" Beauty asked her mother.

"I told you he was the herald of the city and he had gone to bring news from abroad." She tried those words.

“He was?" Beauty asked.

“Yes, he was," she said to her daughter.

“What's he doing now?" Beauty asked.

“Didn’t I tell what he was doing already? How many times do I have to tell you, Beauty?" she replied.

“You said 'he was'," Beauty argued.

“Did I say ‘he was?’ Oh, I am sorry.” She tried to convince her.

“Where exactly did he go to? Japan?" Frank asked.

“Hush now, Frank. You know where he went. Don't you?" Rebecca said.

“No, I don't." Frank denied it.

“Yes, you do. I have told you many times," she said.

“Ok Beauty, dad's been dead for a long time,” Frank blurted, letting the cat out of the bag.

“No, he isn’t. Don't listen to him Beauty?” Rebecca argued.

“Is Hudson my dad?” Beauty then asked.

“No. He's just a friend,” she replied.

“I like him. Is he going to be here soon?” She asked as she swallowing more ice cream.

“Quit it Beauty. I don't want him here,” Rebecca said, lying. They finished their ice cream; Frank went out to play with friends and Beauty wandered over to the television and started watching cartoons with great enjoyment.

Later that night, the phone rang three times and it was not picked up or answered by anyone. Beauty yelled for Frank, but he refused to answer the call and instead yelled for his mother. "Mummy, the phone is ringing," Frank shouted. Rebecca, who had been in the shower, jumped at, wrapped her hair with a towel and rushed into the bedroom to pick up the phone. It was Hudson: "Hi!" he said on the phone. She replied in kind. Hudson cut to the chase quickly and asked Rebecca to go out on a date with him on Saturday. She was thrilled and accepted.

After putting the kids to bed, Rebecca retired for the evening, smiling to herself as she thought about Hudson. On Saturday morning, the mailbox was filled to bursting with bills: water, electricity, phone and credit cards were all inside the box, but there was something else. Rebecca noticed it right away. It was a sweet greeting card – from Hudson. She felt like a princess but she had qualms about the situation she was trying to get herself into, so she called her friends, Mandy first and then Rachel. They both advised her to follow her instincts and move on from Rick's death. She decided then to follow their advice. She went into her bedroom and placed the picture of her deceased husband on her chest. She was then crying alone. She pondered how Rick’s relationship with K.S. had lead to deceit, violence and death.

She wept until her eyes were red. Even though she bathed her face with water, her eyes remained red. The kids asked about her red eyes; they knew it had to do with something and she replied that she was just having bad time. She promised them she was going to be fine. They ate and everything was cool. She picked up the phone and entered Hudson’s numbers and dialed. Hudson answered on the first ring, saying, "Hello?” She told him that she appreciated the greeting card and she loved it very much. He explained that something had come up and wanted to know if they could hang out the next day instead. She couldn't refuse the offer. “Yes! Yes!!” she said on the phone and she kept laughing instead, and that was how it all started.

Three – Two Years Later....Chattanooga, TN

Yes ma'am, I'm coming," Anita replied. Malinda was recovering from a short illness and she lay on the bed waiting for Anita to bring the cup full of water she would use to swallow the medication that she was given at the hospital. Her blood pressure was high. She had suffered blood loss from malaria, and was now diabetic. She was too lean to even walk without a supporting stick, which was Anita. Anita was an excellent care giver; she tried her best even as a youngster, nursing her grandmother exactly as her mother would have done if she had still been alive. "Here you go," she said, giving the glass of water to her. Malinda managed to get up and she took her medicine. "God Bless you, my little princess," Malinda said to Anita. Anita asked Malinda what she would like to eat, but Malinda wasn't hungry. She opted to take a nap because she'd had difficulty sleeping the previous night.

Malinda tried to sleep, but then heard a knock on her front door. Anita heard it, too.

"Let me see who it is," Anita suggested.

"Ok, go ahead." Malinda agreed.

Anita opened the door and addressed the woman standing there as "madam." She responded and was led in. She rushed towards her sister and was terribly depressed by the poor condition of her health. "Carlina, is it you?" Malinda said. "What happened to you?" Carlina asked impatiently. She asked her who about the young lady and Malinda told her she was the daughter of Jamal and Ronke. "It's been too long... you know,"

Carlina exclaimed. Carlina had served twelve years in jail due to a wrongful accusation.

"I heard that you'd been released," Malinda said, "which is why I sent for you."

"Thanks be to God..." Anita offered Carlina a soda and she accepted. Carlina asked how long Malinda had been battling with the sickness and she replied it was quite long. She sat back, set the bottle of soda down, and then felt Malinda's body temperature with her hands. Afterwards, Carlina and Anita helped Malinda to the bathroom. Carlina urged Malinda to take a cool bath to help bring her temperature down. Malinda remarked that the bath felt good and thanked her sister and granddaughter, who then helped Malinda back to bed.

Anita had been delayed going to Nashville to start high school; it was her grandmother's idea to go over there for her high school program. She had to wait around to make sure she was alright before she could go. Since Carlina had come to the rescue, she'd soon be able to start taking classes. She could have waited for at least a week before going, but the letter she received in the mail changed everything. It said that classes would resume the following day, which was Monday. She informed Carlina and she agreed to take her. They needed to go to Wal-Mart for school supplies. It took Anita only twenty minutes to gather everything she needed, then she and Carlina headed home for other preparations; she was extremely excited to be a high school girl.

Monday morning, after Malinda had been bathed and fed, Anita got ready to hit the road. How fun it would be for Anita if she had knew how to drive. She would definitely prefer going alone, playing loud music uninterrupted while driving, but she had yet to fulfill that dream. She put her things in the car, jumped into the front seat and then buckled up while at the same time glancing at the front mirror to see how glamorous she was. Carlina asked her if she had gotten everything she needed and she answered in the affirmative. Carlina pulled out of the drive way and headed towards the highway that led to Nashville, Tennessee.

Less than five minutes after they entered freeway traffic, they ran into a traffic jam; there'd been an accident and traffic was backed up for miles. They both hated this, but they had no options other than waiting along with everyone else. Very slowly, they were able to creep forward, although they were held up in the traffic for almost an hour. They finally arrived and Anita met other young teens with whom she would later attend the University of Tennessee at Chattanooga. These young girls were later known around the school for their beauty, smartness and hard work. She would be told later and after three years of high school that her grandmother had died of hypertension.

Four- Fifteen years later....Return of Bolaji to the US

Anita had grown now to take over her parents' properties; she had everything from their lawyer later when her grandmother passed on to heaven above. She wore some of her mother's nicer clothing, but did not wear Ronke's necklaces; she did not really like jewelry. She glanced in a mirror just like her mother would always do and then sluggishly walked out of the bathroom. She instructed herself to cook and she did. She kept looking at the clock as if she was expecting somebody. May be she was. Was it her boyfriend? She found the envelope again and removed the enclosed letter inside it. She kept smiling as she reread each word from the letter, however, she was impatient to see her brother, Bolaji. He was coming back to America. She was informed that the flight would be at the airport by twelve o'clock midnight. It was only one o'clock pm in the afternoon and she needed to take it slow. "For almost seventeen years I couldn't see my blood brother... what? He stayed in that poor land, Africa. God I've watched and seen Africa, mostly on Discovery Channel programs. They are suffering over there. The first thing I must do is to take him to the hospital for treatment. Then he needs to eat a lot." She kept talking to herself. "I wondered how he even learned to write a letter in English? I'll ask him many questions anyway. Come on twelve o'clock," she urged. Amidst these thoughts, her phone rang. She picked it up and it was her boyfriend, Karl. He was calling from his home town of Louisville, Kentucky. They had semester break from school, so he got a chance to go home.

"Hello, my princess!" He gently pronounced those words as if they were cooking in the oven. "Wow! When did you learn to talk like that?" She asked. He replied, "Just now, baby." "Baby...?" She asked. "You are my baby, babe." He explained. "What are you doing?" Karl asked. "Nothing, I am just getting prepared for my brother's visit."

"I wish I could see you! C'mon. Try. Jump through the phone!"

"You just want to get into my panties!" she declared, laughing.

"No, babe. Trust me it ain't for that, but I'm not ruling it out, either."

Another call was coming from the other line. It was stagnantly peeping and refused to fade away. She had no other choice but to take the call.

"Baby, I've got to go," she said in hurry.

"Why? Is he there already?" he asked, joking.

"Yeah, he's right here. Come on, Karl. There is another call waiting on the other line. Please it's Tasha. Please. I love you. Okay, call me back. Will you?" She asked.

"You bet I will," he answered.

"That's my man. I love you," she added.

"I love you, too. Bye." He kissed the phone.

"Hello," Anita said.

"Wud up, girl…?" Tasha asked.

"Wud up," Anita replied. Tasha asked her and Anita told her that she was getting ready for her brother. She said she was excited and happy to see him again after the seventeen years they spent apart. Tasha promised to inform and invite other friends whenever Anita suggested that they throw a welcome party for her brother. Tasha was delighted.

Throwing the party for her brother would not bother her; she had no problem with money at all. Her parents left hundreds of thousands of dollars in the bank for them along with four cars plus their life insurance money. All in all, it amounted to millions of dollars. She paid her school fees early without even being worried about queuing for financial aid. She was just a lucky girl who was born with a silver spoon in her mouth. Though she was told not to be extravagant, she never denied herself anything that she truly wanted.

She had more than enough clothes and shoes, not to mention underwear and bras. She was such a lucky girl who had been blessed with the life of Riley and she indeed utilized the privilege to the extent that people envied her parents' fortune.

She and her brother would be enjoying the privilege without an expiry date. It is not their fault that they would be enjoying the best of life forever. It was kismet. The money in the bank and those assets would be eternal if they could manage them well.

Three hours later, Anita decided to go shopping at Wal-Mart for her brother. She was then contemplating what to buy for him. She made up her mind not to buy clothes or shoes until after he had arrived because she didn't know what size would fit him. She just went for other things instead. Inside the store, she searched through the wrist watches and chose one she hoped he'd like. She also purchased toothpaste, tooth picks, an electric toothbrush, after shave, lotion, powders, deodorant and a blue sponge. She then moved her nearly full cart to the counter for scanning. "All of this is for my brother," she said smiling. "He's coming from Africa." "Nigeria," she added. She stopped talking, though, when she realized that no one was really listening to her. She paid and left the place. She got home at exactly eight o'clock p.m.

She forgot to buy some drinks but she didn't bother going back. She thought she would go back with her brother when he arrived later. Anita dozed on the couch, but luckily, she had set the alarm, which caused her to jump up. According to the clock, it was 11:45 p.m. She took off like a shot to the garage, where she started the car and made way for the airport.

It was a good thing that Bolaji had sent pictures to her along with his letters, otherwise it would have been difficult for Anita to recognize him. His face hadn't changed; it bore Nigerian traditional one-one marks, which she thought were cute. She introduced herself as his older blood sister and they shared a lovely embrace, then went to her car and loaded his baggage inside. She took him back to the store and bought some juice. Everything was so strange to him and the lights were shining and glowing. He noticed that his sister always stopped at the street lights without even seeing anyone that asked for the stop. He couldn't ask, but later he found out that she didn't stop when those lights were green. Additional confusion then emerged. She stopped again at the four ways stop signs. She told him that one needed to stop to avoid collision. He understood better now.

They emptied the car and moved everything into the house. Everything seemed brand new in Bolaji's eyes. He hit the wall by mistake and it made sound; he hit it again deliberately and the wall voiced out again and he realized it was made up of wood. He was so confused. Nigerian walls were made of concrete. She showed the bathroom to him and he wasted no time to take his bath. He brushed with the electric toothbrush that his sister bought. Everything was so strange to him. She had prepared some scrambled eggs with salad before he could come out of the bathroom. He joined his sister later at the dining table. They shared the eggs and the salad and Anita found that she had many questions that she was dying to ask him.

"How was the journey, Bolaji?" Anita asked, initiating the conversation.

"God, it was long!" he replied, adding, "It took at least twenty four hours more or less."

"You must be tired of sitting, then," she said.

"I survived it at last. Thanks to God we didn't crash," he said, laughing aloud and showing his white teeth.

"Thanks to God! How is everybody back there?" she asked.

"They are all fine. You are talking just like those people at the airport," he said as he was chewing the green leaf lettuce. "We were born here, remember. Half Nigerian and half

American, even though I've never been to Nigeria," she explained briskly. "Sometimes it's hard to understand what some of your words mean.

"The accent is different, yes. I have to pay more attention to hear your words as well," Bolaji confessed.

"Keep talking. I love your accent. Don't worry. You will understand soon. It won't take you long. You will learn fast by watching TV, especially the B.E.T. network. I know you have no clue what I am talking about, but you'll find out soon enough," she assured him.

"I can't believe this isn't a dream. Finally, I have met my blood sister," he said.

"Thanks to God Almighty…" He kept searching through the bags.

Amidst their conversation, there was an incoming call. What? Two o'clock in the early morning? Who was it? It was Karl again. She asked her brother to answer the call and he did. He couldn't understand Karl though, and told his sister that it was somebody that his name started with K because he couldn't pronounce the word right. She sensed it right away and she said, "Oh! It's Karl. Give it to me." She then had the phone.

"Hello!" Karl yelled out.

"What the heck, lover boy? Ain't it too late at this time?" Anita said.

"I knew it. I had been calling for long time and you didn't pick it up. Whazzup? Who is there with you anyway?" He was so curious.

"My new boyfriend... I knew you had one too. I thought it'd be cool..." She was just messing with him.

"What? Are you going crazy? What are you saying?" He was hurt emotionally.

"I was just kidding. He's my brother, Bolaji. I told you, he's joining me today. He had been living with grandma in Nigeria for almost seventeen years. She just passed away lately. He arrived today. Do you wanna say hi to him...?" She was then giving the phone back to her brother when the line faded away. Bolaji said hello repeatedly and heard no answer. They waited again for several minutes and the phone rang.

"Your phone messed up," Anita claimed.

"Not mine, yours. Give the phone to your brother," he demanded.

"Hello, how are you?" Bolaji asked Karl.

"I am fine, you? How was the trip?" Karl asked.

"The journey was long, but I made it here anyway," Bolaji answered.

Then he gave the phone back to his sister and she commenced having a conversation with her man.

"Did you say he came from Africa?" Karl asked.

"Mmmhmmm... Why?" she asked in return.

"He can speak English, though the accent is different," he explained.

"That's how I felt, too. It's a good thing anyway. I am proud of him," she said with pride.

"Anyway, I just wanted to check on my beautiful girl. By the way, don't do what you said earlier. I don't have any other girl besides you. I did before I met you. We broke up for two weeks before I met you. So please don't do anything stupid." He begged her and he was very much serious about what he just said.

"Mark my words. I was just playing, that's all," she said, laughing.

"Sleep tight my angel. I love you. Bye, now," Karl said, kissing the phone again.

"I love you, too. Sweet dreams, all about me, though," she added.

She then placed the phone back on the dining table. Their eyes met at once and they burst out laughing. She told him that was her boyfriend. She wanted to ask him if he had any girlfriend, but she couldn't. Perhaps she was hesitant or too shy to ask. They kept talking for an additional three hours, but then couldn't fight it any longer; they had to go to bed. They did get up from the table and then went to their separate bedrooms.

Anita woke up by eight-thirty in the morning; she rushed to the kitchen and made her brother some breakfast. She set the food on the table and went to knock on her brother's door. She hit it two times and he finally answered. He replied, saying, "Good Morning," and opened the door and then bent down with respect, his knees nearly hitting the floor to greet his sister. She stopped him from doing it and asked, "What was that for?" He explained that it was a sign of respect to elders. He furthered his comments that a younger one must respect the elder and also listen to his or her words. She was surprised by the cultural differences and was eager to learn more afterwards.

Bolaji wasn't satisfied with just three and a half hours of sleep. He insisted that he had to go back to bed and she let him. She then sat on the longest couch in the sitting room, trying to enjoy the morning shows on the TV. She was watching TV and at the same time trying to enjoy some hours of sleep. She was moving into it gently when her phone rang, disturbing her. She should have turned the phone off, she thought to herself. She ignored it first, but then the phone rang again. She finally answered the phone with the laziest voice.

Lamanika asked what was wrong and she told her nothing had really happened, but she was sleepy that was all. Lamanika reminded her that they had a party scheduled for five thirty. The party was just eight and half hours away when she called. She told her she would be getting ready as soon as she could. Bolaji was so tired and kept himself in bed for as long as he could. The only thing he'd done other than sleep during the past six hours was to visit the bathroom. Would he ever get up and hang around his sister? She bought hamburgers from a restaurant and invited her brother to join her for lunch. He didn't care for the taste of the burgers, but ate them anyway because he didn't want to hurt her feelings. He wasted no time again and he went straight back to the bed.

"I am so sleepy," he said. His sister understood how hard it was for him and she couldn't complain or argue about it. She decided to take advantage of sleeping for an hour before the arrival of her party people. She had asked her boyfriend to join them, but Karl was unsure. Maybe he would show up, maybe not. She would find out later. I guess men likes to surprise their women and it works most of the time.

Five o'clock arrived. She had cleaned her body thoroughly, put on some fetching make up, applied romantic perfume and had set food and drinks out on the table. She sat down, watching the MTV music program. She was laughing with no one but herself when she heard the doorbell. She opened the door and they were all shouting welcome to one another and embracing. She let them in and they were making very friendly noises. They were four black girls of different cities - Lamanika, Tamika, Tasha and Jessica and white girl named Tracy; she was a friend to Tasha by then. They were supposed to go home for the break, but they didn't. Anita offered them some drinks at first. They were talking about school and everything else. Anita and her friends were all sophomores at present. She was now twenty one years old and her brother was only eighteen. They were all having a good time, except for Tracy, who felt that she had been discriminated against by Anita because she didn't respond to everything she had been saying to her. She would face somebody else instead of answering her questions.

"Anita, where is your brother? I want to meet him," Tasha said to Anita.

"You know he had a long journey. He's asleep now. Maybe next time. I don't wanna wake him up," Anita replied.

"Okay, cool. I hope he's cute," Tasha said.

"He's super cute. Do you want to see his pictures?" Anita asked them all.

"Oh yeah, let's see," Lamanika enthused.

"Let's see them," Tasha said, chiming in.

"I'll be right back," Anita said as she was walking into her room. She peeped at her brother's room to see if he had woken up, but he was still in bed, fast asleep. She then took the pictures to her friends.

Tracy had stretched her hands out first to collect some of the pictures, but Anita ignored her, which hurt her feelings.

"Here you go, y'all." Anita said as she gave them the pictures.

"Wow! Super cute…." Tamika uttered, completely taken in.

"Thanks to you..." Anita appreciated the comment.

"Not bad at all," Tasha added and she stole one picture secretly.

"What did you mean? You want to go out with him?" Lamanika asked her.

"Nope. I was just saying my opinion about the picture. That's all. Why would I want to go out with Anita's brother?"

Tasha asked. "…because he's cute and very sexy. I know you love those qualities," Anita said, answering her own question.

"Speak or forever retain your silence. If you love the boy or just fall in love, let it be known and his sister would help. Words of advice, from me to you..." Tamika said with laughter.

"Why do you think I would do such thing? I can't help anybody hooking up with my brother, heck no." Anita declared.

She walked up to the refrigerator to grab more drinks. She found some and was taking them to the table. Then a surprising knock was heard on the door. Lamanika rushed to the door and opened it. She smiled as she opened the door and then he entered. Anita couldn't believe her eyes. She was quiet for seconds and then said she didn't think he could make it that very day. They hugged each other and Karl uttered some romantic words into her ears. She spanked him and said he was so naughty and nasty.

"Hum, did you miss me?" Karl said as he kissed her.

"Don't even ask. You can tell." Anita replied, hugging him.

"Get a room, lover birds," Tasha said.

"For what…? You are only jealous; stop hating on us, miss," Anita replied to her. She was then laughing.

"Thanks for coming out today, everyone. Now we will eat and drink, and then later we can dance to some music," she added.

"Perfect idea, I love it. I wanted to shake what my mother gave me anyway," Jessica said as she was heading to the dining area. They all sat at the dining room table facing one another except Anita and her boyfriend, Karl, who sat beside each other.

"My brother brought some African music. We should try it out to dance to. Anyone want to? What do you think, people?" Anita asked.

"No way…! African Music, Mandingo or what…?" Tasha burst laughing.

"Don't mind her. We will," Lamanika said to Anita.

"Speak for yourself, Manika. I won't," she declared.

"I know she's been trying to be funny lately," Anita said against Tasha.

She continued, saying, "I know you all have never seen all of these strange foods before. We call it 'dodo.' It's fried plantain, which is an African name, of course. That's what my baby brother said."

"What's that made from, baby?" Karl asked her.

"Plantains are big bananas; it's not what you're thinking. They're not the same, but they're very delicious. Here, taste it," Anita replied back to him.

"Girl, you're trying to kill somebody. This is too spicy. What did you put on it?" Tasha asked complaining gently.

"Red peppers... Keep eating or drink some water. Quit complaining." Anita said as she was picking up the so-called 'dodo' with her fork.

"Red peppers? I've never eaten them before, but it's all good," Karl added.

Tracy acknowledged the meal even though she was white; she kept the praise to her soul though, because she knew Anita would not listen to her comments anyway. They finished the meal and then rested for some minutes by watching programs on the television.

Then Tasha told them that she brought a disc album of Lil Flip so they could dance to it. They all danced very well and shed sweat until they felt as if they couldn't possibly keep on moving. They enjoyed one another's company and had fun, but they were also ready now to wrap up the evening and go home.

School would be resuming the next day. The four girls left and Karl then kissed his girlfriend before he could finally say good bye. Anita went to bed afterwards.

The following morning, she woke up earlier to get prepared for school. She cooked the usual breakfast and left her brother's meal on the table for him. She then drove off in one of their cars. Bolaji woke up and couldn't find his sister, but he did find his breakfast. He ate everything and then got busy with television programs. He watched BET then MTV and later the USA network. He kept changing channels like a little child. Then he finally stayed with the USA network. He was then enjoying a movie from the channel when a post master rang the bell to deliver a package. He opened the door and signed for the package. The package bore his sister's name; he kept the package in a safe place and kept enjoying the show. Then at noon, his big sister called to check on him; he answered the phone and told her he was doing great. She said she was heading to class and she would see him soon. She asked if a mail delivery man was there yet and he said no, because he thought they called them post men or post masters only. He felt lonely and then flipped the channel to BET to enjoy some new tracks and videos.

Anita was coming out of class when Lamanika yelled her name. They both then headed to the University Center to meet with other friends. Anita's eyes searched every nook and cranny of the place and she could see Tasha and Tamika mocking one innocent boy who was mentally deficient. She stopped them from doing it again and she was angry with both of them. They finally let the matter dwindle into oblivion and proceeded to the cafeteria. They sat there talking about different subjects. Then one of them claimed she was tired of the semester already and she couldn't wait to get out. Anita then reminded her that the school just resumed back today from a week break. They laughed the matter off later. Lamanika and Anita had classes in less than fifteen minutes and they left the others at the cafeteria. Tasha would be having class an hour later. Anita waved at Lamanika when they separated to head towards their individual classes. Anita hated calculus class and wished she could skip it, but she knew she had to take it, so she carried on to class.

The professor happened to be one of the best ones at the University of Tennessee-Chattanooga. He didn't really believe that mathematics was hard to learn or master. He concluded that every topic he taught would be easy and that students would be interested. He greeted the class and began his trick. For many students, mathematics is nothing but a trick. The ridiculous answers that come out at the end of most stressful assignments could be zero or one. Most students believed that mathematics was all a lie and a waste of time. Some claimed that the knowledge of calculus was not needed while calculating how much money one has at hand or in the bank. Maybe they're right.

Anita didn’t really care. The professor was so incredibly smart and fast and the topic was as hard as meat bones. One sample work took over the whole chalk board. She wanted to ask questions, but she was reluctant and somehow felt ashamed. She didn't want to be the only one amongst all of the students who didn't understand the topic. And it's funny that none of them did actually have the whole comprehensive idea of the topic. They just paid mute attention and pretended that it was quite easy and understandable. Anita had lost interest in the whole thing and she was just waiting for the class to end. The professor finished the last examples and asked three times if anyone had any questions. No one dared to say a word and he agreed they understood and he was happy to leave the class after the full ninety minutes that it lasted. As if she had been appointed to head an organization, Anita jumped out her seat and bolted for the door, then went off running towards the Lupton library. She met her boyfriend at the public passage that's connected to the library and begged him to wait for her till she came out. She wanted to check out a book. She was given some assignments from the book and they needed to be completed within two days. She had the book and came out smiling. Then Karl held her hand and they were walking towards the parking lot.

He said that he too had an assignment that should be submitted the next day. Anita was happy to hear that, because she was in hurry to be home with her brother and she didn't want to tell Karl that she had no time for him. She knew he would be hurt emotionally. They exchanged simple kisses and each drove off in different directions.

Rainstorms and squalls scared the motorists and traffic slowed. Most of the day's events were rained out unexpectedly because there were no reports or signs of rain prior to that day. It had just begun after she had joined the main road, about two miles away from the school parking lots. She should have complied with the road signs and regulations and slowed down on the road, but she neglected the road conditions and was speeding to get home sooner.

There was a deluge of rain and she could barely see. This was the case for all of those who shared the road with her. Anita didn't want to slow down, even though the visibility was so poor. That's when she heard the sirens. She pulled over to make way for the ambulance and its flashing lights of red, blue and yellow. Her chest felt tense and she was afraid. That's when she noticed the police car that had pulled up behind her. "Freaking police ..." she hissed. The police officer came to the driver's side of her car. He motioned that she should roll the window down and show him her license and proof of insurance. She did as she was told. He informed her that she had committed a speeding violation. He wrote her a ticket and lectured her about driving in inclement weather. He then informed her that she had two choices to choose from; she could either pay the ticket fee or appear before the judge on the assigned date and contest it. Then they both vacated the scene. She pulled into the driveway when she got home. Rain was gushing down the driveway. She found a stick to push away some trash that was caught up in the water and then remembered to bring her plastic garbage bin to the curb so that the trash service could pick it up early the next morning. She opened the door with her keys and entered.

The first thing her eyes focused on as soon as she stepped in was the package. She stared at it for more a moment then went off to search for her brother. She expected him to be watching television, but found him fast asleep. She put down her bag and then placed the ticket on the table. A loud crack of thunder from the storm startled Anita and woke Bolaji. "When did the mail delivery man come?" she asked him. "What?" he asked.

"The package, the delivery man… Don't you know they mean the same thing? The delivery man, the post man, it doesn't matter," she explained.

"I didn't know that. How was the lecture?" he asked.

"Terrible. I hate mathematics," she replied as she drank some water.

"I don't know why so many students hate mathematics that much," said Bolaji, adding, "I can probably help. What's the topic?" he asked, although he was making his way to the bathroom.

She waited until he returned, then asked, "How are you are going to help?"

"It's calculus," she said.

"That's fine," he replied. "What was it, integration or differentiation?" he asked.

"I don't know. Let's skip it for now. Right now I'm upset about this speeding ticket. I really hate the police," she said.

"Why, aren't they the friends of the city? Don't hate them," he said.

"I know. I've got to go to the court next month," she told him.

"Go to court? For what?" He was scared to hear the word court.

"For the ticket. I mean, I can pay for it if I want to, but I won't. I'll go to court instead. I wasn't speeding that much and he claimed I was above the limit. I wish I could have smacked him!"

"What would happen at the court?" Bolaji asked her.

"Nothing, I don't know. I might be free or forced to pay." She smiled.

"You look just like our mother. I can tell from her picture." He smiled.

"You resemble our Dad more. I miss them a lot," she added, staring at their pictures on the wall.

"It's okay. We have each other," he said, encouraging her.

“Do you have a job? I mean do you work anywhere? You know, a money job?” he asked.

“A job…? Heck no. Neither of us needs to work until after we actually graduate from college, and then you can apply for a job you would like to do but not necessarily for money, though everybody works for money. I mean you can just work if you want, but not because you need the money. Do you know what I'm saying? Our parents were very rich and they left money behind for both of us. I'll give you your documents and account number tomorrow morning.”

She then stood up and walked to the package to pick it up.

“Here you go. I ordered it for you. It’s all yours.” She gave him the package.

“Thanks. What is in here?” he asked, smiling.

“I am not going to tell you. Open it and find out,” she said and smiled.

“Oh my God I love them. God Bless you, Anita.” He hugged her.

“Surprise is good sometimes, but perhaps not all the time.”

The package contained brand new shoes, shirts and glasses, both ordinary and sun glasses. She told him they should go out and eat dinner if the rain stops. He agreed. He packed his gifts back in their box then retired to his room feeling joyful.

“Are we going now?” Bolaji asked Anita. The rain had finally stopped. They entered the garage, got into the car and headed for a nearby restaurant. "Table for two..." Anita told the hostess as they entered the restaurant.

She gave the tickets to them and they were led to their seats. The assigned server served them first glasses of water, and then returned shortly to ask for their orders. Anita told him what they'd both like after consulting her brother.

They conversed, waiting for the food to arrive.

Bolaji hesitated before dining on his fish and Anita dove into her spaghetti. They ate their fill then paid the bill and left a generous tip for their server.

***

Weeks passed by and Bolaji grew ill. He was burning up with fever and Anita rushed him to the hospital. She was grateful that she'd signed him onto her insurance policy when she learned he had a terrible sinus infection and would require hospitalization. She stayed with him, missing her classes. It hurt her to see him ill. She prayed that God would rain abundant health on her brother. Tamika called to learn why she was absent from school and was sorry to learn Bolaji was ill.

A nurse entered the room and administered a shot. She told Anita that there was no reason to cry. Hours passed and Bolaji woke up from sleep, thanking his sister for being such an attentive caregiver. He took more injections throughout the day. They were finally allowed to go home when it was quite late, just after ten p.m.

She made sure her brother made his way safely to bed and wished him goodnight before retiring herself to get some much needed rest.

Morning arrived and it was quiet outside and the breeze was light and scented with jasmine. Anita opened the door and there was Karl, who had been so worried that he came to check on her.

He realized she was upset with him and on his feet, he schemed to breeze through his explanation. She kept knocking back his hands every time he wrapped them around her while talking. He begged her and explained he was too busy at school. Then the anger faded away and she smiled. They happily exchanged kisses and she offered him something to eat. Bolaji had woken up and he was walking towards the living room. When he met his sister's boyfriend for the first time, they shook hands and Bolaji finally rested himself on the longest couch. They tuned into the BET channel, watching previously recorded programs, “106” and “Park Top Ten Live.” Anita finished cooking breakfast and summoned them to join her in the dinette area. Bolaji and Karl both followed her lead. They all got seated at the table, said their prayers and then enjoyed the lovely omelets that Anita had made. The television remained on and rap videos filled with hot babes dominated the screen. The singers who made it to the countdown did so with the help of fans' votes. They were watching the videos and at the same time killing two birds with one stone, eating as well.

“You like what you see, huh?” Karl said, purposely fooling with Bolaji.

“What, those girls in the videos? Heck no…!” He answered Karl.

“Admit it. It’s your fantasy to have one of them girls one day?” Karl said, smirking foolishly.

“Man, I’m still sick from a sinus infection. I’m not going to argue about this. There’s really no answer anyway. Not my fantasy. I hope to meet my soul mate and to be successful in this world,” he told him.

"I forgot that you don't have TV in Africa. My bad..." Karl claimed.

"Karl, would you quit with all that stupid...?" Anita tried to warn him.

"Anita, let him live. Don't stop him. This is man to man. First of all we have TVs, radios, phones, cars, satellites and everything you can think of. And second, I watched many videos while I was in Nigeria, Africa," Bolaji explained.

"Do you know any rappers? Do you know Tupac?" Karl asked, testing him.

"Better than you do. I know him, love him and I am swimming in his legacy. What do you know about Pac? I dreamt about him because I loved him to death. If you want me to play his music and tracks now I can do that. We might be able to know who the true fan really is. I'll rap Pac words just like him, brother. Don't try me man. I'll mime Pac any day," Bolaji said, laughing at Karl.

"What? You dreamt about him? You are such a liar. I don't buy that," Karl said, being cantankerous.

"I swear to God, I saw the man, Tupac, in my dream and we talked. It doesn't really matter to me if you believe it or you don't. Nigeria is not a suffering country at all. We live life just like you people here in the United States," Bolaji explained to him.

"Do you all have artists; singers, rappers, actors, movie stars, paparazzi, and everything?" he asked again.

"You are very slow, I am very sorry to say it. That question is like asking you this: Do your women all have two breasts? How stupid would that sound, huh?" Bolaji asked him.

"Slow down, brother, my African brother, Mandingo." He was hurt.

“Alright kids, knock it off and find something else to do. Go ahead and play pool or tennis or something. I'll go with you all,” Anita told them both. They left for the game house and decided to play pool against each other. Karl won three times and he kept laughing over Bolaji's losses. Karl called it a day and he decided to go home, so he left. Bolaji headed to his room to take nap if he could and Anita went to the bathroom to take her shower so that she could go out with her friends. She took her time getting ready; there was no one waiting on her. She minimized her jewelry and later stepped out after she had glanced into the mirror several times. She looked fabulous.

***

On June 22nd, and around seven o'clock a.m. all of Anita’s friends arrived. This was the day of her court appearance for the speeding ticket she’d received during the storm. They all came in Tamika's car and had decided together that they’d sacrifice their classes that day. Karl arrived later and he joined the ladies who were in the living room with Bolaji. The girls were all dressed to the nines. Anita seemed oddly calm; she wasn’t having any qualms at all. They finally arrived at the courthouse around 7:30 am, and they were heading to the screen, to see which room her name was assigned to, when a guy audibly pronounced Anita's name and Karl looked back immediately to see who it was. Anita gave the guy the ugliest look he’d ever seen. Now she was getting antsy. Karl calmed her down at last and led her to the assigned courtroom. They were passed by sixteen inmates, all with handcuffs and shackles around their ankles, all heading to a different courtroom to face their judgments. Anita and her friends felt uncomfortable passing the convicts and hurried into her assigned courtroom.

The room had been filled up silently and everyone waited silently for Judge Barbara Cathy to call them to order.

Everyone kept communicating with eyes and minds and the silence seemed to last interminably. Finally, at 9:15 a.m., the bailiff announced that the Honorable Judge Barbara Cathy had arrived. Everyone rose and stood silently as she entered the room. Anita and her cohort waited while others took their turns before the judge. At last it was Anita's turn.

Her name was heard and she walked toward the counter. She did the same thing that everyone had been doing; she made her oath and was ready to face the judgment. "How will you plead, guilty or not guilty?" Judge Cathy asked.

"Guilty, your honor…" She answered.

"Did you comply with the officer who stopped you?" she asked.

"Yes, I did your honor," Anita answered.

"Do you have insurance?" she asked.

"Yes, your honor. Here is it," she said, showing the proof of insurance to the Judge.

"What were you thinking that day? Why were you speeding on a wet road? You didn't even care about your life. You are too young to die, you know," the judge advised her.

"Your honor, I was only hurrying back home to take care of my younger brother. He was sick and there was no one to take care of him," she lied.

"Your mother was gone, then?" the judge asked her.

"No, your honor... she and my father are deceased."

"Oh, I am sorry to hear that. Where were you coming from that day?" she asked.

"I was coming from school, you honor," she answered correctly.

“I’ll tell you what. Since this is your first ticket, I'll sentence you to attend driving school in lieu of a fine. You have ninety days to complete the class. It's just a one day class. Now I want you to be careful on the roads and slow down even when the road is dry. Got it?” she asked.

“Got it, your honor.” she was full of happiness at the moment. They all rushed out happily and they exchanged hugs with one another, then took the elevator to the lower level, entered the car and headed back home. After twenty minutes on the road, they finally got to her crib and all departed from Anita's house with their cars after saying their good-byes.

After drinking some juice, Anita announced that she needed to get to work on her calculus homework and shared that she had an exam at the beginning of next week. I want to make sure I at least pass with a C,” she muttered if she was so scared to face the examination.

“Why not earn an A, sister…? Why set your sites so low?” Bolaji asked, challenging her.

“…because I know my capability, my brother. I know that I will barely make a C even if I work hard...” she declared.

“What if I can help? I know the subject, and most topics in it,” he claimed.

“Get out of here. You haven't even started college yet. How the heck would you know freaking calculus? I don't even trust your knowledge of algebra. Maybe you have got magic though. That's the only way you could do it on this earth and I heard you are all very good at black magic in Africa. Is that true?” she asked.

“I don't know. What's magic anyway?” he asked in return.

“I don't know. How would I know what magic is?” she answered incompletely.

“You should know because you're saying something about it. Why are you talking about it if you don’t know what you’re talking about?” he asked.

“Well, you win. Let me go and bring the text book. What do you say?” she asked.

“I say nothing. Go ahead and bring it. I’m not scared.”

She brought out the book with optimistic faith that it would overpower her brother's confidence. She placed the book on the table and opened it to the pages her professor had assigned. Bolaji seemed undaunted and simply smiled.

He solved all of the questions quickly and she was flabbergasted. She could barely believe what he’d done and she was simultaneously proud of him. She then made herself busy with different examples and the practical questions that her brother solved for her. He didn't have any exam to face, so he kept watching television programs for the rest of the day.

Monday morning happened to be the D-day for Anita and the other students who would be taking the examination that she faced. She realized that she had no appetite and decided not to bother with breakfast before heading to school. However, her brother surprised her by making breakfast, which she suddenly realized she was very hungry for, so she cleaned her plate and headed out the door.

The stereo car was left tuned in to Power 94.3 FM; the morning show was airing at the time, but she didn't really pay attention to it. She only had one thing on her mind and that was her examination. She edged up, speeding above the legal limit, but this time there were no police en route to catch her, so she rushed to park then ran to the assigned room even though she’d beaten the ETA time she’d established for herself. She quickly found a seat and sat down in it. Other students continued to straggle in. It seemed, finally, that the auditorium was full and complete silence reigned for some time before the professor's arrival.

"Morning everybody!" the professor greeted all of his students at once and without wasting a second of the useful minutes, he distributed the papers to them all. "Read the instructions very well and don't you rush; you have two solid hours to complete the questions," he advised them.

"If any one has any questions to ask, please don't be hesitant. Okay, everyone, please take a look at question number seven. I wanted to write 'square root of x to the power of negative x over two-thirds. You should all change it now. Can you all see it?" He asked again. "Ok, start everybody." He began walking to his seat after getting his students started on the exam.

There she was, full of tension before turning the paper up to see each question distinctly. Suddenly, though, her anxiety turned to happiness. She blessed her brother quickly with prayers; everything he'd taught her surfaced unexpectedly and she began battling each equation with strong confidence. She was given two hours to finish the questions, but she was almost done with them all in just thirty-five minutes; it seemed that the harder the question appeared to be, the more her confidence increased, multiplying to overcome her initial trepidation. She couldn't help but smile. Her eyes met the professor's and they both smiled. She stood up afterwards and every other student believed she could not understand any of the questions and that might be why she was leaving early. Although she was reluctant to stand up, the first amongst hundreds of students, it wouldn't help her to sit around doing nothing, plus the professor wouldn't let her anyway. She gave the paper to him and he asked her to go through the paper again to make sure there was no mistakes. She insisted that everything was perfectly answered. The professor opened a page of the answer sheet just to scan through it; he couldn't support his eyes with everything that was written on the paper. He called her back immediately after she had made it to the edge of the class room wall. She listened to the call and she was suddenly scared. She crossed quickly back to the professor's desk, eager to hear what he had to say to her.

"What's your name?" The professor asked while he was still dazed by the unexpected brilliance she'd exhibited on paper.

"Anita, Jamal... Jamal is my last name." she answered. "Who is your tutor?" he asked.

"No one in particular, but my brother just taught me some things yesterday," she replied.

"What level is your brother? Is he schooling here?" he asked. "He will be. He hasn't started yet. He's at home right now. Maybe next year though..." she replied.

"You actually dazzle up those questions impressively. I thought you couldn't do it, but that's why you finished so early, about fifty minutes. You are very good." He was so proud of her. He later let her go and she left with optimistic belief of having at least a C or B if not an A-minus.

Anita headed to the University Center for lunch and she met her friends there. Some had just finished with their papers as well. She ordered a hamburger from the cook when it was her turn. She filled up her cup with orange juice and walked towards the place where her friends already saved a seat for her. Tasha had some French fries which she was sharing with Tamika, Jessica just drinking her soda and Lamanika was halfway divided between dining and reading a book she held open on the table. The conversation was flowing smoothly, not only among these friends, but with the all mouths present at the

University Center; the entire place was full of laughter, which gradually dissipated tension from the exam. Perhaps it would emerge back immediately upon entering the examination rooms. Karl was heading to the UC center as well when he had just finished with his first paper. He would be tackling the second one in less than thirty minutes. He joined the girls after exchanging friendly words with each and helping himself to bites from his girl's burger. He told his girl he had to leave soon because he would be facing yet another examination. She agreed and he was left, waving to her with a smile as he departed.

"I love your man," Lamanika said innocently without lust. "Excuse the heck out of me! What did you say, Manika?" Anita said, almost losing it.

"Not that kind of love. I mean I have respect for him. Not that I wanna date him or go out with him. He is your man," she emphasized, clearing the air.

"Oh, my bad... I can't play like that," she explained.

"I hear you. I told you I wanna meet your brother, didn't I?" Tasha asked.

"What do you want me to do? Didn't you all meet several times already? I can't tell him that my friend wants to meet him. He is my younger brother," she replied.

"Well, I guess I have to come over one day. He's very cute," she declared.

"Suit yourself old friend. You are more than welcome anytime," Anita told her.

"Can I come too?" Tamika asked Anita.

"I should come, too; what do you think?" Lamanika asked, voicing the same question.

"You know what I think? I think you are all crazy. My brother ain't no playa. He's for real and he only needs one lucky girl, just one," she declared briskly.

"You know I love everything about your brother! That's why you need to back me up, his cutest marks, his cheeks, his accent and everything. I love me somebody like that. He should be a male model," Tasha remarked, fantasizing.

"Well good luck to you. You have got to be honest with him because he doesn't need a lying girl that will be sleeping around with different men," Anita said.

"Trust me. I am a virgin, Anita." Tasha laughed as she said it.

"I can tell. Perhaps you meant you were once a virgin, but not anymore," she said.

"Anyway I am single; I am honest and very pretty." She added. "I am beautiful and sweet to boot. Why are you always so full of yourself?" Jessica challenged Tasha.

"I am just saying it. I know everyone here is beautiful, relax!" she replied.

"You all need to keep your voices down and let me concentrate on my book. Why are you all acting like a bunch of kindergarteners at recess?" Lamanika asked, then faced her book.

"Well, Miss I -am-busy-reading-my-book, this ain't no library. You need to get on your pretty butt and find your way to the designed area for reading, which is the library. You aren't the only one doing exams or tests; we're doing it too," Tasha replied jovially.

"Why are you all constantly caught up in drama all the time? How about we talk about something else? Maybe funny movies or commercials, anybody?" Anita threw out the question.

Then suddenly it came to suppress the hullabaloo, a fatal beating of a male student by gang members on a boy who was caught flirting or had slept with one of their girls.

Cobra butted his head with a hammer and Leo continued striking him in his belly repeatedly. The victim made a calling-for-help noise and hundreds of legs ran to the scene and they could not believe the public spectacle, the eyesore they were witnessing. Their hands were automatically and temporarily paralyzed by fear. They all stood there happily unhappy, watching the extreme three on one beating the gang was giving to this helpless boy. Cobra, as the leader of the other two gangs-members, Leo and Samuel, ordered them to continue the beating till the victim would have not a single breath of life left in him. The news was luckily spread to school security officers and they came exigently to rescue him from the gang. The gang members vacated the scene as soon as they heard the sirens blowing and the boy was rushed to the hospital. Anita told her friends she would be leaving for her next class and they all departed the place and headed to their classes to face the next paper.

Bolaji opened the door without being instructed; he had peeped in to see her pulling into the drive way. She entered rigorously, her eyes severely altered and sunk deeply into their sockets; her lips betrayed her suffering and she was experiencing complete soreness throughout every part of her body. She was so tired. Her brother was curious to know what was wrong with her; she dropped her bag, rushed to the fridge, grabbed a soda and she was enjoying it after when she had laid down on the couch. She removed her upper clothes to take advantage of the air coming from the fan and she shut her eyes for just a minute. She then turned on the TV. Bolaji kept quiet and watching the dramatic role she seemed to be was exploring, then he decided to interrupt and ask what happened to her.

"Anita, what the heck happened to you?" he asked.

"You won't understand, brother," she replied.

"You should tell me. I'll understand," he said.

"Too much work at school, my brother," she said and began drinking the remaining soda as if the can was already empty.

"What did you all do, break wood or something?" Bolaji asked her again.

"What did you mean break wood? What wood?" she asked him back.

"That's the only thing I know would be heavy on someone," he said.

"Shut up! You are being crazy lately," she said again and she set the can down to the table. She was then staring at the pictures on the television.

"How were the papers anyway?" Bolaji asked again.

"What papers?" she asked, trying to provoke him.

"You know what I mean. Quit being silly..." he said.

"Nope, I won't. You might wanna explain better," she jested. "I meant your examination," he explained with a single word. "What examination, my little brother…?" she mimicked his accent with the purpose of making fun of him.

"Forget you, then. Don't even worry about it," he said.

"Now you're getting angry, aren't you? I'm just playing with you. The exam was perfectly fine. And the mathematics examination was totally unbelievable. Even the professor couldn't believe it and he asked who my tutor..."

"And what did you tell him," Bolaji interrupted.

"I said 'my brother.' He asked further if you were attending UTC already and I said you haven't started yet. He was impressed with your work; I know he would be happy to meet you," Anita suggested.

"I don't know about that. I love to be anonymous. I don't want that sort of attention. How did you do then? Do you think you nailed it?"

"I am pretty sure I will get C or B, perhaps an A minus."

"So you didn't even know how well you did, do you?"

"Shut up! I finished the all of the questions in fifty minutes."

"How long did he give to you all?"

"Two hours. That's why he was so surprised with my quickness and..."

"You better get a straight A!"

"I think I will. Just wait!"

"Good for you. I just want you to make me proud of you, in everything."

"You know what, I'll be done with my tests next Friday and we can go out together like big sister, little brother. I almost forgot that there will be a stage play for the public at UTC after the exam. I hope it won't change. Would you like to go?" she asked.

"As long as it's staged, I'll be there. I have never watched a live play before."

"You are going to love it. I haven't seen it yet, but it'll be good," she promised.

"Well, how about ID? I don't have one yet, remember?" Bolaji reminded her.

"What ID are you talking about?"

"School ID of course. Isn't it going to be needed at the gate?"

"Nah, it's for both our school and the public; no ID is required, my brother. We will pay less though with our school IDs and you all will pay more." She stopped with a smile.

"Oh, that's how it's going to be? Discrimination! That's right. That's exactly what I call it. Why do you students have to pay less? This ain't no Payless Shoes," he joked.

"We don't call it discrimination; we call it prestige or something of that kind."

"Prestigious admittance, huh..?" he asked.

"Sort of…" she answered.

Anita looked up at the wall clock and it displayed: 4:03, along with the day's date and current temperature.

"Shit," she said, "the program already freaking started." She picked up the TV's remote and changed the channel from BET to TNT prestissimo- she loved the program tremendously. It charmed her. Bolaji told her he had cooked some rice with beans and also fried plantains; she asked him to please bring some to her since she was so engrossed in her program on TV. She didn't want to miss anymore than she already had – the first three minutes. He complied and the two enjoyed the show. She kept laughing and having conversation with the program like a mad woman. Her brother just stared at her and he was wondering what might be causing her weird behavior. She didn't really pay any attention at all to her brother's presence. The program kept distracting her with different tricks and she was utterly rapt in amusement. She barely responded to her brother's words while he was asking her some questions, then her phone rang. She picked it up to say hello and it faded away. She was happy it happened because she knew it would disturb her concentration on the program she was watching anyway. Five more minutes had added to those that had been spent and the ring tone sang again; she felt some annoying pains inside her womb, down beneath her belly and she switched off the phone quickly to keep up with the program; it had been one of her friends calling. Bolaji asked why she had to switch off the phone, but this led to an argument; he ignored her and he left angrily for his room. She sat there until the end of the second round of the program. She walked towards her brother's door and knocked on it repeatedly.

"Open the door. Come on Bolaji! Open the door. I am begging to you. Please... Bolaji!"

"Go away, you irrational lady. Leave me alone."

"Pleeeeeeeeeeese Bolaji, open the door. I just want to apologize"

"...apologize for what? You didn't do anything wrong, did you?"

"I know I was wrong. See? I am on my knees begging you to forgive me."

"You are forgiven. You know you are the queen and you have ultimate power. I forgave you without a thought. Go on with your arbitrary rule. You shall reign longer than you could ever imagine possible. I'll say my piece any time I feel that you want to abuse your power and it would be nice if you would listen."

"Okay, open the door."

"I am on the bed; I can't get up."

"Get up and open the door, Bolaji. Please..."

"See you tomorrow."

"Open up the freaking door! Now!"

"No way… Not with that attitude. I can't, sister, I am sorry."

"I am just playing. I don't mean it that way. Open the door."

"I'm naked, I can't open it."

"So what…? Open up the door. I'm your sister."

"You are my sister, not my girlfriend. This is a grown man now, not little baby Bolaji anymore. Don't you understand? Only my girlfriend is allowed to see me nude now, provided I have a girlfriend."

"You are going to make me cry. Please open the door. You said you forgave me. Didn't you?"

"That's right I said it."

"Then open it if you mean it."

"Lady, you are so persistent. I'm coming."

"Thanks and I love you."

"Yeah, right... " He opened the door for her. "Stop lying to me. This ain't no two year old kid anymore. What did you mean you love me?"

"You are so silly. You are my brother and I love you very much more than everything in this world. You know that, don't you?"

"What about Karl?"

"Stop being silly, Bolaji. That's different. My love for you has no comparison to anyone. We came out of the same womb; we shared the same blood and parents. I have you forever as my lovely brother. Karl is my boyfriend, maybe my future husband. You know friends; boyfriends or girlfriends could be gone and never come back, but siblings are forever. I love you."

"And I love you, too."

They hugged each other and she told him she would be going out soon after when she finished with her bath.

"Say hi to him for me," he laughed.

"Who…? You are so crazy Bolaji. I am not going to him. Who is him?" She was laughing. "Aren't you talking about Karl?"

"That's exactly where you are going to. Ain't nobody talking about no Karl. Did I? I didn't remember saying such a name."

"You are stupid. I'm going to hang out with my friends."

"And I said, 'Say hi to 'em.'" He quoted his own words.

"Whatever. Do you wanna go?"

"No, I am good. I don't want to be a disturbance. Have fun and don't fight. More importantly don't forget to use it."

"Use what, Psycho?"

"Condoms of course ... I should have said don't forget to use them instead of saying 'use it.' Perhaps you would go more than the necessary rounds I could ever think of."

"What are you? Nuts? Quit being nosy about somebody else's business…who told you we are having sex with each other?"

"Nobody. Your actions revealed it and I am not so young as to not notice it." Bolaji was rubbing his hands against each other.

"I can't believe I am actually discussing this with you."

"Neither do I. It's a good thing though; you know sharing is caring."

"You have lost your mind. I am going to be late, Bolaji."

"I understand. Peace out, big sister."

"Understand what?" She smiled.

"Nothing, go ahead and take your bath. He should be waiting now."

"You are so impossible. I don't care what you think. See ya," she waved and walked away from his door.

She then jumped into the shower room, took her bath thoroughly and applied some glossy make up on her face. Like mother, like daughter; she looked so beautiful. She was then contemplating what kind of dress she should put on. She knew that Karl always loved seeing her in tight, but snug jeans, or any other long pants that would squeeze her buttocks together to pop them up in a sexy and fantastic manner. She changed into three different pairs of pants before she finally made up her mind to wear a striped pair. An hour later, she finally got ready and drove off in a Chrysler Sebring convertible. She was listening to her favorite artist's song when the phone rang. She should have placed it where it would be easy for her to grab, but she forgot to do so and she almost hit another car while searching for the phone. The caller had left her angry messages complaining that he was left in limbo and he was losing hope for her attendance or appearance. It was too late for her when she later found the hidden cell phone; she burst into laughter when she listened to the messages and she called him back urgently. The guy was seriously angry with her and he didn't pick up his phone. She thought he had gone out or something, but she then changed her mind and she was heading to her friends' dormitory instead.

"Oh my living G.O.D..! Look who is here." Tamika uttered in confusion.

"Girl…! Turn around. Let me see that thing. Wow! He's a lucky man." Tasha said as she was squeezing Anita's butt with her hands.

"Quit it Tasha. You are gay," Anita said.

"No, I am not," she said defensively.

"Why are you grabbing my booty now? Don't you have your own?" she asked.

"By the way, Karl called. He said he was waiting on you or something," Jessica said while playing with her teddy bear.

"Are you for real?"

"Why must I be playing like that? I am dead serious," she replied.

“Okay, everybody... Nice seeing you again. I’ll holla at you all later. I've got to go. My man will kill me for not showing up," she said as she was opening the door to step outside the dormitory. They all walked her to her car and she drove off after she had waved adieu to each one.

Anita arrived at Karl’s to find him outdoors in the waning light. He accompanied her inside and took his place on the couch. He was dressed up and had been waiting for the phone to ring, but the phone didn't ring anymore for the golden girl who showed her beautiful face was the one he’d been waiting to hear from. She apologized for the delay and promised to be a changed woman. He let her romantic words and kisses dissipate his anger and they both wasted no time stepping out. First they went to a restaurant and then finally to a cinema to watch one of the latest releases, which had received rave reviews.

***

Three weeks later and a week after final exams, Anita took Bolaji to watch the live play she had told him four weeks ago. She paid for seven tickets at the entrance - hers, Bolaji's, Karl's and her friends'. They were then heading into the theatre to find their seats. They sat lined-up one after the other and each was idly busy with popcorn and peanuts before the arrival of the actors. Ten minutes prior to the beginning of the play, three thuggish looking men entered the theater and the whole room was forced into silence. These men were Cobra, Leo Martin and Samuel Edie, the gang members responsible for the beating death at the university. Everybody was afraid of them and no one would ever dare to confront them on any action; they were labeled as both untouchable and invincible.

"Who are these people?" Bolaji asked curiously.

"Shush! They are very bad, Bolaji. Keep it quiet," she warned him.

Then one of the actors came out to give a welcome speech before the play began. Justin Milan, the actor, gave an impressive speech that foretold the excellent story of the play. Everyone had the belief that the play would be good provided the guy was actually in it. Cobra, on the other hand, noticed something different in Justin; he saw the quality of being a thug in him and he had it in mind that he would invite him to join his club. The lights went down and the whole room was totally dim and the dim lights then cast a shadow on the first actor who stepped out to the stage. He spoke words of mourning, very poetic, and he was indeed with a mournful face that could easily convince anyone's sensibility to discern that he'd suffered a recent familial loss.

He pretended that he was in his room on the stage; he was slamming some invisible items against an imaginary wall to exhibit the pain he felt for the loss of the person. The audience felt pain as well in responding to this actor; he was a fine actor. It didn't stop there, however; it started from its storage and sprang from his face down to the chest to wet his singlet. The tears made the situation so real and so convincing that most of the female audience members didn't even realize their tears had worn the make up from their faces. The lights faded again and a woman was tied down captive on a chair with strong ropes and tight knots before the lights went back up.

What a surprise! The audience wondered how fast they did this. She was helpless and at the same time hopeless; she would never think that a single soul could notice her being in the hidden place. It was sometimes hard to get the picture right on the stage; each attendant would have to find ways of visualizing the incidence in each act or plot. They imagined that the place would be somehow both dark and unsafe. To that, a blind man who was then working with the aid of rod towards the place he couldn't see as the audience sensed it. The blind man heard the voice of the crying woman and he paused to listen more carefully, to be sure that he was not deaf but blind. He was guided by her voice and he untied the lady safely. The man told the lady he was just a wandering man and he had accepted his kismet. He asked the lady to help him to the nearby motel or any gas station. The lady didn't do what he asked for, though. She took him straight to her house where she was then treated as a ghost. The first actor who staged his role happened to be her husband and he thought she had died, which was the reason for his words in the beginning. She had been kidnapped by his friends who were willing to demand some amount of money from him by threatening him with his wife's soul. He kept stepping back as she moved closer to him. She was so angry that she wished she could simply kill herself straight away. The closer she got to him the angrier she grew. Afterward, he admitted her being a living soul other than a ghost. She told him everything and she added that she wanted him to accept the blind man as their roommate. She called the man in and it was another bombshell that the blind man was actually a brother to her husband who had got been lost for several years. The play ended well and the kidnappers were arrested and sentenced to twenty three years in prison.

The lights faded again and then lit back up again with an assemblage of all of the actors on stage at the same time and the audience gave them a round of applause. The audience’s rears were all sore from such long hours of sitting. Everyone finally stood to step out of the theatre and find his way home.

Cobra kept applauding as Justin walking towards the door to step out. He told him he displayed a brilliant performance on stage and he didn't beat around the bush before letting it be known that he was hoping to recruit him as a new member in his gang. Leo added his words as well, and Samuel also tried to convince him. Stupidly, Justin accepted their invitation. He didn't realize he had just made a bad decision that would change his life negatively forever. They all left to have drinks and party.

Bolaji had been dying to learn how to drive since coming to America, but his sister's schedule thwarted his plans. He persuaded her that he was going to learn how to drive right now or she should forget about it forever. She agreed and grabbed the keys to one of their cars and she was ready to show him the way.

"The first thing you do is to put your leg on the brake pedal. Then start the car," Anita said pointing towards the ignition. "Okay, the ignition is rolling. What else?"

"Always make sure that you check mirrors, front, right and left and make sure that there is nothing behind you like an upcoming car before you can pull out of the drive way," she advised.

"Everything is being checked, then. What else?"

"Then apply gas."

"What gas?"

"On the right side of your foot, press it." "Okay, I've got you."

"Then remove your leg slowly from the brake pedal. Not so fast! I said slowly!"

"Okay, I got it."

Then he continued driving on under the supervision of his sister. He completed about eight miles drive before returning home and he thanked his sister for the support. The next thing he needed to do was to study for the computerized road safety test. She already had the book that he needed and right away he busied himself with it. He temporarily divorced watching television for six hours to study the book and he felt like he would be named the king of a war after just six hours of study. He kept reciting and repeating each word from the book like someone who had been busying with the support of a team of coaches. Anita took the book away from him lest he be distracted. She was helpful and eager to take him for his test. He told Anita that he was ready to go take the test the next morning and she didn't argue about it. Her co-operation exhilarated his mind and he felt that he couldn't wait for morning to arrive.

Anita then decided to cook something for the lunch. She pulled yams out of the cupboard, peeled off their skins, washed them and sliced them, then put them all in a pot that was half-way full of water and set the pot on the stove. She sprinkled some salt on the yams. For the best combination, she cooked beans with them and she mixed them with palm oil. After two hours of mixtures, everything was deliciously ready to eat. With a rare but delightful face, he verbally complimented his sister for spending so much of her time in the kitchen and giving him that delicious meal. He joked that he would pay her for the cooking and they laughed it off. They had got seated at the dining table and the prayers had been said as well before a knock out storm blew with lights unexpectedly; the windows were left opened and Bolaji rushed out to close the car's windows. Before he could step out of the car, it had caught him and doused his clothes. He didn't have to rush anymore and therefore took his time to close the windows. He was so soaking wet outside that Anita had to ask him to come inside. He took off his wet clothes and joined his sister back at the dining table.

"Gosh! This food has hypnotized me..."

"Save your jokes, Bolaji."

"I am dead serious. You are very good at cooking. I should hire you to teach my girlfriend how to cook." He continued to drink. "Thanks, anyway. Tell me something, who is your girlfriend?"

"You of course... I told Karl already that we were going to fight over you one day."

"You are always being funny. Seriously, who is she?"

"Seriously, it is you, my dear sister."

"Not on your wish list."

"I'll show you. It's my number one item on my wish list. Why are you asking me this anyway? Have you seen me going out with somebody? You know I am always indoors with myself or sometimes with you. So who do you expect to be my girlfriend? You, of course and you said it already that you love me, didn't you, darling?"

"You are stupid. I love you as my brother, not as a lover. And would you be my boyfriend if...?"

"I would if I could..."

"You must have lost your mind. Why would you want to do such a stupid thing?"

"...because you are beautiful. And to do stupid things with a beautiful woman it actually worth it. I had made up my mind that I should choose you as my lovely girl."

"You do need a therapist for real. I can't believe this."

"I have already talked to a therapist and he told me to do it if that was what my mind wanted to do. And I decided to go for it." He pretended to be very serious.

"God, can somebody help me out here with this psycho brother of mine? You are not serious about this, are you?"

"I told you before and I'll again, I am in love with you."

"Okay, I should go into my room now before you totally lose your mind." She was disturbed by his attitude.

"Why are you running from me? You don't want me? I thought you loved me."

"As my brother, psycho... I can't sit with you anymore. You need to go out and find your own girl, not your sister. I have friends you can choose from."

"I don't want them. It is you I want, no one else. Will you marry me?"

He knelt down with a playful intention.

"Not in this life. Get up and quit being a foolish boy."

"You have turned into a psycho. I am going to call psycho therapist tomorrow"

"For what exactly…? That ain't necessary. I am ok. There is nothing wrong with me."

"That's what you think. Your behavior makes no sense. None at all."

"I am just playing with you. You know that's against the will of God."

"You sounded far too serious to me. I thought you really meant it. I was like what had gotten into you? Good thing you didn't lose your mind."

"That would be the most stupid thing a man would do, you know. How comfortable will it be for a man to be sleeping with his own sister? That's so disgusting."

"Some people would, my brother. There is nothing rare to living in this country or many other parts of the world. You know, things like that have been known to happen from time to time," Anita declared.

"May God never turn me into something I don't want in my life," Bolaji prayed.

"I will say amen to that. And me too, I pray for myself," she added.

"Well, I am going to take a nap. Tell her I am sleeping if she comes," he joked.

"Tell who?"

"My girlfriend of course, the pretty girl who came here the other time... Don't you remember that beautiful face?" he asked.

"You wish..."

"Not that I wish sister. I already have. Can't you see the difference?"

"I know you have been hypnotized with the sleep not with the meal. You are acting like a drunken man now. Go ahead and have your nap," she counseled him.

"I am sane not insane, adviser. Thanks to you anyway. I'll be going...to bed."

"Sweet dreams..."

"...about what, you…?"

"There you go again, stupid. Just go inside and shut up."

"Alright, see ya tomorrow morning. I love you!" He shut the door.

"I love you too." She then walked into her room.

At twelve midnight, he woke up and he couldn't go to sleep anymore, so he turned on the TV and tuned in to MTV to watch some music videos. Then for some minutes, the network aired a local commercial that featured one of his future girlfriend's friends, Tracy. He didn't know this yet, but he wished he could meet her one day just to tell her he was a big fan of hers. The clock rolled for three and half hours and he was now sleepy again. He went to bed and this time he was far gone for good. He dreamt of a beautiful white girl three times and they were both having conversation when his sister came innocently to interrupt his dreams by knocking on his door to reveal that the morning had arrived outdoors. He jumped up at once and he was trying to recap the déjà vu; it was late to recall everything. The only thing that was still living in his brain was that the girl was white, though extremely beautiful in his dream. He was full of excitement. He took his bath, observed prayer and he was ready for the driving test. His sister also had a score to settle; she needed to go to driving school for the ticket she had some weeks ago. They both dressed up and drove separate cars, following each other. She drove ahead of him so that she would be going to her class after showing the place to Bolaji. She blew horns and pointed to show the place to him. He waved at her and they mentally exchanged good luck wishes with each other.

He presented his photo ID and social security card to the front desk attendant and he was given some paper work to complete prior to taking the examination. He filled out the papers and took them back to the lady; he was then given his number to listen for. He waited for another ten minutes and it would be his turn next. He went to the assigned window for second identification and was asked if he was there only for a single test or both the computer test and the driving test; he answered that he would love to take both. He was tested on vision first and he passed above average. The lady set the screen for him and he was let alone to tackle those questions on the screen one after the other. He did all the questions with his own ability and it stopped when he reached number twenty-four because he missed nothing from number one to the former number. He was then taken to the road for his road test. Luckily, he passed the test; he was so tense he feared that he would fail. He was then given a driver's license with his name and picture being inked indelibly and laminated. He left with joy and drove like he had been cruising the roads for decades. His sister got home before he did. He pulled into the driveway and parked his car. He checked the mail box and picked up its contents. Searching through the mail with his eyes not looking up, he accidentally hit and tripped over a stone on the pavement. It was painful, but it did not bleed.

"You're back already?" Bolaji asked her while he was sitting down.

"Yes, about thirty minutes ago. I thought you would call me. What happened?"

"Nothing. I know my way home. How was your class?" he asked further.

"Perfectly fine, everything had been cleared. Yours…?"

"I failed. I have to go back in three weeks..."

"Three weeks! How many questions did you miss? I don't believe you."

"You shouldn't. I passed it," he said, grinning.

"And the driving too?"

"Everything, sister... Aren't you proud of me.?"

"Of course I am proud of you. Good job. Now you can go to where ever you want or be dying to go."

"For real…? What about strip clubs?" he asked jokingly.

"I don't care. It's your choice. You have grown up now," she said.

"Okay, I will make sure I utilize my newly given prerogative. I'll be partying like I want, dressing as I wish; I will have total freedom in every way. God Bless America and every other part of the world." He jumped up and down.

"Well, don't abuse your freedoms. That is my advice to you."

"Word…? Thanks my big sister. I love you so much. I mean as my sister." He smiled with a sardonic look.

"I appreciate it. I love you too. What do you say if we go out and celebrate your success? Do you want to go?"

"Hell, yeah, I wanna go. Why wouldn't I? I would be stupid to object."

"Okay, give me a minute to get ready and..."

"I understand ladies' things. Go ahead, do what have got to do and don't rush. Take your time, lady. I'll be here," he burst out laughing.

"You are very funny. I know your girlfriend will be madly in love with you and your silly mouth. She would be sick every time she couldn't see you. That's my guess."

"More like a confession to me. I am glad."

"Who confessed? Me?"

"Huh, no. Me Not you at all. Would you please jump your butt into the bathroom and let's go? Hurry up now, big sister."

"Mind your speech young man. Watch yourself, little brother."

"Okay, your royal highness. But I said please..."

"Yeah, I heard you. Just give me a minute."

"I give you a minute and now it's twenty minutes. Can't you tell time?"

"Whatever! I'll be right back." She left for the bathroom. She let him take the control of the vehicle since he had received his driver's license now.

They spent about fifteen minutes at the Tennessee aquarium in Chattanooga and later went to the zoo. She suggested that they should stop last at any restaurant of his choice and he agreed with her. They visited Ryan's Steak House on Brainerd Road just off of Lee Highway. They got seated for a minute then they stood up back to serve themselves. Each found his plate to put food on it and headed back to their seats. Two minutes later a server came to ask if they were doing alright and suggested ways she could better help them enjoy their meals.

"How you guys doing tonight? Is everything ok? Can I get you anything?"

"No, thanks... We're fine," Bolaji answered with smile on his face.

"Quit being such flirt," Anita said, messing with her brother.

"Cute couple... Enjoy your meal." The server commented.

"We are not a couple," Anita said with a very satisfying smile on her face.

"Why, are you trying to deny it? The man is cute, isn't he? Be proud of him."

"Thanks to you... I tell her all the time." Bolaji added.

"We are not a couple. We are siblings. He's my brother can't you see the resemblance? Look at him. Look at us both," Anita explained to her.

"That's what makes you both a great couple. You know cute couples sometimes resemble one another sometimes. I admire you both. Enjoy!"

"You just don't get it, do you? He's not my boyfriend, ok?"

"Oh, I get it. He's your fiancé, my fault," the server said.

"How did you know? You must be psychic," Bolaji said to the server.

"You both are getting crazy now. Quit it Bolaji. We are fine ma'am and we'll call you when we need something. Is that alright with you? Anita asked the server.

"Oh yeah. I'm cool with that. I hoped I didn't offend you at all?" she asked.

"No, you are straight. I just think others might need your service, you know?" Anita suggested as she was putting a slice of bread into her mouth.

"Thanks for being nice to us, miss," Bolaji joked.

You are very welcome, sir," she replied while walking away from them, and then Anita passed bread over to brother's side to share with him. He thanked her. She stared at him and laughed with no words of explanation for such laughter.

"Why does everybody think you are my boyfriend?"

"I don't know. Perhaps I am too cute or something," Bolaji responded.

"She is too crazy just like you. She was talking about something she doesn't know."

"The lady is psychic. She knows before she talks." Bolaji said.

"She needs to go back to school then because she's woefully wrong.

The server came back again to add water to their glasses. She asked further, "...everything alright? Where are you from, sir?" She faced Bolaji.

"He's from here..." Anita answered.

"I am from Nigeria. Why do you ask, anyway?" Bolaji was curious.

"I noticed the accent, though slightly. I thought you are from Virginia Island."

"He was born here..." Anita said again.

"Yeah right, the server said.

"I am telling you the truth. He lived in Nigeria, though, but he's from here originally," Anita replied a bit sharply. She felt the server had overstepped her bounds. Nonetheless, she still tipped her an even 20%

"Are we ready to go, my darling?" Bolaji asked as they stood up. "You are super silly. Come on let's go. I'll kill you when we get home."

***

They finally got home that night and waited in the living room to watch TV for a little while before each would finally leave for his and her respective rooms. Bolaji suggested that they should both pray for their parents' souls and ask God to continue His peace on both of them. It was nineteen years already that their lives had been stolen away by guns. Anita said her prayers with tears making rivulets along her face, trickling down her prominent check bones, coursing down her face and splattering the collar of her shirt. These words brought back sad memories to her. Bolaji acted like a man and he boldly said his own prayers with dry eyes. He told his sister to rinse her face with water and let the bygone pass to oblivion and said that they should only be remembering them with prayers, not with tears.

Five – Three years later....Atlanta, GA

A fetus thinks it is held up for being in the womb for nine months prior to its arrival in the world, but instead of it being smart enough to house itself inside where it will have free access to nourishment provided by its mother's body, it would never listen to any mouth that could be saying;,"

Don't go, stay here, it's safe here and you will be protected."

It would probably respond, "I am grown enough to see the world and everything it conveys."

She was too excited to get prepared for college and she couldn't wait any longer to leave her city for Chattanooga, TN where her brother Frank had been studying for two years now. She was by herself inside her room glancing into the mirror with different bikinis and at the same time she was accessing her own booty and the entire body. "Damn, my Mama gave me something good," she said to herself. She then opened the door that connected the bathroom and her room together and she entered the bathroom to wax her body completely. She was too much into starting college and it was four weeks away. She now promised herself to be waxing her body at least twice in a week. She took a shower after finishing with waxing and she applied lotion to her body to increase the skin's firmness and glow, the beauty which was her name, Beauty. Every one wondered how Rebecca knew she was going to be super elegant to name her no other name but Beauty.

She walked into the living room to join her mother and brother; they were both amazed with her newly revealed beauty. She didn't utter a word, but she sat next to her mother on the couch instead. Frank rolled his eyes over her couple of times and he could not say a word either. Then Rebecca asked her to bring three apples for them to share and she did as she commanded.

"Here you go," she said, handing her an apple.

"Did you wash them?" Rebecca asked.

"Where are you going, anyway?" Rebecca asked without facing any one in particular as she sat back down.

"Are you talking to me or to him?" Beauty asked her mother. "Yes, it is you of course. Who do you think I am talking to?"

"Frank?" she asked.

"No reason. You didn't face any one in particular, that's why I asked. I am not going anywhere. I am just trying to be..."

"Why are you so dressed up, then?" Frank interrogated her.

"Nothing... It ain't your concern any way. I dress for my own purpose."

She replied by clutching her eyes closed.

"Why are you trying to be rude to your brother? You should be nice to your brother. Apologize to him right now!" she ordered.

"I am sorry, Frank," she begged with laughter.

"It's ok. I'm not mad at you." He forgave her like a brother.

"You are bad, Beauty. Is that the proper way to apologize?" Rebecca asked.

"I said I was sorry, Mom. What else do you want me to say? He forgave me already, didn't he?" She was annoyed.

"You should keep your voice down, young lady. What's your problem?"

"Nothing Mom, I am not yelling at you or anyone else. Gosh!"

"Mom, it's cool. Knock it off," Frank begged.

***

At 9:30 am, Hudson was let in after knocking twice on the door. Beauty gave him a very suspicious embrace that conveyed a sense of unease which Hudson quickly picked up on. He thought perhaps something had happened between her and her mother. He greeted Frank and then checked on his own girlfriend, Rebecca. Hudson asked what was wrong with Beauty and she lied, saying that nothing had happened to her. Frank let it out by saying she was just having some issues with her mother. Hudson begged her to let it go, forcing her to smile and laugh.

“How was school, Frank?” Hudson asked as he was walking towards Rebecca to join her on the couch.

“School…? It was fine. We're done with this semester. So much stress, you know?”

“Stress you call it, huh? Hang in there. It won't seem that way once you begin to reap what you’ve sown. I mean when you graduate and start making money, big money.” Hudson encouraged Frank to succeed.

“Too many freaking assignments every day; I hate that a lot. I understand it's just for four or five years, but it seems eternal to me. Did you go through the same experience while you were in college?” Frank asked Hudson.

“Everybody has to go through that; trust me. I did. Your parents did, too. Be cool and have fun with it. You'll live.” Hudson replied.

“He’s being lazy lately. This ain't no Frank I knew some years ago who always busy with his homework and assignments and who made good grades to make his mother proud. Where is that Frank? He ain't living here anymore," Rebecca threw that question to Frank.

"Mom, you just don't get it, do you? High school is different from the so-called college. I am still making good grades if that is what you are so concerned about. I will always make you proud of me, and she will too, definitely," he said, pointing to his sister.

"Of course, I will. We will make her proud. I can't wait to get into college," Beauty said.

"So you are getting prepared for college, too?" Hudson asked.

"Yes, I am all ready for it. I am excited," she replied with glee.

"When do you start? I mean when are you going to start?" Hudson asked further.

"Fall semester, one month away. Four weeks of course." She replied.

"Oh, congratulations then. College students, too many dramas..." Hudson said.

"My baby is so much into college and I don't really understand the reasons for the excitement. I know it is progressive. Don't get me wrong, but why all the 'I can't wait motivations'? She acts like she had been dying to get into it for the past decade," Rebecca commented.

"Nothing is behind it. I am just excited to go. Aren't you happy for me, mom?" Beauty asked with a sympathetic face.

"Oh my dear poor little angel, of course I am happy for you and I am excited too," Rebecca said as she was embracing her.

"Sometimes you act like you don't want me to go," Beauty criticized her.

"No, don't. Don't be ridiculous. You know I am happy for you both."

"Helloooo? Why ain't nobody giving me any attention? Am I not here anymore?" Frank said as he stood up to pick up the magazine that had fallen onto the carpet.

"What did you mean we aren't giving you any attention? You didn't say anything, did you? Everybody is having conversation and you've just been silent." Rebecca was then interrupted.

"I *am* speaking, Mom. You all just kept talking amongst yourselves and left me outside. I feel like I have been left out of the conversation," Frank said, clearly annoyed.

"Don't get it twisted, young man. We are here to listen to your words," Hudson said. "He's just jealous of the love I get from you both. He wants to be embraced too. Maybe you should hug him and tell him you love him like you did to me, mom." Beauty suggested.

"You shut up, Beauty! I am not jealous of anything, ok?" Frank denied it.

"Well, let's call it a day. What do you all say we get out of here and go shopping for your school needs? I mean both of you," Hudson said, addressing both Frank and Beauty.

"It sounds good to me. Let's go." Frank answered.

"Shopping? Is that necessary?" Rebecca asked Hudson.

"Mom, I wanna go. Come on let's go Uncle Hudson," Beauty said.

"Then go. I am not holding you back. You all have fun and don't fight, ok?" Rebecca warned them both.

"What did you mean have fun? And you too, pretty lady. We are all going together," Hudson told Rebecca.

"Are you serious? You are playing, right?" Rebecca asked.

"You're damned right, I'm serious. Come on let's go," he urged.

"Okay, gimme a minute to use the lady's room. I'll be back soon." Rebecca said.

"Don't you mean twenty?" Hudson joked.

"...twenty what…? You are being silly." Rebecca asked.

"You knew what I meant. Twenty minutes to get ready," Hudson said, somewhat impatiently.

"I know it already. I'll be right out. Keep him busy, Frank," she said.

"I will, Mom. Please hurry, though!" Frank urged his mother.

"Shut up, silly boy! You are supposed to side with your mother not oppose her."

"I am not opposing you. I said hurry. You are wasting time now talking."

"I'll be done soon. Gosh!" She then entered the bathroom.

"I know you should have..." Hudson began then paused.

"You are all keeping me late. I'll be right out, I promise," she said, then shut the door.

"You have no excuse, just hurry up."

The sky was grey blue, pale blue and dingy white; the sun arrived early at10:33 a.m., which made the face of the day to seem older than its actual age. It was going to be a sunny day, Rebecca thought. They all jumped into Hudson's newly purchased car and they were all going shopping. He put on a CD of his favorite rock star and they all began singing with the artist. They finally got to the mall and headed for Macy's first. Hudson told Frank and Beauty not be hesitant, to grab whatever they wanted. The colors of the shirts competed with one another in Beauty's eyes, so that she couldn't choose at once which color was her favorite. She decided to gamble and choose one with her eyes being shut. Frank didn't waste any time. He chose five different shirts of different colors. He knew, as a man, what he wanted even before they got into the mall; therefore, there was need to waste time on it. "Don't you see what you want?" Rebecca asked Beauty who had had her eyes shut. They were forced to open and she was embarrassed with her mother's voice that made her into a bit of a spectacle.

"Stop it, Mom! You're embarrassing both of us," she said testily. She then began walking away from them.

"Easy young lady; don't walk away." Hudson said.

"I'm sorry, Beauty. I didn't mean it that way. I was just asking. Maybe I could help you to choose," Rebecca said.
"Why didn't you say so? I thought you loved me." She kept walking.

"I do love you and I'll always love you both. Please stop walking for God's sake." Rebecca then begged.

"It's okay, Beauty. She has realized her mistake and she won't do it again." Frank held her to stop her from walking. They settled the matter and headed to the shoe displays. They got what they wanted and Hudson paid for everything. They exchanged thanks for it and he appreciated their words with a smile on his face.

***

After three hours, they got back home and Rebecca cooked lunch for them. She knew they were all hungry. They circled around the dining table, said their prayers and began eating. Then Mandy arrived, joining them. She had come intentionally not only to spend time with Rebecca, but also to meet Hudson for the first time. They greeted each other when Rebecca had introduced them to one another. Rebecca then grabbed an extra plate to honor Mandy's visit. She accepted the food and they all continued eating.

"You look absolutely fabulous, my friend," Rebecca said to Mandy.

"Oh, how nice of you to say…? Thanks and so do you."

"Oh, stop kidding. I am good, though," Rebecca added.

"You are beautiful. That's what your friend just said. Why deny it? You're beautiful and we admire it," Hudson boldly told Rebecca.

"I heard you, nice man. Men lie to you all the time. They lie just to lie..."

"What kind of line is that? They lie just to lie? What does that mean?" Hudson asked her.

"I mean you men lie to us just to steal from us. What I meant to say is that you men lie to lie down with us in the bed. You all are liars," she claimed.

"but right now the kids are listening. Let's change the subject."

"Who are the kids? These two? They're both grown up adults. They're now eighteen and twenty-two years old; they're not kids anymore. And I'm sure they would probably gain something from this conversation. Beauty, men are pigs. You need to be careful and be smart at the same time. Do not open your thighs for a liar. I am serious. I don't know who your boyfriend is, but be careful. Frank is a man and he has no problem.

"He's one of them. One of the pigs," Rebecca said.

"Mom, stop it. I don't have a boyfriend. Stop embarrassing me," she whispered.

"I know you will one day, young lady..."

"Are you calling me a liar, mom? I wanna know, are you?" Frank interrupted with his question.

"Oh my poor little boy, nope... You are not a liar, but you are a man and men are liars. You should prove to yourself that you are different from them, meaning be nice to your girlfriend; don't lie to her and always listen to her. Women love men who listen to them. That's what we love and cherish. Life would be better if all of you men could do it for us, but I doubt it. Ain't that right, Mandy?" Rebecca inquired.

"You are absolutely right, my friend."

"So you are telling me that only men are liars, but that women aren't? I have seen many movies and live television programs that show women lying and sleeping with different men and they would still be claiming that they love you, and that ain't no lie."

"I don't know about that one, not me," Rebecca said.

"Me neither. I have never seen those movies or realities. What channel are they on? I wanna watch them," Mandy asked Hudson.

"Oh, you have got jokes, huh? I don't know. You should find out for yourself."

"Shall we talk about something else, guys?" Frank asked, trying to change the subject. "Ok, like what exactly?" Hudson asked.

"I...don't know. May be you can think of one subject, like a place or something fun –
perhaps history or anything else," Frank said.

"I am not very good in history. But maybe I can try a little bit," Hudson responded.

"It sounds good to me. We are listening. Go ahead." He couldn't wait to hear it all. "Hudson is not very good at it.

He's the most terrible story teller I have ever seen or known in my entire life. He's good at something else, though," Rebecca said.

"Mom, be nice. I want to hear it, Uncle Hudson."

"Don't worry. I'll help him out. Have you all read the paper today? They said a woman gave birth to a bird. It was aired on the news last night. It was late though." Mandy just lied to them all.

"Gave birth to a bird? … a bird?" Beauty asked, confused.

"That's right, a bird. I think it was a pigeon or something," she added.

"How is that possible? I can't believe it. A bird…? We are talking about different species here. Human being and avian – a bird. What a fallacy. The reporters must have been drunk or something. That simply isn't possible. Nope. I don't buy that. No way…!" Frank argued.

"Don't you know that money is now being used as a weapon of destruction? Women are sleeping with animals now because of money. Those whores could sleep with anything: snakes, horses, bulls, dogs and so on. She might have slept with birds, who knows?" Mandy tried to convince them.

"You might be right on that. I heard that, too." Hudson agreed.

"Maybe scientific technology could be used to collect sperm from birds and test it in the human body. The result might come out to be a bird then," Frank suggested.

"That could be true. You may be right – except … Gotcha! I am just joking, y'all. How in the hell would a woman give birth to a bird? It'll never happen. I even pray that it'll never happen. But you all fell for it though," Mandy came out clean with laughter.

"You are very good. I had begun to believe you," Hudson said.

"Me, too. I thought you were serious. You deceived me," Frank said.

"...and me, too..." Beauty added.

The clock must be moving very fast that none of them actually knew they had spent ninety minutes since they got back in; weather people never lied, their presuppositions not always accurate. They'd predicted rain by 4:00 p.m. in the weather forecast; it was now 4:20 pm. Not a second later did it begin raining. She smiled; she knew it that she could count on the weather forecasters. She mostly scheduled her things to do around it. Hudson was upset that it was raining; he had wanted to leave before the rain arrived. Now it would he would have to wait at its mercy for it to disappear, which he didn't really plan for; he unhappily managed to spend the rainy period inside with them.

PART TWO:

LOVE SEES NO COLOR

Six- Months passed....School Campus

At exactly 1:30 a.m., Bolaji woke up from sleep, headed to the bathroom, used the toilet, flushed it, then glanced into the mirror. He thought to himself that his face looked almost mean after such long hours of sleep and then he walked back into his bedroom tried to fall asleep again. Suddenly, however, he remembered he'd been dreaming about the same girl he had been dreaming about some weeks ago. Was this déjà vu or fate? He stood up and thought deeply about the situation; every time he had a dream about this white, lovely girl, it seemed to him that he had had that experience somewhere before, perhaps in his first life, if and only if the theory of reincarnation was true. The dreams were somewhat difficult to classify into a given category. It would best fit into a paradigm of premonition or déjà vu. This is fate, he thought to himself.

Then by 3:33 a.m., and after he had gone back into sleep, the dreams returned. It was the same girl again. She captured his senses and engaged him in playful conversation. There were attending school together; they hooked up and were having a good time with each other. Every word Beauty spoke in his dream hypnotized Bolaji and the same thing was happening to Beauty. They were simply perfect for each other.

Anita knocked on the door and woke him. He tried to get back to his wonderful dream, but his sister kept knocking on his door until he answered it and she told him to get ready for school. He told her he had heard that and he would be preparing right away. He sat on the bed and recaptured the sense of hypnotic déjà vu. He tried to recall a distinct narrative but was unsuccessful so he headed to the bathroom to take a shower. He applied lotions when he had done bathing, brushed his teeth, put on jeans and a shirt and then he was heading to the living room where Anita was.

She had made breakfast for both of them. He had his and ate it. She asked him if he needed help with school, but Bolaji told her he would be fine. He wanted to share his dreams with his sister and opened by telling her that he'd had recurring dreams about a beautiful young girl, but Anita didn't want to hear it. She told him that everybody could possibly have dreams and they meant nothing sometimes. She didn't even listen. Perhaps Bolaji would reveal to her that the girl was white so that she would tell him immediately that they shouldn't mess with white people as her grandmother had raised her to believe.

She rushed him instead and asked him to forget about any silly dreams. She stood up and closed the door after landing her feet on the porch and told him to be careful and hurry.

Bolaji resented that Anita wouldn't listen. The girl is beautiful; he wanted to tell her that. She was so caught up with school starting that day that she rushed her brother. much into going to class. After all, new classes were starting today. Bolaji wished her farewell and remained hurt that she didn't want to listen to him in earnest.

He drove off in his brand new Mercedes; he tuned in to the local radio station, the so-called people's station and the only artist that was airing at the time was Usher, the native born performer who hailed from the city of Chattanooga, Tennessee. He started miming the songs from A-Z till he approached the general school parking lot; he pulled into it and then parked his car. "Ladies and gentleman, you are now listening to the people's station, power... power 94.3 all day every day, you all heard? The best station of all time, believe that you all..." the statements he uttered fooled no one but himself. He remained in the car, turned off the ignition and wanted to practice asking for guidance around campus before he stepped out of the car; he was self-conscious about his accent and feared being mocked. He knew that people with African ancestors expected to understand them and when they couldn't they would deliberately ask him to repeat himself just to mock him. He knew that his large vocabulary and unusual accent also interfered with his efforts to communicate. He vowed to check this today in order to make things easier.

He finally exited his car and began walking towards the theatre department. He approached a small group of guys and asked directions. They were straight forward and helpful. They pointed him in the right direction and he was pleased. The building was simple – a rectangular plot that was longer than it was wide. Once again he was assailed by a sense of déjà vu. He pondered how fate or destiny might be linked indelibly to one's kismet and knew that there was nothing on the face of earth that could possibly stop it from happening. As he walked along he was conscious of his color and felt like a king. Girls of all colors smiled and waved at him – following his path with their eyes. He cut a dashing figure.

He came across Tasha on the way as well and she smiled at him with lust on her mind. She had seen Bolaji every day and knew he was very attractive, but today she realized he was the most handsome man she had ever seen in her entire life time. She felt like kissing him right away, but she fought the thoughts and managed to be a grown woman. She walked by him after exchanging friendly hugs and words. She asked about his sister before proceeding and he answered that she should be in her class now, otherwise with Karl. From one side of the building that could be labeled as its breadth, along came the object of his dreams, Beauty.

She was fabulously dressed in brand new jeans, which were moderately tight enough to showcase her booty. She wore a modest pink blouse and glowed with her sense of joy at starting school. She walked along as if she were auditioning for a modeling contract; she'd just departed from her brother Frank who had just pointed out the theatre department to her. Bolaji was on his way to Theater 111- Introduction to Theater. He was also wearing blue jeans, white Nike shoes, a shirt with blue, black and light yellow colors in a striped to design and blue sunglasses. All the girls he strolled by took notice of this handsome man. Some feet away from the class, Bolaji shifted his book bag. Beauty held her books in her right hand; they weren't very heavy. The two walked towards one another. She did not notice him at first, but when she looked upward and forward she realized that he was the most handsome man she had ever seen. She thought to herself that he had been deliberately placed before her like the angel of paradise; he appeared like one of those stars up in the sky and she forced herself to think deeply in order to be friendly to him if that was her limit.

Suddenly, she was on her feet and presto, she breezed out some skills to gain his attention. She had been totally captured by his appearance, lost deeply in day dreaming and romantic thoughts that she didn't even know when she finally collide with him and her books fell to the floor. They both rushed at once to pick up the books. She was down there looking at his handsome face and she remained utterly silent. Perhaps she had used up all of her words. Bolaji broke the silence, asking her if she was okay or not doing alright.

Bolaji carefully picked up her fallen books. He couldn't help but stare at her as he returned them. He was glad he was wearing spectacle as he was picking up some of the books. He searched through her body with his eyes that were hiding under the sunglasses.

"Oh, yes. I'm fine she insisted. It was just an accident. I'm sorry if I bumped into you. Do you forgive me?" she asked him.

"Absolutely, I do forgive you. Get up." He offered his hand to help her.

"You are so nice." She moved towards him with the thoughts of wanting to kiss him right on the spot, but she didn't.

"Is today your first day at school?" Bolaji asked with smile. "Yes, I am a freshman. Perhaps 'fresh lady' I should say," she joked with a smile.

"Freshman is a general term. I am a freshman, too. Actually, I am looking for this theater class." He showed his printed schedule out to her.

“Theatre 111…? Me, too! I guess you and I wound up in the same class. How perfect that will be. I am full of excitement right now. You are the first person I’ve met in this area and you are very cool to hang with,” she said.

“Nice complement you gave me. I’ll take it. And thanks though. She placed her hand on his other idle shoulder as they were walking to the class. They entered the class after being known and the whole class turned facing the door to see who was coming in because the door made a loud noise as if it were protesting.

They apologized to those seated nearest and made their way to two open seats. She sat in a nearby front seat ahead of Bolaji because she was short and he sat immediately next behind her. The professor, Dr. Thomas, continued his lecture. He was just reading from the play, “Raisin in the Sun.” Beauty then found herself a piece of paper to write with and she wrote:

Hey cutie,

The moment I saw your face, I swear

I was enraptured with love. Do you think I

am pretty? Do you find me attractive at all?

Please answer me with honesty.

She then put it in front of him secretly in order not to disturb or interrupt the lecture. He glanced at the paper and smiled at the words in it. He then took his time to read through it carefully. Then he replied by writing:

Find you attractive, do I think you are pretty?

Are you kidding me? You are the most

attractive and beautiful woman I have

ever seen in my life. That's the truth.

I don't want to get into trouble here.

Following her lead, he carefully and surreptitiously passed the paper back to her. She smiled and she wrote back at once. She waited another minute before placing it on his desk because the professor was walking towards her seat. She thought he had discovered her game, but the professor was just walking according to his own purpose to make sure all the students understood the lecture well. She felt relieved and then proceeded to place her reply on his desk; it said:

Getting into trouble? I don't understand.

Why do you think you are going to get into

trouble? Never boy! You are like a rare king

to me. You are free to say whatever you like

He couldn't believe her reply and at the same time he felt the freedom and he was trying to use it, but something kept telling his brain to be careful as well. He wrote back:

You know women are so unpredictable,

if you know what I mean. I don't want to be

charged for harassment or that sort of thing.

I guess I should watch my tone here.

I hope you will understand me.

She didn't like his reply because she felt that he didn't trust her. Despite that, she gave him confidence in her words. She then acted like it didn't hurt her feelings and she looked behind herself and their eyes met, both of them smiling. She turned back facing the chalk board and she pretended as if she was the most serious student amongst all the others who had been listening to everything the professor had been saying since the first minute of the lecture time. She waited another minute, and then decided to write again to let him know she was willing to give him the ultimate freedom towards herself and she wrote back instantly:

Well, I am not going to charge you with

anything, harassment or whatever you called it.

Don't you trust me at all?

He was reading it when the professor spoke up to get his attention, although he didn't know what he was reading. He stopped reading it for the moment and then proceeded. He wrote back without wasting any time:

Trust you? How would I? We barely even know

each other, now you are talking about trust.

I am not trying to be rude or anything.

I think you are trust worthy anyway.

She read it, smiled at once and she kicked him with her leg then she wrote back:

I told you and I gave you my words

I swear to God I am cool with you and anything

you say. Trust me... well after the class, ok?

He loved what he read from the paper and smiled, but he didn't reply since she had stated that they would discuss it further after the class. Dr. Thomas gave them some homework to do about the play, *The Glass Menagerie* and he asked them to read the next play, *Romeo and Juliet* before the next class on Wednesday and then dismissed the class. Bolaji stood up just as she did and wrapped her arms around his waist. Different thoughts ran through his mind and he didn't really know what she was up to. They stepped outside the art department and she began her questions. She really wanted to be his girl provided he didn’t already have one.

“So do you have a girlfriend? I mean friend... friend, like a lover?” She prayed secretly with her mind as she threw that question. She would be hurt if he had had a girlfriend or lover.

“A lover…? I am afraid not. Why did you ask anyway, do you want to give me one?” He smiled as he uttered those words.

“I would be more than happy to give you one. Do you want one?” She pushed his chest.

“If you give me, I'll take it. Yes, I want one.” He was only joking though.

“What if I give you me? What about me?” Beauty asked him, though she was shy.

“You, huh?” He kept laughing without saying yes or no; he thought she was just messing with or testing him.

“What, you don't want me because I am white or not pretty enough for you? Oh, I get it. I’ll see you later.” She was hurt and she began walking away from him.

“Wait! Come on. Not that I don't want you or because of your race or color. I don't discriminate when it comes to anything, especially love. You’re not serious about this, are you? You are joking, right?” He asked her with smile.

“Joking? Why do you think I am kidding? I am very serious. We are talking about our future here. I am not the kind of girl who would be lavishing all the attention in our lives for stupid games. I want you as my man, my main man and if God grants it so, I would be glad if you happened to be my husband. And please don't make fun of me.” She spoke her mind.

“Why did you think I would be making fun of you? I have great respect for women. And I respect you, I mean very much. I think we are getting somewhere now. By the way, what's your name?” He asked her, reaching out to hold her hand.

"Beauty, what's yours?" she asked in return.

"Yeah right, I can tell you are beautiful. Seriously, what's your name, Beauty?"

"I am serious; my name is Beauty." She replied.

"Bolaji, My name is Bolaji. B. O. L. A. J. I. My mama gave me that."

"Sweet, my mother gave me Beauty too. What kind of name is Bo.la.je, anyway?"

"It is Bolaji, not Bolaje. You need to say it right." Bolaji told her jokingly.

"Yeah, whatever… So what do you say, you like me?"

"How could I say no to Beauty? The first thing man should seek from a woman. Let us give it a try and see what happens..." Bolaji replied.

"Are you serious? I don't like it when somebody is mocking me or lying to me. If you think you don't want me we can still be just friends," she said.

"I am not joking. I have never dated anyone before. You are the first girl I have ever felt this kind of affection for. So ain't nothing holding me back. Let's go for it and we should pray. I know you wouldn't believe this, but I have been having dreams about you for weeks. It is kind of déjà vu to me. Perhaps we were a couple in our past lives or something. Perhaps it is our fate to be together. You think I am crazy, don't you?" he asked.

"No, you are not crazy at all. I had the same dreams too about you. That's why I am so crazy into you just like I was in the dream. I am having another class soon. I'll see you tomorrow or later," she drew herself into him.

"Okay, I'll see you then."

Beauty wasted no time and she kissed him on the lips when they were hugging each other affectionately. They separated and headed for their next classes. She kept smiling and waving until he was out of sight. Each of them was rapt, filled with happiness and joy.

Bolaji was then entering the next class; the lecture room had been filled up, waiting for the arrival of the professor and Bolaji joined the class quietly. Adam, a Brazilian student, sat next to him in the front row; he asked for his name and they exchanged greetings. The class was Economics 101 and it was one of the mandatory courses that each student was required to take prior to graduation. Tasha was in the class, too. Although she was a senior student, she had waited until her last term to take the course. She sat in the last row, staring at Bolaji's back. Even though he wasn't aware of it, she was smitten with him. She was only making a mistake by not letting him know how she felt for him. It was too late now, though, because in such a surreal and inexplicable way, Bolaji had just met his life partner, a lovely girl with whom he'd already fallen deeply in love.

Soon, the professor entered the classroom and greeted everyone. He distributed the course syllabus that contained: class schedules, test dates and rules, the do's and don'ts of the class. He read through the papers and he explained verbally to let each student know what might lead him or her to either fail or to pass the class. He announced that cheating would lead to an automatic zero score and would require the student to repeat the class. He then began his introduction to the subject. After sixty minutes of lecture, he let them go. Bolaji and Adam walked side by side, talking to each other and they wanted to work together to get good grades in the subject. They became friends at once and they exchanged digits as well before each finally headed towards his next destination. Bolaji was happy to have him as a friend.

At the University Center, Bolaji was eating his sandwich when Anita wrapped her hands around his eyes; he struggled with them and finally took them off. He looked baffled to know who it was and he found out that it was his own sister. She took bites from his food and sat down facing him; she smiled before continuing her words.

"How was everything so far? You think you can cope with it?" Anita asked.

"It's alright. We've had two classes already. That's how they're rushing you here?"

"UTC doesn't waste time. It's the best school, you know," she replied.

"Where are you going now, home?" Bolaji asked her.

"No way. I have three more classes. I won't be able to go home till 5:30 p.m."

"5:30 p.m.? That's too long. I can't do that. I have two more classes and that's all. And I'll be through today. My next class is Calculus II and Introduction to Statistics."

"Calculus II, are you kidding? How in the world can you get start with Calculus II? You're not a senior student yet. You are freshman."

"Well, my level passes of all required preliminary courses. I heard some of the people who took the placement test together started from Algebra but my level was so high, even higher than geometry, pre-calculus or Calculus I. Don't hate me. I'm proud of it."

"You are silly. I am always proud of you," she replied.

"I saw your man five minutes ago. He was walking like he'd lost something..."

"Where did you see him at? ...he by himself?"

"No, he's with a girl. I am just kidding. I saw him at the book store, just passing by."

“Don’t worry about it. I will call him later. I can't wait for the weekends. We are going to party all day on Saturday and going for the new movies on Sunday,” she said happily.

“Are you talking about the weekend that just passed yesterday or the one that's seven days away? Women, you are all so full of parties and shit. Let me have twenty dollars from you,” he asked.

“What happened? Are you broke? Didn't I tell you about the new car you bought? You didn't listen. Now you are broke,” she criticized him.

“I am not broke, lady. I will never be broke. I just need twenty dollars for my gas. Would you be kind and give it to me?”

“Yeah, I will give it to you. Here you go.” She gave him the money.

“I appreciate it. Love you. I'll see you when you get home.”

“I’ll see you then. Be careful and don't fight, Bolaji.” She was then walking out of the University Center going to her next class. Beauty entered the class for English 121 where she would later meet with her friends Tracy and Mickey. Bolaji would have started the class with Beauty, but the school’s protocol required him to take 'English as a Second Language' and passing with a C grade or better was mandatory.

Dr. Maya shut the door to stop any late comers from entering the class, and then she introduced herself to the class. She also instructed them on the required text book for the class after reading the course codes like any other professor would do, and then she asked each of the students to stand up and introduce themselves to the class. Beauty lent one of her pens to Tracy when she couldn't find hers to write with and she was thankful and lucky – otherwise she would have been sent out by

Dr. Maya. After forty five minutes, the class came to an end for the day and the students walked out of the class.

“Thanks to you, gorgeous...” Tracy thanked Beauty while walking out of the class.

“You’re welcome,” she responded.

“My name is Mickey; Tracy's friend. We are both models."

Tracy introduced herself to Beauty.

“Are you serious, you guys are models?” Beauty asked.

“Yes, we are. You’ve seen our commercials, haven't you?”

“No, I haven't. I don't watch TV that much,” she responded. “That could be the reason. So what's your name?” Tracy asked. “Beauty and I am from Atlanta, Georgia.”

“And I’m from Savannah, Georgia, not too far from Atlanta as you probably know. “How cool. So where are you from?” Beauty asked, facing Tracy. “Kentucky, but I’m living in Chattanooga with my grandmother now.

“It’s nice to meet you both. We should be friends,” Beauty suggested.

“Good thinking. I’d love to. Here is my cell number.” Tracy gave hers to her.

“Here is mine, too.” Mickey did the same.

“And here is mine for you both,” Beauty said.

“We have other friends as well. We will meet at UC center one time soon and get together. What do you say?” Tracy asked her.

“Perfect idea; I'll call you guys. I guess I should get going now.” She then waved.

As freshmen, all you have in mind is that school is going to be fun and worth attending every day. Once you have started, then you will realize that it is somewhat stressful. You will think that all you have to do is sit down in a class, listening to the instructor, but it will become boring as time goes by. Perhaps it was her fate to wait until that time; Tasha should have been finished with her introduction to statistics class, Stat 101, a long time ago. Jealousy took up residence within her mind for seeing Bolaji talking to Beauty. They met again for Stat 101. It surprised Bolaji that the same professor who taught them Calculus II would also teach Statistics 101. Bolaji told his girl that he had just had Dr. Duane for Calculus II a while ago. Looking at him talking and laughing with Beauty heated Tasha's body rapidly; her skin's surface became moist with sweat springing out from her body, and she felt like hitting Beauty's head against any available hard object. She wanted to move close to their seats but the whole room had been filled up and the professor wouldn't permit it even though he was still waiting on them to settle down before he could proceed.

Tasha's feelings were hurt, which ruined her concentration on the subject; she kept fighting it until she couldn't take it any longer and she had to step outside. She asked the professor if she could use the restroom and she was pardoned to go. She left for good that day and she never returned to the class. Beauty gave pictures of herself to Bolaji. She wanted him to keep her in his mind and to feel the same way she had been feeling for him. He accepted those pictures even though he didn't have some to give in return and he kept them in his *Star Magazine*. They were lucky that day they didn't get caught talking while the lecture was still ongoing, otherwise they would have been forced out of the class. The class was dismissed after fifty minutes and they were happy to step out.

"I'll call you tonight. You better pick it up or I'll cry on you," Beauty said.

"Ain't no need to cry; I'll pick it up. Hold on a second..." His phone was ringing and it was Adam. "Hello," he said showing one of his fingers to tell Beauty to hold on for some seconds. "How is it going? Having fun with those classes? Well I... am with somebody in here right now..."

"Somebody..." Beauty interrupted madly.

"I am with my girl here. Her name is Beauty. I am serious, that's her name. Well I'll see you tomorrow or maybe Wednesday. Be cool man."

"Why are you ashamed of me, Bolaji?" she asked.

"Hell no…! You have made me curse now. Why do you think I am ashamed?"

"I don't know. I am just checking. I am sorry if that makes you angry."

"I am not going to get mad at you. I never will. Was it because I said I was with somebody instead of saying my girlfriend?" Bolaji asked curiously.

"That could be it. Forget about that and I'll see you tomorrow."

"I'll miss you." She kissed him twice and hugged him tightly.

"I'll miss you, too," he said as his eyes met with hers.

"Oh, how sweet... You have no idea how deeply and madly I am in love with you. I feel like we have been together maybe hundreds of years. I don't even know how to explain it. Please Bolaji! I beg you in the name of your God and everything, don't break my heart. Let me know if this isn't going to work before it's too late. I swear to God the love I have for you is more than the volume of any ocean or sea. I loved you long before I even knew you or met you in person. Do you really have feelings for me? I mean it's okay if you don't. We can still be friends. Know this, though; I am going to kill myself later on if we separate after having become a couple."

"Well, thanks for speaking your mind. I have feelings for you. I love you and I'll never break your heart and you shouldn't break mine. Come here." He then kissed her and then parted, each of them waving and smiling until they lost sight of one another.

Bolaji got into his car and he was looking at the pictures that Beauty had given him while they were in class; he loved them all and he felt like the luckiest one on the face of the planet. Good thing she was close to her eighteenth birthday, otherwise it could lead Bolaji into trouble; she was seventeen and Bolaji was now nineteen. He started the car by turning the ignition with the key and the car stereo started automatically; he loved Tupac Shakur that much and he could not afford to let off of his memory; he kept miming his rhymes till he actually pulled into their drive way.

Seven – Another Month Passed....Chattanooga, TN

Sunday morning, Bolaji was in the living room listening to Tupac as usual and placed the *Star Magazine* that held Beauty's pictures in between the pages on the coffee table; the front cover of the magazine was very intriguing, beckoning every eye and inspiring everyone who beheld it to read it. Ergo, Anita grabbed the magazine without even asking to and then came across something she never expected to see, picture after picture of a white girl. Anita was disturbed emotionally and could not continue with the story she'd initially meant to read. She looked at the pictures again and her eyes confirmed the color of the girl to be white; she thought it was a dream or some sort of imaginary realm and she was willing to ask her brother some questions about the pictures and the girl in them.

"Who is this, Bolaji?" Anita asked impatiently, her heart hard.

"Who is who?" he asked in return while reducing the volume of the disc player.

"…the white girl in the picture, is she a classmate or what…?" she frowned as she was sitting down on the couch before asking further.

"…white girl, huh? Yeah, classmate. Hey wuz up with you? She is my friend."

"Friend, what kind of friend…? Of all the beautiful black girls at the school you are too blind to see one. I will give you my words and if you are smart enough, you'll take 'em…" she spoke with agitation.

"Why are you trying to be hateful about white people now? Is there something for you in that or is anything I am missing that I need to know because I don't get it. Why are you angry now? Ain't she a human being?"

"Oh, I get it now. You all still have that mentality…"

"What mentality, you psycho?" she said as she was walking angrily towards the kitchen. "I don't know. You should tell me right now. Slave mentality… I know is one of the reasons, isn't it?" he asked her.

"What, are you blind or you are dull, or are you both? Don't you know they discriminate against us all? You know that, don't you?" she asked convincingly.

"No, I don't and I don't believe that, either."

"Well stupid, you don't have to …"

"We all know that God doesn't discriminate. He only distinguishes amongst us to test human beings. He wants to know who will pass, and who is going to fail His test. That's why he creates different colors. It's a test and by you seeing color-differences, you are on the edge of failure. You and anybody else, that's right I said. I am cool with anybody on the face of the earth; it doesn't matter if such is black or white, green, purple …. Whatever, a human being is a human being; they're ain't no difference…We all bleed red."

"You are stupid and slow. You wouldn't talk that way if you knew what I know. Don't you know who killed our parents?"

"How would I know? Oh, let me guess, white people, am I right? Bullshit!"

"Do you think this is bullshit? They killed them both. You were too young to know by then because you were there with granny in Nigeria before she died and I was with Dad's mother here in America; she later died, too. Now you came back here and you are trying to date a stupid white girl? Think about it, Bolaji…" She began to cry.

"Think about what, sister? I have nothing to think about. I do things on my own terms and in my own ways. You have to learn how to accept and deal with that…I cannot be your puppet!"

"Because of that stupid white girl you are trying to disrespect me, that stupid witch!"

"She is not stupid, okay? See, keep on crying. I don't have time for this kind of conversation. I am going out, now. See you." He walked towards the door and slammed it behind himself after stepping out onto the porch outside.

"Go ahead stupid boy. He is mad because of that stupid devil witch. I don't even know why he is so stupid to not notice things around here. We know different here in America." She was angrily talking to herself in his absence.

Meanwhile, Adam had called Bolaji's cell phone and left him a message. He called him back immediately as he entered the car and he was heading to his house when he learned he was at home. He knocked on his door and they exchanged friendly greetings as Adam opened the door for him. Adam offered him something to drink and Bolaji accepted a can of Grape Fanta. They worked on the assignments that professor Duane had assigned and then started watching a movie. After hours of visiting and when the movie had finished, Bolaji decided to head home and Adam walked him to his car, waving goodbye as his new friend drove off.

Before he'd even driven a mile drive his phone rang; he picked it up and this time it was the lovely Beauty, she wanted to hang out with Bolaji the next day, which was Sunday. He flipped the phone with his right hand while the other hand was battling the steering wheel to balance the movement of the car.

"Hey baby, I thought you went home this weekend," he said.

"No, I didn't. I stayed because of you. Frank went though." "Frank? Who is Frank?"

"Oh, don't be jealous. Frank is my brother."

"Oh, I'm sorry."

"That's not necessary."

"When do you want me to pick you up tomorrow -- I mean what time tomorrow?"

"You know what I mean. Yes, what time tomorrow?"

"Any time, baby… I am always here for you."

"What about five o'clock in the morning?"

"Oh, five is too late. How about three o'clock in the morning. I mean three on the dot. Sound good to you?"

"It sounds great to me."

"Quit playing, Bolaji. What time will you be here?"

"I'll pick you up by ten in the morning. What are you doing?"

"Just lying in bed and thinking about how handsome you are."

"Oh, sweet imagination… What do you have on?"

"That's my man; he's always trying to get nasty with me. I just have panties and a bra on. That's all."

"You are going to make me lose control of the steering wheel now. What kind of colors are they?"

"You didn't tell me you were driving. I have to let you go now. Please be careful on the road. I love you, bye."

"I love you too, boo. So you don't want to tell me the colors?" She rang off not hearing this last. Their conversation over, he continued driving home.

He entered the house with red eyes and his sister asked him where he had been all that time. She was relieved he was just visiting his friend, Adam. Bolaji told Anita that he would have to go to bed early because he had somewhere to go the following morning and she kissed him good night.

He woke up at six o'clock in the morning and he was getting ready to spend the whole day with his girl, being the first time he didn't really want to mess up at all he had taken his bath, brushed his hair to let those waves shine and he brushed his teeth three times already; perhaps his girlfriend might be doing exactly the same thing he was doing now. When the clock reached 9:00 am he went to the refrigerator and had some bananas, apples and drinks he bought on the way home last night. He had cooked rice with beans and dodos and also some turkey wings and thighs, and he placed these things in the cooler and he took them to his car. His sister was still in her room sleeping and he didn't want to wake her up; he left a note that he might be back and this time he drove in his brand new yellowish butter Lamborghini, and he was heading to Beauty's apartment. He kept dancing happily with his favorite rapper, Pac's, rhymes and he got there after a thirty minute drive.

Three knocks had been cast on the door and his girlfriend was in the bathroom battling with her make-up, but she looked just fabulous to him. He knew she was in there and he kept his patience till she came and opened the door, he smiled.

She dressed in a fabulous dress that her mother, Rebecca, had bought for her; it was a deep ruby red gown that did not require either a bra or panties beneath it. She was glowing even more than fresh roses and her body scents were more fetching than those of nectar to insects during pollination; her lips were soft and better than any others; her grey eyes were so sexy that could make any man lose his continence with lust if he wasn't careful, but Bolaji tried hard to overpower any such of aims and he kept smiling as Beauty moved closer to him. Beauty had been looking forward to the day and she felt like she was on the top of the world and she had to dress just like the queen of the globe. They held each other's arms as they were counting the steps down from the stairs. Beauty was much more proud to be seen with such a young and handsome rich guy with a brand new Lamborghini; neighbors were jealously looking at them as they approached the vehicle. Bolaji opened the door for her and he then went to the other side to start the car. She couldn't believe what was happening to her right now and she did not even know that the poor guy named Bolaji happened to be one of the few haves in a world of have nots. Some people even thought that Beauty might well be a gold digger.

***

"Are you okay, Baby?" asked Bolaji, the first words he threw her way.

"Yes, I'm alright. Where are we going exactly?" Beauty then asked.

"Do you ever trust me?"

"Do I trust you? Yes, I do."

"Okay, I am taking you to a very romantic place. It ain't going to be a restaurant, not a theatre, none of that but it will be a quiet place, just me and you nobody else. There we can spend a perfect romantic time with each other. Does it sound good to you, my dear?"

"It sounds good to me. But …"

"Ah-uh, no but…"

"Would you hear me out first, please?"

"I am sorry, what is it, honey?"

"Don't you think we are going to be starved?"

"Not that I think, I know we will starve that is why I …"

"I wanna spend the whole day with you and if we just spend thirty minutes at the place just because we are starving it might mess with my emotions and I am not going to like it."

"You should have trusted your man. Look behind you; the cooler contains everything we are going to need. I have got food in there, fruits and drinks."

"You're kidding, right?"

"No shit baby. I'm serious. We are going to have fun."

"Oh, I love you so much. I am so lucky I found you."

"Stop kidding, I am the luckiest one to find you. That is the truth." He then made a right turn at a corner that led to a beach; he drove for two additional miles before reaching their destination and parking their car.

***

It was so quiet and somehow scary that only birds and some creatures in the water were the only inhabitants at the place. They settled under a tree that provided shade and blocked the sun's rays to make the place comfortable and habitable for them both. Bolaji did not scare; he took out a wide piece of cloth and stretched it on the face of the grass to accommodate him and his girlfriend, and then he placed the food beside them with disposable plates he bought the other night. He filled the plate for both of them and they began nourishing each other with food and drinks. She put food into his mouth and she requested the return and he did the same. She enjoyed the food and the game and she was deeply in love with him more than she could ever imagine and the love between them was now totally eternal.

"Do you enjoy the meal, my lady?" Bolaji asked her.

"I loved the meal, my lord. What is this called, my lord?" she asked, pointing to the dodo.

"It's called dodo, my lady. Dodo is a Yoruba term, one of the languages spoken in Nigeria. It's made from plantains, I fried them though. And the meat was turkey, my lady."

"I noticed that, my lord," she said smiling.

"Let me asked you a question. If I died today, who would you be going out with?

"What kind of question is that? Don't be playing like that. I don't want you to die."

"You do know that I will die one day, right?"

"That's for sure. Everybody will die."

"So answer my question, my lady?"

"I am not praying that my man should die at young age. You are going to live life to the fullest together with me. Stop playing like that, Bolaji. If you die, I am not going to forgive myself and I will kill myself."

"Promise…?"

"What, Bolaji? Are you okay? I am serious; I'll kill myself if something happens to you."

"Why would you do that?"

"First of all, not that I would kill myself, I will kill myself for sure. You need to mark the difference and the only reason that would make me do that is because I love you with every bit of my life. If the only love of my life has gone why would I be waiting? I have to go with him immediately so that we could be together again and ever after. Would you do the same?"

"I swear to God, I will for you because I love you deeply."

"Wow! Okay let's talk about something else." She said as she lay on the cloth and placed her head in between Bolaji's thighs. "Okay, amongst fear, trust and love, which do you think is the greatest?"

"Oh, that is kind of tricky. I am going to say love because if you love someone dearly you will definitely learn how to trust him. And you should have fear for him because you didn't want to do something that could make him mad. Am I right…?"

"Bravo! You are so smart. Some people are smart but not beautiful and some are beautiful and not smart, God gave you both. You are smart and beautiful. I am very blessed and lucky to have you as my girl, my future wife."

"Future wife, are you serious?"

"What did you mean am I serious? I am very serious"
"A lot of people don't think that way; they just want to fuck and that's all. They would run when it comes to commitment."

"I don't like dating. I choose you to be my wife even though we have not married yet. I respect you and consider you as my wife."

"I don't believe this. Are you serious with all you are saying?" "Yes, I am. Don't you like it that way?"

"More than everything in this world, baby."

"Now open your mouth…" he had peeled up a banana and he was trying to feed Beauty with it.

"Yummy! Thank you very much. My turn, open yours…" she fed him in return.

"I love you, baby."

"And I love you more."

"And I love you more and more."

The movement of the breeze was advantageously freshening and shining the surface of their skins, perhaps temporarily, and blood had moved close to their bodies' surface to balance the temperature between them and their surroundings. The tree they sat beneath danced with its branches and fanned the bottom to disperse all the debris away leaving nothing behind but the clean spots to play on and this motivated these young couple to stay some hours more.

"How did you know this place?"

"Somebody helped me with it," Bolaji answered.

"Who might that be?"

"The power of love," he chuckled.

"You are very funny. Let's play something fun."

"Like what exactly?" He was curious.

"Something like singing, chasing and so on. Do you like that?"

“With you, I love everything.” Bolaji smiled while mouthing those words and he stood up, lifting Beauty up as well.

“Who is going to start first?” Beauty asked.

“You know what they say, ladies first.”

“Whatever. You should go first, please.”

“I love you, I love you. Wherever you are, I’ll be there with you. Nothing in this world would come between us wherever we go.” He sang with lovely satisfaction.

“I have loved you before I even knew you. Wherever you go, I shall be there with you. Wherever you stay, I’ll stay there with you. Ain’t nothing in this world would come between us wherever we go.” She smiled.

“I’ll give you my words. Baby, I am promising you. I’ll give you my words. Take them as I give and nothing in this world would come between us baby, I promise you.” He then started running, expecting her to run after him romantically.

“And I’ll give you my heart, but baby don’t break it. I’ll gift you with my soul, but baby don’t lose it. Nothing in this world could come between us I swear and I promise you,” she said as she chased her man playfully.

“In my dream, baby or my day life, I repeat in my dream or my day life, 24/7 and 365, I’ll be thinking of you,” Bolaji said while hugging her.

“Surely, in my dream, my love or my day life, I said in my dream, baby or my day life, 24/7 and 365, I’ll be kissing you.” She laughed quietly and then kissed him.

Then the late night and the darkness of their surroundings forced them to vacate the place and he took her home. She felt like she did not want to be even an inch away from him and she tied herself to his body while hugging him good night. This moment could have done something to both bodies; they might have been wet underneath with excitement. She later released herself and she walked up stairs with sobering eyes and Bolaji then drove off when she had climbed up all the stairs and waved good night.

A minute had passed ten o'clock, and Bolaji then entered carelessly with rhymes flipping in between his upper and lower lips. Anita was angry and she stared at him without even saying a word. Bolaji kept rhyming unknowingly and he did not say a word of greeting to his sister; he walked towards the refrigerator and grabbed a bottle full of water, and he was sipping it down until he was fully satisfied.

"What's good sister?" he broke the silence at last.

"What do you mean what's good? Where have you been all these hours?" she asked demandingly.

"I was out ..."

"...out with whom, Bolaji?"

"I was out with a friend," he responded.

"Like the person ain't got no damn name?" she asked further.

"Why do you wanna know anyway? What do you care?"

"I hate your dumb ass questions sometimes. I have the right to know where the hell you are because I am your big sister."

"Well thanks big sis...I am a grown man now. Got it?"

"Whatever. I will continue looking after you as long as I can.

"That was my promise to our parents. Gosh! This isn't Africa. You need to be careful about where you are going and who you choose to roll with."

"Aight thanks."

"And stop saying that stupid word. It's alright, not 'aight.'" You didn't grow up in the 'hood.

"Are you done lecturing me now, Professor Anita? That sounds great."

"Whatever. Take my word and follow it. I read your note on the table since ten o'clock this morning and it took you twelve hours to get home? What have you been doing for twelve hours, anyway?"

"Quit being nosy, sister… I am not telling."

"Keep it to yourself then…"

"I will and it won't hurt."

"That's for sure."

"Thanks and I will be going to bed if you don't mind, do you?"

"Why would I? You must be tired anyway."

"I'll see you tomorrow morning."

"Maybe you will. I have to get up for an early class. I'm going to bed now, in a minute."

"See you in the morning, then."

"They both then walked into their respective rooms and locked the doors behind themselves."

The sun came out too late the following day -- not until after 1:00 pm. Bolaji was still in bed dreaming about the past that occurred between him and his lover and he couldn't get out of the bed until the sun's rays forcefully came through the window screen. He opened his eyes confusedly and he couldn't believe the time; he'd missed all of his classes for the day. He remained in bed for some minutes and left his mouth hanging open. Finally, he got up to brush his teeth and cleanse his dirty body. The first in-coming call was his sister's and she curiously wanted to know if Bolaji was missing from school due to illness. He lied that he had driven to school but then had felt so sick to his stomach and nauseated that he had no choice but to go home. She pitied his condition without knowing that she had been fooled. Then another call came to Bolaji from Adam, his best friend.

"Hello, brother what happened to you?" Adam asked.

"Nothing man."

"Why didn't you come to class, then?"

"I stupidly overslept."

"What, you were drunk?"

"Heck no; that's forbidden."

"Forbidden? By whom?"

"God of course. I will never, ever do that in my life and I pray not to by His grace.

"Alright, so what the heck happened then?"

"I told you I couldn't get up from bed. I just got up now. What happened in class? Duane came or he didn't?"

"Man, he did and he gave us a test today."

"You are kidding, right?"

"I am not kidding, brother."

"Stop playing…"

"I swear to God."

"How…?"

"I don't know, but God saved me."

"Gosh! That was too risky. It could cost you everything man. I owe you!"

"You don't owe me shit. I know you would do the same for me."

"That's true. Hey man, I've got a call waiting on the other line, I will hit you back."

"Alright, holla back then. See you."

Bolaji was walking out of the kitchen and then heading back to his bedroom. He preferred talking to his girl alone in his bedroom where nothing would rudely ruin their romantic conversation.

Beauty was saying hello while Bolaji was just trying to lay on the bed so that he could concentrate better on the conversation; he put Beauty on hold, turned off the television and then turned the fan on to cool his body.

"Hello! How's the most beautiful woman in the world"

"You always make me feel special," she said on the phone.

"You are special should you doubt that."

"Thank you, darling."

"You are very welcome."

"I didn't see you or your double at school today. What happened baby?"

"You didn't? I saw you walking away from university center with your friends."

"Why didn't you call me?"

"I thought you were looking at me and I waved at you but you had been buried in the conversation you all were having by then."

"Wipe off your lips, brother. I didn't go to UC center today. I had four tests and I sought every nook and cranny of the school…"

"…looking for what exactly?" He interrupted.

"I was searching for my missing baby, my darling."

"You wouldn't believe this. I was dreaming about us and I way overslept. Guess what time I got up?"

"What time…?"

"1:00 pm, I swear to God. I couldn't believe my eyes."

"Are you kidding? One o'clock. I know you don't drink, or I would have said perhaps you drink too much. What caused it anyway?"

"You caused it."

"What did you mean I caused it? How…?"

"You hypnotized me into sleep and I was drunk with your love, so I couldn't get up at the right time."

"Now you are trying to put it on me. I admit and that's a good thing as long as it is me and it's not somebody else."

"Not a chance baby, just you and me and nobody else. I promise."

"Oh, I love you so much."

"And I love you more."

"Where are you now?"

"In my bedroom lying down on my bed and I am doing nothing but thinking of you."

"Can I come over?"

"I would love that. I'd love to see you and welcome you to my crib."

"You wish. I am just playing. We will hang out next Sunday." "I can't wait till Sunday. I feel like it should be tomorrow morning."

"Me too, baby."

"Where are you?"

"The same place you were and I…"

"Where is your brother at?"

"He is at school I think. And your sister…?"

"She ain't back yet... I am glad she ain't. She always gives me a hard time."

"I thought I was the only one with Frank here. He asked too many questions already. Baby I've got to go. My mom is on the other line. I'll see you at school tomorrow and don't oversleep. I love you."

"I love you, too."

"Bye-bye." Beauty said.

Eight - Six months later.....School Dormitory

Frank had got prepared for school, but he could not find one of his textbooks and then decided to search for it in his sister's room. He entered the room and began searching while his sister was still in the bathroom, taking her shower. He ran his hands into a book, but accidentally, and some pictures were flung out as the book fell onto the floor. They were the pictures that Bolaji and Beauty took together four weeks prior to the day. They seemed like nothing but a fluke to Frank. He glanced at them and he detested what he saw; his sister hugging and kissing not only just a man, but a black man in those pictures. He noticed that he had been seeing the guy in the pictures around the school's premises and he planned to chase him off. He secretly left Beauty's room, and before she could notice his presence. When Beauty came back into the room she had the feeling that someone had been there, but she didn't take it very seriously.

Beauty, ever since the day she got hooked up with her boyfriend, had been taking extra special care of how she looked, including her clothes, which she always chose with Bolaji's taste in mind. She knew he loved her in sexy jeans with hot tops and hence she naively wore a blue jean with a red top and then covered her hair with a face cap after she had had tennis shoes on her feet and she walked to the nearby bus stop to take the public bus.

While she was heading to her first class, she came across Tasha and she innocently greeted her as student to student. Tasha bristled instead, which surprised Beauty.

It was breakfast time and was a very sunny day; Beauty with her friends was at the cafeteria eating and at the same time joking and conversing before Tracy grabbed one of Beauty's books and began searching through it. She then found pictures of this cute black guy and shouted, "Wow!" this attracted the others' attention and they were eager to know what had happened.

"Wow! Every one, look at this… look at what I found…" said Tracy.

"Give them back to me." Beauty was fighting over the pictures, but not too seriously.

"Come on Beauty, let's look at them," Mickey said to her.

"What is his name?" Tracy asked.

"His name is Bolaji." Beauty answered.

"Cute name, too," Mickey added.

"Oh, thanks" Beauty said, thanking Mickey for the comment. "What? Thanks or what did I hear? It looks like somebody is in love," Trish interrogated.

"So is he a friend or more than that…?" Faith asked Beauty. "He is more than that to me. Whatever…" Beauty was trying to explain.

"It's okay. I mean he is really cute and everything but…" Faith added.

"…But what or because he is black…? Answer my damn questions somebody." Beauty felt the pain of discrimination.

"Well…" Tracy was then forced to stop by Beauty.

"Well what…? We are in love, he loves me dearly and I do back. What's the big deal? Or is it a crime to be in love?" Beauty asked angrily.

"Not at all girl, we are living in free world. You get to choose whoever you want to be with and that's not a crime," Mickey encouraged her.

"That's my man and I love him with my heart. No one could take him from me because I love him so much," Beauty said while kissing the pictures.

"Alright miss love, shall we talk about something else? I mean something good and expensive such as shoes or something?" Tracy asked.

"What time is it right now?" Beauty asked Tracy.

"It is quarter to eleven," she answered.

"Oh, shit! I've got to go. I have class in less than five minutes." Beauty stood and packed her belongings and they all left the place for their classes. And Bolaji and Adam were both walking to the cafeteria for an urgently needed breakfast, but they came across Beauty and her friends where they greeted one and another but the suspicious embrace that Beauty and Bolaji gave each other made Adam impatient and curious. He set his eyes on Tracy immediately when he saw her with others.

"So tell me something here, brother. Am I missing something?" Adam asked Bolaji.

"I don't know what you are missing." Bolaji replied.

"What's going on between you two?" He asked further.

"Do you mean me and Beauty?"

"She is my girl." Bolaji replied.

"Seriously, Bolaji I am not playing."

"And I am not playing, either. She's my girl. We're dating each other…"

"Date…ooo? I know you are playing, right?"

"What? We can't date each other because she is white and I am black? That's your point, isn't it?" Bolaji threw the question out angrily.

"I am not saying that. Did I say that already?"

"I don't know. Maybe you are trying to say it. You hang around with me and you are, I don't know, may be white or brown whatever..."

"I am man not a woman, brother..."

"I see what you are saying..."

"You know what? Go for your heart. Hey do me a favor. Hook me up with one of Beauty's friends."

"Which one of them do you want?"

"The one who looks like a model. I like her. She is very..." Adam said.

"She is white, remember..." Bolaji said to him. "So am I. I am white too."

"Are you white? I thought you were black that's why you're rolling with me?"

"Don't get me wrong, I am white and I am black as well. I can fit into both categories."

"Oh, smart ass."

"You are very crazy, Bolaji."

"Thanks."

At noon, Bolaji was on his way to class, sweating from the beating rays of the sun and he was in hurry to take advantage of cooling down when he came across Frank. He did not know him yet, but Frank knew him from the pictures and he hated him already. Frank deliberately hit him and refused to ask forgiveness for his action. Bolaji was amazed and he asked him for an apology and that was something Frank would never ever do to anyone, especially to Bolaji. He stepped back and asked Bolaji what he had just said.

"I thought you were going to do something about it, coward!" Frank said.

"You have got that right, punk. I am about to do something right now," he fired back at Frank.

"Okay. Bring it on…" Frank said while holding up his fists. "You're in the wrong man. You hit me and didn't say a word to apologize."

Bolaji reminded him.

"You are damn right, I ain't said shit. What are you going to do?" Frank asked again.

Several students burst into the scene to break things off before it got physical between Frank and Bolaji. A small crowd gathered, but ultimately, nothing happened. Some of Beauty's friends witnessed the scene and Bolaji then left for his class. Adam was so concerned with Bolaji's red eyes. He felt that he knew something had gone wrong with him. He impatiently asked what happened to him and he whispered the details into his ears because the class was still in progress and none could afford to lose the class by bending the rules and being forced out. The class ended and they stepped outside. Adam was then tightening his loose shoes while also removing dust particles from his pants. They walked to the students' refreshment area and then got seated to have a talk. He urged Bolaji to do something soon before it was too late. Bolaji replied that he would be alright and there would be no problem at all.

Bolaji was heading to the parking lot where he parked his car at; he was ready to call it a day and head back home when Beauty grabbed him from behind and wrapped her arms around his waist; he was so scared but he turned gently to see who she was and he was glad to find Beauty. She asked him how he was feeling and told him she heard about what happened between him and Frank. Bolaji was shocked and he was willing to know how she even knew his name.

"So you know him that much?" He asked furiously.

"Know who that much, Frank? Is my brother, remember," she replied.

"Ho, Frank. That was him, your own brother. Why was he acting like he hated me already? He was curious to know.

"I guess from the pictures," she suggested.

"…The pictures! Did you show them to him? Why would you do that? Don't you know that no man would love to see his sister with another man? It's almost automatic. They feel too overprotective. Why?" He was afraid.

"Calm down Bolaji. I didn't. He snuck into my room or something. What are you afraid of? He is not going to do anything, relax!" she urged.

"Well, I am feeling sleepy right now and I'll call you tonight." "Okay, my darling. Sweet dreams, all about me." "You bet. I love you."

"I love you, too."

He entered the car and drove off; she would have gone with him but she still had more classes that day and she walked back to the next class. He could not describe how deeply he was in love with Beauty. All he knew was that the volume of all oceans would not be in anywhere close to the volume of his love towards her and she was so much in love with him too *only God knows* who had the greatest one between the two of them. He placed her pictures beside the driver side to occupy the seat in replacement and with a satisfactory smile and white teeth he looked at the pictures one after the other. He had sent Beauty a love letter about two days earlier and he expected her to have received it and talk about it, but she did not have it yet. Perhaps she would have it later on.

After classes and when she had stepped out of the public bus she went to their mail box to check her mail and she found the letter that Bolaji had sent to her. She opened it impatiently to read through and she momentarily suffered words to describe her emotional feelings at once. All she wished for was that she should remain to be his golden girl. The letter was not actually a letter it was a lovely composed poem and it touched her soul that she cried happily, the letter contained this poem:

Golden Flower

I use a golden pen to write my golden words to my lovely golden girl
That comes to change my life into a golden one.
Her eyes are the most golden eyes I have ever seen in my golden life.
The eye lids and the lashes are woven to give a golden blink each time.
And her golden white teeth explore the golden smile that illuminates my face.
Her nose is perfectly sculpted and nothing it breaths but the golden air.
The lips are very soft, better than nectar with the golden scents.
The entire face is beautiful and worthier than the golden prize.
The hair is always shining and more fetching than expensive golden jewelries.
The arms fit the golden clothes.
And the legs are sexy and touchable to fit all the golden jeans.
The entire body shape is indeed perfect like a golden sculpture.
I don't fancy a golden car nor do I fancy a golden house
I don't fancy a golden shoe nor do I fancy a golden watch
All that I fancy is my beautiful golden girl
She is the very golden flower in the beautiful golden garden.
She is the best sugar to make a golden tea.
She is the perfect mayonnaise to make an excellent but golden sandwich.
Can anybody help to call a photographer to take the picture of this golden image?

The only golden photo that should be framed within golden glass
She is the golden prayer that could beautify one's life into a golden one.
I am in the bushy land to pick but a golden flower
My friends are in a hurry and have no patience to search further for the golden flower
I bear the pains and continue my odyssey alone, only for the golden flower
I am beaten by the sun's rays and as well as unfriendly heavy but golden rainfall
I never quit searching because I value the golden flower
I laugh last because I finally get to meet the golden flower.
She asks me why I sacrifice my golden life for her golden face
I answer that the golden life would not be perfect sans the golden flower
She smiles with the golden teeth and jumps into my golden hands
I am very much glad and proud to have the golden flower in my golden life
My friends are jealous to see me with the golden flower afterwards
It ain't my fault because I am patient and focus to get the golden girl
I pray that if God gives me a second chance to live a golden life again
He should please bless me with your golden soul and face again
I love you my golden bird with my golden heart
I cease my golden pen here with the golden smile and we shall meet on the next golden day

Your golden man,

Bolaji.

She picked up her phone and dialed his numbers with extreme emotion. He was in the restroom and could not hear the phone ringing. She decided then to leave him a message.

"Hey, baby. It's me your golden girl. I got your letter, I mean poem rather and it was well composed. I love it very much. I didn't know you are also a poet. There are a lot of things I didn't know about you and I am glad that you had those qualities. You are smart, brilliant, a genius, sexy and lovable. I swear to God that I didn't know you were born with the silver spoon in your mouth and I felt like people might be thinking that I am a gold-digger. I want you to know that I love you for you and not for your money, and I have loved you even before I even meet you in person. Well, I am going to frame this poem and I display it in my bedroom with pride. I love you and will see you on the next golden day. I love you very much and bye for now." She then hung up.

When Bolaji was done using bathroom he noticed that he had had one missed call and a voice message, he listened to it and he laughed out loud. He called her back immediately; it rang twice and she took her time before picking it up.

"Hey, baby…" Bolaji said to her.

"Where were you?" She asked instead.

"I was using the bathroom. I got your message. Did you like the poem?" He asked her. "Are you kidding me? I love it very much. I didn't know you were a poet. You are very secretive, Bolaji."

"And secretively, don't tell anybody. I love to be anonymous," he said.

"Maybe you should write a poetry book," she suggested.

"I don't know yet my lady. I am thinking to wait till I graduate. I will have plenty of time to write whatever I want to write."

"Good idea, baby."

"That reminds me. What the heck you were talking about that people might think you are a gold- digger? Don't give a hoot about what people be thinking about you. Just continue to follow your heart. Don't listen to them."

"Okay, baby. I was wondering if you would love to take other pictures with me tomorrow. I know a photographer who is very professional…different from the first amateur and I want you to add poetic words at the bottom of each picture, what do you think? "

"That's great baby."

Nine – One Week Later ….Chattanooga, TN

The outdoors forbade bare legs on the streets at the moment; everyone remained in his or her home without even being instructed to do so; it was too hot and over a 100 degrees Fahrenheit. Cars were the things the only things that dared to brave the sun, wheeling drivers around on the driest and most dangerous of the nation's hottest roads. People could only handle the heat with the comfort of air conditioners.

Frank was there in the living room working on his assignments that were likely to be due soon. He had been working on them since 7:00 a.m. and it had been some hours of work already that he felt like taking a short break.

Beauty jumped out of her bedroom and she confronted her brother. Frank was so confused and he thought, “Wasn’t she the one who prepared breakfast for both of us?” Beauty hated to fight with her brother or any of her family members, but whoever offended Bolaji had indeed come caused her to be ready to fight with both her heart and mind, provided that she would not be physically able.

“What’s the matter with you, young girl?” Frank smiled.

“I’ll tell you what’s wrong with me. What happened between you and Bolaji today?” She frowned.

“Bolaji…? Ho, the black…” He stopped before he would say something offensive.

“Go ahead say the word. You are so stupid, Frank. I don’t appreciate you picking on my man. I am eighteen years old and I can take care of myself. What’s your problem?” She was furious.

“Stop seeing him. As long as you stop seeing him there will be no further problem. We were told to stay away from black people, remember?” he reminded her.

“Nobody told me anything and I will not stay away from him; you might want to jot that down now. I have seen you too with black guys and friends; what do you have to say about that?” she asked him.

“I am a man and I am very smart at what I am doing,” he said.

“And I’m smarter than you. You should think about that, too,” she argued.

“I don’t want to hear all that nonsense you are saying, girl.”

“Fine, don’t listen. Nothing will stop me from seeing him and whether you like it or not, we will get married one day.”

"You are out of your mind. Maybe you have lost it and I will help you to find it back. Get married? Bullshit! Not in this life. I know what I am going to do..." He was then forced to stop. "What are you going to do? I'll tell you what, if you do anything to hurt him I swear to God I will never forgive you."

"Like hell I care. I have got a million perfect ideas; first, I am going to call mom and tell her. That could stop you," he taunted.

"So what…? I will tell her myself and she will accept him because she loves me that much," she said confidently.

"We will see. Tell him to stay away from you, otherwise I will deal with him."

"Don't you dare lay your hands on him again otherwise I'll press charges against you myself." She was trying to shock him.

"Oh, that could be better because the only way I can stop dealing with him is to get locked up. So call the police right now, lover bird."

"Leave me alone! You are so stupid. And do me a favor, don't fight my boyfriend again."

"You keep calling him your boyfriend and that irritates me and it will get him into trouble. I'm telling you…" he warned further.

"No one is going to get into trouble. This is America, brother. Don't be stupid like I told you earlier."

"You are the stupid one dating a black guy…" he said back to her.

"…black, yellow, red and white it doesn't matter. Love is what matters.

"I am not stupid like you were and I have more experience than you do. Why must you date a black man?"

“Are they not human, psycho? Answer me, Frank! All I know is that we are equal before our creator and all made by the same creator,” she explained.

“And who might that be exactly?”

“I don’t know. Perhaps God, Allah, Lord. I know there is God up there in the sky who creates everything and especially human beings with one and only one single blood. He covers bodies with different skin colors. Think about it, Frank.

“When did you become a preacher? I feel like I am wasting my time with you here arguing. I am going out. Call mom and tell her. By the way, you really need a therapist…” He smiled and walked out through the door.

Beauty wasted no time and decided to call her mom who was there in her car driving back to her home town. She was looking into the front mirror as she drove. Her cell phone rang twice and she picked it up on the second ring.

“Hello, my little angel,” Rebecca said.

“Mom, I am not little any more. I am almost eighteen years old.” “Well, even if you are fifty years old, you’re still little to me.”

“Okay, fine you win. I am having my birthday party next month, Mom.”

“Are you coming home for your birthday?”

“No, Mom. I wanted to do it here with friends.”

“Okay, I will send you presents.”

“Thanks Mom, I love you.”

“I love you too my little angel. How is the education, my baby?”

“Everything is fine, mom. I can’t wait for break,” she kept smiling with each word coming out of her mouth.

“Why, are you tired already?”

"No, mom... I just miss you that much."

"Oh, poor baby I know you won't miss me anymore when you get yourself a boyfriend."

"Thanks to you…I was going to tell you that…"

"What, you have got one already? That was too early, you just got there. Somebody is growing up now. Where is Frank? Put him on the phone for me."

"He's not here, Mom."

"Where did he go to?"

"I don't know, maybe to his friends or something. He is mad at me though," she revealed.

"He's mad at you, for what?" she asked curiously.

"He doesn't like my boyfriend."

"That's childish. He is not going to be your boyfriend, is he?" "I tried to explain that…"

"I'll talk to him. Hold on Beauty, will you…?" she was trying to pull into a convenience store's parking lot.
"Hello…are you still there?"

"I'm here, Mom," Beauty answered.

"So tell me about your boyfriend. What does he look like?" She was initially happy to hear about him.

"I know you are going to love him. He's smart, very funny, cute, black…"

"…Black! Oh no way…" She hung up immediately.

"Hello! Mom…!"

The phone had faded away and she felt depressed but that would never stop her from seeing Bolaji because she had made up her mind that she would continue to be with him even if it took away her life.

Four o'clock in the evening her phone rang and the depression faded away immediately when she heard Bolaji's voice; he was there downstairs to pick her up for a ride around the town. She invited him upstairs and he did and made himself comfortable while waiting for her to dress up. She tried hard to dissipate the feelings away from her heart so that Bolaji would not know that something was bothering her, but he knew something might have happened, so he planned to lift it off of her chest by telling jokes to reveal her pearly white teeth. He didn't ask what happened. He only wanted her to forget about it. She appreciated his sense of humor and his personality and the love grew even more in her heart. They were just driving around the city of Chattanooga and with no aim for any particular destination. Bolaji was such a good mimic that he could dress like a thug sometimes just like he did that day; he had bandanna on his head and he thought he looked just like Tupac. He turned on the CD and Pac began rhyming. He did not see Beauty as just a white girl and he neglected that Pac might even say something offensive in her hearing so he kept miming the track. Then he gained the other side of himself and changed the rap music into something that could suit his girlfriend, he mimed that too and he further amazed Beauty.

"You know every song, don't you?" she asked Bolaji.

"…Some of 'em, not all of them. I listened to most artists-singers and rappers when I was in Nigeria."

He answered. "…Nigeria? Don't you mean Nigeria-Africa?"

"Yes, you are right. Why, you don't believe me?"

"Of course I do, baby, but I am amazed. I thought people were saying there were no conveniences in Africa - things like radios, satellite or TVs. I hope you are not offended…?"

"Why would I be? I am not offended, but let me explain to you. First of all, Africa is a huge continent not a country. People think all of Africa is suffering. Nigeria is a blessed country and to make comparison it is just like the USA. It comprises about thirty something states that are united as one – Nigeria. I have seen the Discovery Channel. You all are talking about hunger in Africa. There is hunger in every one my lady. Not all American lands are that rich. In South America for example, and so on. Talk about people living in the jungle, running around naked, living with animals…"

"Isn't it true?"

"Heck no it ain't. Nigeria has everything that the USA has, talking about the government, celebrities, artists, amenities, luxurious cars, industries, money, wealth and so on. And some of you think we do not speak English. The only thing that's different is the accent."

"Really…? I thought you could speak English because you were born here though you stayed over there."

"You know what's funny though? One lady asked me at the airport when I was coming from Nigeria where I came from and I replied that I came from Nigeria and she asked further how long I had been to the United States and I replied, "today is the first time since I was born." "She was like, 'how did you learn to speak English?' I told her we do speak English and she didn't believe me."

"Can I ask you a question?"

"You are my girl. Ask anything."

"Those marks on your face . . . where did they come from? I'm sorry to ask. I'm just curious. I want to know everything about you, my love." She was afraid that she may have embarrassed him.

"You are very funny." He burst into laughter.

"What's so funny, Bolaji…?" She joined in his laughter.

"Are you expecting me to say that I procured them from fighting with a wild animal?"

"I don't know. I've heard that in Africa people hunt wild animals for fun. I am very sure that no one would dare put those marks on your face here in United States," she explained.

"It's a cultural thing from my mother's side. Remember? I told you my mom came from Nigeria, right? See you are all crazy. During all the years I spent in Nigeria, I never came across a single lion or tiger in my neighborhood."

"So Nigerians don't do that?"

"No..."

"...running around naked...?" She laughed.

"We said the same thing about you all. You all are the ones who strip and dance around nearly naked, not us. We saw videos of women and even young teenage girls dressed in the smallest bikinis and we thought that was how the all American women would be dressed. Now I know differently. I want you to visit Nigeria so that you can learn firsthand how it really is."

"Would you take me there?"

"Would you love to go?"

"I'd be glad to go with you, baby."

"Hey girl, do you mind if I ask you a question?"

"I don't mind at all. Ask me anything you want to."

"Do you promise you are not going to get angry with me?"

"I promise, baby."

"Why are you so beautiful?"

"That's your question? You're not serious, I hope."

"You already promised to bear with me. Is it because you are Beauty?"

"Oh quit. I'm not *that* beautiful. Quit teasing me." She smiled and twice gently struck him on his well-muscled shoulder.

"Shall we enjoy some music, ma'am?" He laughed and soon they were miming the track together.

***

Inside Cracker Barrel, a popular southern restaurant, Anita and Karl were waiting for the server to bring their orders and Karl had it in mind to ask Anita about her opinion on her brother dating a white girl. Cracker Barrel is one of the busiest restaurants in the south if not the busiest, especially on Sundays or during any public holiday. The couple visited the place on the busiest day, which was Sunday and Independence Day for Americans. The waiting time became unbearable and they took one of the keep-you-busy games that the restaurant provided and began playing with each other for almost an hour and the half. They would have left the place but they loved most of the food served in the restaurant so they kept their patience and battled for an additional half-hour. Their orders finally arrived and they began eating and then Karl remembered what he had been going to ask his girlfriend about Bolaji and Beauty. He was about to open his mouth when Anita was not and someone deliberately kicked the chair and water spilled all over the table. The server came horridly, wiped off the table and got them another cup full of water and this time she put lemons on top of the water for no particular reason. The couple did not ask for lemons, but made no complaint when she brought them; they kept laughing and refused to tell her what went wrong when she insisted on knowing what she had done wrong. They asked her not be worried and she felt relieved with the words. Karl dove in with his straw and began sipping water. Anita kept watching but she could not do the same because she was embarrassed because people were staring at him; he did not care. Then he stopped to discuss the main subject that had been rolling in his mind for days. He paused silently for minutes without a single word; he was having second thoughts before opening his mouth.

"Anything wrong, baby?" Anita asked when he paused. "No baby, everything is fine. So tell me something, is everything cool between you and your brother?" he asked as he set the glass cup down to the table.

"What do you mean?" Anita asked surprisingly.

"I am sorry but him going out with a white chick…" he couldn't finish the line because he was interrupted.

"Oh, that's your reason. We are cool. I talked to him already and he didn't listen to me. How did you know by the way?" She was curious to ask.

"I have been seeing them both together for months around the school premises. I know something was going on. I don't think black folks are going to agree with him, especially women, you know what I am talking about?" he said.

"I tried Karl. I don't know what else to do. If you would be kind and be of any assistance then call him and talk to him. That might help. What do you think?"

"I don't think that's a very good idea. That is what we call trespassing. He is not my brother and he is free to do whatever. I am only concerned about what might be the consequences later on. I know somebody out there might have problems with them. It ain't me, though, I swear. You will need to talk to him again," he replied to her.

"He told me he was in love. What else do you want me to do now? He will be okay."

"Did you mean as in L.O.V.E? Okay. Let's continue enjoying our day." He smiled with his glass cup being raised up to Anita's.

After thirty minutes of chatting between Anita and Karl they were just a minute closer to leaving when the two golden birds popped through the front door of the restaurant and headed into the lobby. Bolaji greeted Anita and Karl by waving to them from across the room where he would be sharing a meal with his lovely girl, Beauty. Karl and Anita stood up and got ready to leave only because those people at the restaurant began staring hatefully at Bolaji and Beauty, which Anita was unwilling to tolerate. Bolaji thought differently and he believed Anita and her boyfriend were leaving because they did not like Beauty. The assigned server happened unfortunately to be a black girl and she was unfriendly when she asked what the couple might like for drinks or appetizers. Bolaji looked at her face and it recognized her negative attitude. He frowned back at her and told her they would take water and nothing more for an appetizer. The server came back and deliberately splashed water on Beauty's top; it was totally wet and so soaked that she could not sit a minute longer for the embarrassment. This irritated Bolaji so much that he asked Beauty to leave with him. The jealous server burst into laughter though she apologized afterward and she should at least get suspended for her unfriendly behavior if not terminated, but nothing happened to her, because the manager in charge was also a black man who thought Bolaji was a sellout. The whites and the blacks, present at the moment, were all happy for the disgrace that befell Beauty and Bolaji; they had no mercy on them at all and hence they left in shame. Beauty insisted that they should call the home office and report the incident, but Bolaji on the second thought realized what might later be the result and he begged her to let it go and she accepted at last. They drove to McDonald's and ordered burgers with drinks. He made sure that she was happy before he took her back to her apartment. As they approached the apartment, Frank's very rude voice could were be heard from upstairs hollering for Beauty like she had been missing for years. He walked downstairs popping questions at Beauty with not an atom of respect. Beauty decided to make him even angrier and gave Bolaji very romantic kisses before she untied herself from him and headed upstairs with a very satisfactory smile on her face. She did not answer a single question out of the many that Frank threw at her. She knew he could yell at her because he was the elder but he would never dare to lay his hands on her, never! Frank felt disrespectful and he schemed to deal with Bolaji further.

Ten – Two Weeks Later....School Campus

School had resumed after Independence Day and every student was reluctantly ready although happily unhappy to start classes again. The University Center was filled with students. Some were eating, some were chatting and embracing one another and most were staring and listening to school news from the big screen centered at the lobby, and the news aired that the school policy had changed lawfully and every student was advised to maintain peace and harmony towards others and their professors as well, but to gang members the news meant nothing. They hissed and laughed it off.

Then classes forced most students to vacate the place and few remained except for a group of curious students and the so-called thugs. Cobra, Jug, Samuel Edie and Leo Martin were all there at a corner and were high from smoking weed. Frank was making a beeline towards them despite harboring some fear.

He did not know what might happen because these thugs were all black and he was white. Cobra raised his head up and exhaled a heavy cloud of smoke in violation of the school's no smoking policy. He didn't care about rules. Cobra was scary, everything about him- his eyes, hair and especially voice. He smacked Jug and told him to look up, showing him the white boy who was coming into their direction. They were all at once ready to give a deadly beat down. He could only escape if he publicly claimed he had no beef with the thugs.

He then finally approached with tension and he could barely stretch out his hand to exchange greetings when Cobra gave his hand to him first, he was just shaking and felt relieved when they accepted him and smiled at him. Cobra, the leader of the gang members then asked him what he wanted; he knew he could never want to be part of them not. He tried talking like he was black, which made them laugh.

"What is happening with you all?" he asked.

"We are good. You know we are just chilling. You want some weed?"

Leo Martin offered him some smoke.

"No thanks…" He was panicky when he said now, but said it anyway.

"What do you mean, no? I am just playing with you. Wassup with you white boy?" He asked, smiling.

"I'm good. I came to ask you for a favor…"

"Oh, ok. What would that be, whitey?" Cobra interrupted him.

"You all know Bolaji, right?"

"How should we know him if not he is famous? Are you talking about the dude with marks on his face?" Jug asked.

"You've got it. Yeah him…"

"African mother… I hate that boy. The last time I checked on him he was with a white chick…" Cobra said.

"I heard he was born in America, but he grew up in Africa. So what's up with you and him, Frank? …Frank, right?" Samuel Edie asked him.

"Yeah, it is Frank; you said it right. The white chick you saw him with is my sister and I want to stop them. I don't want them together and I want your help. I mean, I want him to feel lucky to be alive and to never mess with another white girl again."

"You have no reason to be scared" Cobra reassured him.

"Please. I want them to stop dating."

"Come one Frank, relax man. We have got your back and we are going to deal with him tomorrow. That's what we do and we enjoy doing it every day. Ain't no need to beg…" Cobra added.

"Did you ever talk to your sister? I meant did you warn her?" Leo asked him.

"I did. Above and beyond the call of duty. I got nowhere. She is so stubborn and too wayward. She didn't listen to me," he answered.

"Yo Frank, don't even worry about it. He ain't nothing…" Cobra said.

"We will deal with him tomorrow. See you man." Jug said to him.

"Alright guys. I'll holla…" Frank joked with the word.

"Later man… and be careful. "Hey, don't mess with black chicks…" Cobra warned him.

"Trust me; I won't do that…see you." He laughed.

He left the place with such a happy face and he thought he had attained the golden prize of life by stopping his sister from going out with Bolaji. On his way out of the corner, he ran across Bolaji and Beauty holding each other's hands and chatting lovingly while heading to the cafeteria to find something to eat. Frank did not say a word and he could barely even look at them. He was eagerly waiting for the next day to come so that Bolaji would receive the severe punishment that he had planned for him. He walked past them in a hurry and pretended not to see them. Beauty didn't want Bolaji to find out that her brother was a racist.

The following morning, Bolaji had been feeling out of sorts and was thinking of not going to school, but his girl called and told him she would love to see him on campus. He, unfortunately, agreed to be there for her. He would have followed his heart and remained indoors for the rest of the day and kept enjoying his safety and privacy but he loved his girl that much and he would do anything to please her all the time, so he got up at once, trying hard to be a strong man and did twenty push-ups and sit-ups to ignite his body, then he jumped into shower without dawdling. He dressed up only to impress his girl. He loved to hear Beauty's comments from he knew she appreciated his compliments about what she wore and that she dressed to please him. He felt very lucky and blessed.

After twenty minutes of driving, he finally arrived at the reserved parking lot.

Adam was already in the class and doubting Bolaji's presence. Adam confessed that he thought he would not be able to come because he told him he was having bad joint pains. Bolaji just smiled.

Dr. Duane, one of their favorite professors at the time, was then coming into the classroom as if he was disturbed. Perhaps he had had something that killed his emotion and made him late to the class. He did not apologize for his lateness and he frowned before announcing the cancellation of the class and that it would be rescheduled to later hours in the afternoon. No one dared to argue with his decision. Adam told Bolaji he would have to run home quickly and be back late. Bolaji loved that and he was ready to spend the given hours with his girl provided that she would not be having any class sooner. He called to ask where she was at and she replied that she could see him coming towards her direction at a distant place; he hung up when he could see her too and they both walked into the cafeteria together to order some delicious food.

Although many students just ignored them, they also drew some hateful and disturbing stares cast by fellow students who frowned on interracial relationships. The students wanted to see black with black and white with white not Asian chick with black dude or white boy with Latino girl. Bolaji happened to be a very stubborn man who didn't care about what other people thought about him or what he did with his life. Beauty noticed the hateful looks they were giving and she felt so offended she was nearly on the verge of tears. Bolaji starting to joke with her to take her mind off of her heartache. It worked like magic. Their world seemed to narrow down to just the two of them – Beauty and Bolaji. She kept laughing and having a good time with him and that continued irritating most of the black girls near them and it forced them to vacate the place with hatred and hisses, none of which bothered Bolaji a wit. Beauty suspected the patronizing of the gang members as they were walking up and down the University center. She knew they meant business on somebody but she could not make a conclusion regarding who the business would rest on. The gang remained calm for the presence of many students and secondarily, university security. They continued walking around for hours and paused several times to sit beneath a tree outside where Bolaji read her romantic poetry in the beautiful weather. Security patrols continued perusing the area. Beauty was scared by the gang's presence and she instructed Bolaji to leave with her immediately; he agreed without an argument.

The next class was Psychology and Bolaji, Beauty and Tasha were all taking this class together. The class was going to be taught by Dr. Duane just for the day. No student knew this because the class was being taught by Professor Martin, a female professor who was also a UTC alum herself. She had called in sick that day and when Dr. Duane entered the class, about one-third of the class population was left in a daze when he instructed them to take out their psychology text books. Some students knew he was very good at mathematics and statistics to mention just two and now psychology? They couldn't believe it.

"Hello everyone and sorry I was two minutes late," he said, apologizing for his tardiness. "Ok, everybody, open up your book and turn it to page 167. Also, as you all should well know, you have an assignment due today. Please make sure all of your pages are stapled together and that you have your name, my name, the course number and today's date in the upper left hand corner of each page." The students shuffled their papers and Dr. Duane wearily pulled a stapler out of his briefcase because he knew from having taught for so many years that his students probably wouldn't have followed directions and stapled the papers themselves before coming to class. "I'll pass around this stapler in case any of you forgot! Just make sure I get this back and please notice that my name is on it, so don't walk off with it!"

"Everyone pass your assignments down to the end of your row where I will pick them up from the last student in each row.

C'mon now, let's hustle. I told you the paper was due at the *beginning* of today's class. Dr. Duane fidgeted about with his lesson plan as he waited for his students to comply. A student in the back of the room raised her hand.

"Can we get an extension on this, Dr. Duane? It's really hard and I'm still working on it."

"Well, why didn't you come to my office hours or go to the Writing Center for tutoring help?" The girl just shrugged and rolled her eyes.

"Young lady, I suggest you read your syllabus. Unless you are hospitalized there are no extensions for anyone, period. The syllabus also states that for each day that an assignment is late I will deduct ten points from the assignment's final grade. These rules are for everyone, so please, I don't want to hear that I'm unfair." A few girls in the front of the room giggled. They'd all finished their work the night before and had had many cups of coffee to keep themselves awake. They were now a bit sleepy, but also happy that they wouldn't have points deducted for tardiness.

The door whooshed open and Tasha came rushing into the room, schlepping her bag over her shoulder. She was late. "Thank you for joining us, today," Dr. Duane joked and laughter ensued. Tasha frowned as she stepped further into the room. She noticed that Beauty was sitting in the seat she usually sat in – a seat she chose specifically because it was right next to the chair occupied by Bolaji. Tasha'd had her jealous eyes set on him from the first day of class and she envied Beauty's fresh good looks and flawless appearance. She walked over to where Beauty was sitting and said, "That's my seat. Get up." "You can't be serious," Beauty replied. "Oh, I'm serious, all right!" The edge of her voice cut through the room and there was silence as Tasha continued to glare at Beauty with the expectation she would abandon her chair for Tasha. "I'm not moving, Tasha."

"What's going on over there, ladies? You're holding up the class. Tasha, you are the one who's late, so it's your own fault you don't have a chair now and I suspect I know where that chair is. Tasha please go across the hall to room 132A. There's no class scheduled for that room this hour, so go grab yourself a chair and come back and take a seat at the back of the room so you don't disturb all these students who had the courtesy to be here on time."

Tasha stormed out of the room, then came back into the room lugging a chair that, just as Dr. Duane had told her, was in an empty classroom across the hallway.

Bolaji squeezed Beauty's hand and they both stifled their giggles. Tasha had just made a grand spectacle of herself and she knew it, too.

"Okay, hush, all of you," Dr. Duane said as he gathered the students' assigned work.

Finally, the papers were gathered, everyone was seated and Dr. Duane shifted into his professorial element and began to lecture. When he had finished nearly two hours later, he dismissed the class and the students began to hustle out the door. Dr. Duane sighed when he noticed his own stapler atop the desk furthest from the door. He strolled over, retrieved his stapler, organized his briefcase, and then headed off for his next class.

Once out in the hallway, Bolaji and Beauty exchanged hugs and some serious French kisses before parting ways with one another.

The gang members were still out there waiting for Bolaji's appearance and they were glad to see him standing up there while kissing Beauty and they were ready to give him a beat down he could never imagine. Bolaji was clueless about the gang's plans on his head and he continued walking towards the library, where he intended to get caught up on his assigned reading. He was trying to psych himself up for the task ahead, but found little to look forward to as far as the assigned readings were concerned.

Bolaji did not notice that on the way to the library, he was being followed.

"What did I do? I didn't do anything wrong." Bolaji kept repeating the statement.

"We will tell you outside. Get up, mother lover!"

They dragged him out and started striking him seriously; he managed to escape and they were seeking every nook and cranny of the building for him. He took the available elevator to the third floor and was finding a safe place to hide; the gang members were still searching in different directions. Leo took the elevator as well but to the fourth floor, Samuel took stairs, Cobra stood at the door waiting for him to pop out and Jug was just running up and down, yelling for Bolaji to come out.

"I swear to God you are dead man. Come out now. Where are you, punk?" Cobra said angrily.

"There he is…!" Leo yelled out as Bolaji snuck out from his hiding place.

"I swear to God, I will kill this rat," Jug uttered.

There was Bolaji trying to mix himself with the crowd settled in front of the Lupton Library. The gangs never gave up and continued searching for him in the crowd.

"Excuse me; excuse me, coming through…" Cobra said as he was passing through the crowd.

They finally caught him and began giving heavy blows. He threw his too, but four against one was overwhelming and the gang beat the crap out of him. They did not stop beating him. He passed out unconscious on the ground. The gang scattered when they heard sirens coming from the campus police car. A small crowd gathered around Bolaji who was then hospitalized at a nearby clinic for two hours. Anita didn't know what happened exactly. She was told that a male student was severely beaten by gang members and she felt sorry for him without even knowing that it was her brother. Beauty's friends reported the incident to her and they all went to the clinic together to see Bolaji.

Bolaji gave his car keys to Beauty and told her she should go and bring the car from the school parking lot; he knew she would be fine to drive the car because he'd taught her himself. Her friends did not know and hence they had some fears for her sake. She did as she was told and drove Bolaji home. He told her to go home with the car. He said that if she wanted it she could have it, which made her happy even though she had no intention of actually following through with his joke. What she loved is that he made her so happy and she was so glad he was getting the care he needed after the beating he sustained on campus.

"Make sure you have plenty of rest. I will make sure I deal with the gangs" Beauty said pitifully to Bolaji.

"No. Don't do that. Leave them alone." Bolaji warned her. "I can't let them get away with what they did to me."

"Baby, I will be fine. Just leave them the hell alone."

"Okay, fine. I will come back to see you."

"Don't worry. I'll be fine."

"I love you" Beauty then kissed his forehead.

"I love you too, bye."

Beauty then left him alone and drove away with the brand new Odyssey; she loved driving the car but of course, she loved Bolaji far more than she loved his car. Anita was speeding seriously while heading back home from school when she learned later from Karl that it was her brother who had been beaten by the thugs at school; she was deeply disturbed and very sad and by the time she got home, Bolaji had already come home and had gone to sleep. She decided not to wake him up and hoped to see him in the morning. She entered her own bedroom and changed her dress for indoor wear, and then she heated up some leftover chicken for dinner.

Her phone rang while she was ready to eat and it was her boy friend who was calling to check on the status of her brother, perhaps his brother in-law. She picked it up and the conversation was flowing till they were temporarily out of words; they talked for almost four hours on the phone. At midnight, Tasha called to speak her mind, too, but by then Anita was exhausted and told Tasha she needed a good night's sleep. Anita finally made it to bed and wished every living thing a good night sleep.

Eleven – The next days

Wednesday morning following the incident of Bolaji's beating, he got up from bed and lay on the couch watching television. His face was wrapped up with bandages and he had a floating cheek on the left side of his face; he was tired and worn out completely. They beat him so hard he hurt everywhere even a week later. He was in terrible pain. He even had a broken bone in his left foot. He had to wear a boot and use crutches.

Anita could hear the television and she walked out to join him in the living room. She had no idea of what happened to her brother until she saw him lying on the couch with his face in bandages. She felt sorry and at the same time was furious that he had to take the beating just for not listening to her counsel. She did not know what to say or do at the first approach; she walked up to the fridge and took a bottle of chilled water out, then poured two glasses out – one for each of them.

"Here you go, my brother. Are you okay?" She threw that question while serving him the water.

"Yeah, I am fine thanks." He answered respectfully.

"And they did this to you because of her…? You need to leave Beauty, or whatever her name is, alone. I am warning you..." She cared that much and warned him further.

"So what else would I be looking for if I left Beauty alone, ugly? …can't do that, sister."

"This ain't no joke, my brother. She thinks she is pretty, doesn't she?" she said angrily.

"Hell yeah, she is pretty, gorgeous and more beautiful than you." Bolaji shot back to her.

"Yeah right," she smirked.

"I am not kidding. She is beautiful and that's my baby. I don't care what others are saying or doing to me. We will never part. That's my word…" Bolaji said.

"What the heck is the matter with you? You gonna get yourself killed, but I ain't going to let it happen as long as I am alive. Can't you find any other girl at school, I mean black and beautiful?" She was outraged.

"Numerous of them but ain't no one like my beautiful Beauty. She is so unique and I'm a lucky man to have such a special girl like her. She's one of a kind. We are blessed with our love and nobody stop us." He gave his sister a smile.

"What tha…are you insane? Blessed, huh? Blessed to have a white chick, sucker!" She hissed at him.

"Did you just call me a sucker …did you?" Bolaji was mad.

"Hell yeah, I called you a sucker. I can call you whatever I want as your damn big sister," she said proudly.

"All right big sister, I'll tell you what, you can date who you want and I am free, as is every American citizen to date or marry whomever I wish to wed. I don't care if she is Japanese, Chinese, Mexican, Caucasian, and African, or African American, Black American, White American, European, Canadian, Latina, and so on. This is my life and my choice. You don't tell me who I should choose to be my life partner. I've already decided that she's the one. End of discussion.

"Do what you have got to do. I am very sure that mom and dad would be watching us now and see that I said mine. If you were smart, you'd listen to me."

"You are my sister and you are supposed to back me up."

"You are right. And as my brother I don't want anyone or anything to hurt you. And that's exactly what I am doing; I don't hate you or her. I just didn't think it seemed right, both of you together because people didn't' like that either…"

"You know what? Fuck other people! What does anyone know about love? I love the girl and she loves me back; isn't it wonderful? All I need is true love and with her that's what I have. I love her and I trust her."

"Shut up, stupid. Trust her? I guess you know what she is doing right now; she might be out there fucking one of them brothers. How do you know that she's not cheating on you right now? How can you be so stupid, Bolaji?" She felt like hitting him.

"You know what, therapist? Forget you. I trust her and she trusts me. And by the way she is not fucking anybody, ok? I can't sit here arguing with you. I am going to bed." He stood up and headed toward his bedroom.

"You come back and sit your behind down. You don't walk away from me, young man." She was calling him back.

"I am sorry, I can't come back." He entered and locked the door behind him.

"Go on with your stupid head. I'll call you when I get done with the cooking."

"Thanks, but I am not eating today. I've lost my appetite." He was talking from inside his bedroom.

"Whatever…" She then left him alone and made herself a chicken sandwich with gravy. Three hours later, Bolaji had fallen into a deep sleep. Adam called to check on him and Anita answered the phone and told him he was asleep, so he left the message that she should tell him that he was going to Texas for immigration issues and he would be back the following week. She promised to deliver his message to him and they exchanged good-byes.

The only person who was due to stay indoors was Bolaji because of his broken foot and therefore, Anita took her bath and left for her boyfriend's place after she had finished with everything she was doing at home.

Pain woke Bolaji up from sleep. He tried hard to fight the pains but it got up to a point that he could not take it anymore and started crying like an infant. He called out to Anita, but she'd already left to see Karl. Her phone was turned off intentionally, though.

Bolaji ached. He could not stand or walk, but lay on his back on the bed. He replayed the beating in his mind. He'd never felt so awful. He felt helpless. He couldn't stand having such limited mobility and such severe pain.

He knew Beauty would not be there at his place for the foot surgery was scheduled for the next day and it was late already. He would probably need to think twice again because the magnetic power of love had pinched her to get up from her bed and drive to his house, even though it was after midnight. She arrived at his door and knocked three times, but he'd given her a key to the house, so she let herself in.

He was amazed and happy to see her at that late hour and he told her to help him to the bathroom first. He took his time for while and eventually got back to the bedroom; he didn't know what to say to her, but was silently thanking in his mind.

"I couldn't sleep at all because I was worried about you…" she explained while rubbing his chest.

"…but it's too late now to be out at this time." Bolaji said.

"I know and I don't give a damn." She laughed.

"What about Frank?" he asked.

"What about him? Forget Frank…"

"So he isn't going to ask where you go or …"

"You worry too much. You need some rest and I'd appreciate it if you could get some now." She then rested her head on the other pillow and let her hands play on his chest.

"Thanks darling. And what time will you be heading back home?" Bolaji asked further he was scared for the late hour and her safety.

"Heading back home, are you kidding…? I am not going home tonight; I will sleep here with you" she proudly replied to him.

"Sleep here with me? You are joking, right?" He was trying to make sure she was joking with him.

"I am serious Bolaji. And to prove it to you…" She was then removing her clothes leaving on only her underwear.

"Well, we need to take it easy. We needn't rush. We have to plan for the future as well," Bolaji said tensely.

"What are you talking about? Sometime your words need more thought before one could have a clue about them. Let me ask you one question…" She was totally relaxed as she lay down beside him.

"What is it?" Bolaji asked interruptedly.

"You know it has been a while that we become husband and wife if I could say it that way and we have been joking, kissing, and having a good time with each other…"

"Is anything wrong with all these…?"

"Not at all but when are we going to have sex?" She asked him with very pleasing and relaxed eyes.

"Sex…? So you came here for sex tonight not for my condition?"

"Don't be silly Bolaji, I didn't come for sex. I was just asking. You are very silly, you know that?

"Let me ask you question," Bolaji said to Beauty.

"You are my man, go ahead," she responded.

"Are you yet a virgin or not? It has nothing to do with our relationship. Trust me."

"I don't know."

"Why don't you know? Have you had sex before with anybody?"

"What does it matter to you, anyway? Maybe I have, maybe I haven't."

"Some men don't even like virgin girls anyway, so don't bother yourself. It is wide open for you." She was just messing with him.

"What did you mean it's wide opened for me? I didn't open it, did I? Well, it's okay though. That was in the past before we met and I have no problem with that. All I have to say please be trustworthy…" Bolaji said.

"My turn smart mouth, how many girls have you had sex with in the past? I am very sure you are not a virgin yourself," she asked jokingly.

"Zero. You are my first and I pray that you will be my one and only. I couldn't bear not to be with you!"

"You are lying."

"I am not lying. How many guys have you been with?"

"Only one and his name is Bolaji. And here is right next to me." She laughed.

"Are you really a virgin?"

"How can you even ask me that? Of course I'm a virgin. It's all new to me. I love you, but this is all new to me! Everything, kissing, foreplay, sex, you name it. I listened to people when they were talking about sex and everything. I have no experience with sex and I always think one day I will have the experience with my man. I don't know. Maybe you don't like virgins, which frankly kind of scares me now a bit. I heard most men didn't like virgin girls because they're more difficult in bed."

"Well, I appreciate your being a virgin girl and it is something that I cherish, so don't be ridiculous."

"So when are we going to have sex?"

"You haven't forgotten yet? Okay when we get married, I am talking about three or four years away."

"I can't do that Bolaji. That's too long." She frowned.

"What are you going to do then, have sex with another guy?" He asked curiously.

"Hell no, never in my life. I am going to have sex with you whether you like or not," she said, laughing forcefully.

"What, are you going to rape me or something…?"

"I don't know." She threw a pillow at him but jokingly.

"We are going to kiss and play but let's practice celibacy for a while."

"We are going to be celibate, for how long, Bolaji?"

"Do you know what time it is now, baby? We need to have some sleep. Tomorrow is my foot surgery; shouldn't we be worried about that?"

"I am sorry. Good night honey." She kissed him on the lips.

"Sweet dreams my lovely girl," he said with smiling face.

The following morning, Anita planned to be home earlier and with the thought that she did not want her brother to know she slept over at Karl's place Anita did not know that Beauty slept at their place, too.

Beauty took a shower with Bolaji. They were both sitting on the couch in the living room watching early news when Anita opened the door and she was shocked to see Beauty at such an early hour and at the same time she was ashamed to find out that her brother knew at last that she did not sleep at home even though he was not going to say anything about it. Bolaji told her that Beauty would be taking him to the surgeon that very morning and she should not be worried about taking him and he suggested that she might need some rest as well. She appreciated it and she lovingly agreed with him.

Hating to see Bolaji on crutches, Beauty's heart went out to her man. In the car she put his favorite CD in the player. She was always going to please her man no matter what. He appreciated the ultimate submission, and he prayed secretly with his mind too that God should please let him have her for the rest of his life. He wanted to be with Beauty always and as long as she was at his side he knew he'd never be anything other than the happiest man alive.

They kept smiling and laughing till they approached Memorial Hospital. They parked at the GR level and they took the elevator to level eight and headed to room C84 where they were going to see Dr. Keith, the foot surgeon.

The lobby was teeming with people already and many had already been there for several hours. Although the joking and music had mitigated Bolaji's pain, it came back to him with a vengeance unexpectedly. Beauty tried to be of help, but he could not take the pain any longer and he had to be cynosure of the many eyes in the lobby. He didn't care. He cried out in pain, which was fortunate, because the receptionist was moved and managed to help him to see Dr. Keith earlier than he thought he would. His foot had been mangled and needed to be reconstructed. It took three hours of consecutive works before it actually got fixed and that was amazing at last even though Bolaji was instructed not to walk on it for about a week. He and Beauty were on top of the world for getting his foot back on track. They bought the prescribed medicine at the Eckerd store and then went to Sonic Burger before finally heading home.

They met Anita sleeping on the couch in the living room and they decided not to wake her up but going into his bedroom in lieu to have romantic lunch. After finishing with the burgers and the drinks and when he had swallowed his medicine too they headed up to the bed and lay down beside each other naked.

Bolaji knew he could be with his continence if he wanted to and being disrobed with his lovely girl gave him no second thoughts at all, though she might be thinking about sex in her mind. She loved the magnetic call between their bodies and she could not resist the essence of his body. She clung unto him, magnet to his steel. At this point she had no intention about sex. She just wanted to enjoy rubbing her body against his and she would definitely love some kisses and foreplay if he was able.

He smiled underneath her and did not hesitate to give her the first three kisses and then began caressing her hair with romantic words whispering into her ears. She was madly into him and felt that she was about to lose control of herself and she was now in need of it, but she did not want to force him. He kept laughing and smiling as she was kissing him while he was playing with her…then he paused and asked her if she had seen the movie he bought two weeks earlier. She replied that she had not, but with intention of slapping his face bloody. He'd killed the moment and had derailed everything. She was furious, got up and got dressed quickly.

"Are you getting angry at me?" He knew something was wrong.

"Why would I be getting angry at you, did you do anything wrong?" She asked in return.

"I don't know. What was with the rush then?" He asked again.

"I am not rushing, I am just going home. I left home since yesterday and I should be going home now." She frowned.

"Well, I am sorry. I don't mean to hurt you or your feelings." He apologized even though he did not know exactly what she was angry for.

"You are sorry, for what?"

"I don't know, Beauty. So you don't want to watch the movie with me?" he said with sympathetic face.

"Look here, Mr. I do not want to watch any movie now. I was having a good time with you and you killed it. I had you in mind. If you want to watch a movie, then watch it, but I'm not in the mood. You should know that when two lovers are having a good time hugging, kissing or whatever, neither party should ask a stupid question that would kill the emotions. I wanted to play with you, not watch any stupid movie with you at the moment. Maybe later when we get done. You definitely hurt me, Bolaji." She wept.

"Oh, my bad. Come on, let's continue then." He offered the romance again.

"You're never going to understand or get it. Once it had been ruined it would never going to be recovered. Not today anymore. Just don't do it next time. I am going home, I'll call you later." She then walked up to the door.

"I swear to God, I didn't do it on purpose and I did not aim to hurt your feelings. You know I love you very much," he explained.

"I know you love me but you are scared. Don't deny it. You need to let go of fear Bolaji. I understand and respect your words, your thoughts, your orders. You said no sex and I agreed. I am not going to force you to do what you don't want and plus I know you want me to be your wife so I respect that and I know that I am all yours. That doesn't mean we cannot play with each other, damn it. I want to enjoy your body and have a good time with you. There are numbers of ways we can enjoy each other than having sex…and I know that from reading books and looking online before you ask me how I learned that." She laughed with her wet face.

"Wow, bravo! That is my girl. Are you sure you don't want to continue?" He smiled.

“You are stupid and very mean.” She then opened up the door and ready to step outside.

“What are you going to tell Frank?” Bolaji asked.

“I knew it. I am eighteen years old and I am a free girl as an American. He has no business about me. I can tell him whatever I feel like telling him.” She smiled then walked back to Bolaji to kiss him.

“What was that for?” he asked happily.

“To let you know that I love you and I forgive your innocence.” She smiled again.

“Well, I’ll love you forever more. I hope to see again tonight,” he said.

“Yeah right, I am not coming tonight. I’ll come to see you tomorrow morning; I love you.” She then closed the door as she stepped outside.

“I love you too, darling.” He was with happiest face.

As she stepped outside finally and headed to the car who but Tasha pulled in; she waved, but didn’t say a word as Tasha waltzed up to the door to visit Anita. Beauty did not say a single word; she drove off instead to avoid trouble. Tasha proceeded to knock persistently. Her knocking woke Anita up, she then let Tasha in.

Anita asked Tasha what she was doing at her place unannounced, although she was welcome any time Anita emphasized. But she’d been caught by surprise and was curious.

She told Anita she was worried about Bolaji’s condition and that she came to check on him. She asked Anita what Beauty was doing at their place at such time in the morning and she told her that she was the one who took Bolaji to the surgeon for his foot surgery earlier. Tasha asked Anita to excuse her and with the promise that she would be back soon and she headed towards Bolaji's bedroom. She cast three knocks on his door and she added one more.

"Who is there?" Bolaji asked while lowering the volume of the television.

"It's me, Tasha, but you already know."

"Who are you?" He asked again.

"It's me, Tasha, your sister's friend." She smiled.

"Anita was out there on the couch about three hours ago, hasn't she got up yet?" Bolaji said.

"I saw her already. I came here for you. Can I come in?"

"Sure, come on in." He then covered his exposed body with a blanket.

"Are you okay? How is the foot?" She kept walking towards him as she opened the door.

"Everything is fine. I got the foot fixed this morning. Beauty took me there and she just left about fifteen minutes ago. Perhaps you saw her." He said, pulling Tasha's hands off his body.

"I met her at the lot leaving... Why she got to drive your car anyway?" She was being nosy.

"I ain't trying to be disrespectful, but that I think is my business," he answered her.

"Cool. Have you eaten anything this morning?" She was trying to touch his head.

"Thanks for asking, but I ate lunch an hour ago. What do you care anyway?" Bolaji asked with caution.

"God should be my witness; I care a lot about you. And obviously you don't seem to give a damn, and that I need to work on. I can't let a tramp or stupid wench steal you away from me…"

"That was the most bizarrely awkward remark I had ever heard in my life. I don't know if this English is correct, but that's awfully awful," Bolaji said angrily.

"What was bizarre about it…?" Tasha asked.

"Everything Tasha and if you don't mind, you are being excused already." He was mad and wanted her to leave.

"Are you asking me to leave?" She said confusedly.

"You are damn right I am…your friend is out there in the living room waiting for you. Thanks for stopping by and I appreciate it very much, see ya." Bolaji waved at her.

"Okay, fine. I am leaving." She walked out angrily and slammed the door.

"Ain't no need to break my damn door, gosh!" He then turned up the volume to continue enjoying the movie he was watching earlier.

Tasha told Anita that Bolaji was rude to her and Anita begged her not to be vexed and that she would talk to Bolaji afterwards, she then dressed up and they both left for party. Knowing that they both had gone for good, Bolaji then decided to give Beauty a call. She picked it up after one ring with the word 'hello.'

"You know who this is?" Bolaji asked her.

"Yeah, I know who that is, my man," she replied.

"Frank got mad at you when you got home?" Bolaji asked.

"How many times I have to tell this coward not be scared anymore? Frank did not get mad at me. He was not home. I don't even think he slept home last night, either. Stop having fears of him, Bolaji," she said, playing with her hair.

"So what are you doing?" Bolaji asked.

"…right now…?"

"Yeah, right now…" Bolaji replied.

"I am just resting and trying not to remember your bizarre changing of the subject."

"Baby, I said I was sorry. Are you thinking of coming tonight?"

He smiled as if she was watching him.

"No, I'm not coming tonight. We aren't going to do anything but talk anyway. I think I should sleep in my place tonight … maybe I'll play with you in my dreams."

"Oh, you have got jokes. That's very funny." Bolaji said.

"Why don't you laugh then? If something is funny then it needs laughter. Guess what, I called mom today…"

"What did she say? Is she still upset with you?" Bolaji asked. "Mad at me for what? She has no reason to be mad…" Beauty replied.

"What about the whole black and white thing…?" he asked again.

"Last time I checked I was an American citizen and I remembered you were too and as the citizens of America there exists freedom. We are both free people and we've chosen each other. It's that simple. Really it's not a big deal, Bolaji. She'll come around. Let your heart be at rest my lover and nothing can stop us." She delivered this speech with full confidence.

"Okay tough girl. I am scared though. I have got a broken foot already, you know," he said laughing.

"Well, I should let you rest and I'll call you tomorrow when I wake up."

"Alright my darling. I love you very much." He then hung up to have some sleep if he could.

The case about Bolaji's injury had been investigated and it became known to school authorities that Frank was involved in the seemingly mysterious beat down Bolaji had sustained. He was arrested and taken in for questioning along with all of the gang members save Cobra two days after the beating.

That was the reason Beauty could not meet him at home. She wanted to call her Mom and explained the whole situation, but she thought twice and decided to call Bolaji and ask for his opinion. It was seven o'clock in the evening, Thursday night, and she felt hesitant to call Bolaji, because he might be getting ready to go to bed, but she picked up the phone at last and dialed his numbers. The phone rang three times and she was about to give it up when Bolaji answered sleepily. Her news about Frank's arrest shocked to him and he could not believe his ears, although he was angry at the moment.

He asked Beauty how Frank was going to be bailed out and she replied she had no money to bail him out and that he'd given her the go ahead to use his Visa debit card that he gave her for emergency or personal use. He had lot of money in his account, but he hadn't told her how much he had on it. He knew she could not spend the balance on it no matter how much she shopped.

She didn't know what to say to him, but she rushed to the police station to bail Frank out. Frank was surprised to see Beauty and he was wondering if she had told their Mom. Beauty asked him to come to the car, the Odyssey, and they headed back home. He remained silent for a long while, but as she parked the car he broke the silence, thanking his sister and then asking if she had called their Mom.

"I did not, but you were very cruel to my boyfriend," she said.

"I owe you more. I promise to be good as of now on," Frank said, lying.

"As long as you are going to be nice to him, I'll keep your secret, but don't you disappoint me. You're my brother and I love you, but I love Bolaji," she said, threateningly.

"I promise I will." He left for his room.

Beauty was so happy that she called Bolaji and told him that she would be on her way to spend the night with him. Bolaji seemed resistant, but she insisted on seeing Bolaji though and he acquiesced. She was trying to take advantage of the situation. She knew Frank would not have the guts to tell Rebecca that she did not sleep at home and if he did, then she would reveal his secret. She knocked when she got there and Anita opened the door with an unfriendly expression. Beauty greeted perfunctorily and wasted not a single moment to leave for Bolaji's room. She opened his door and jumped into his bed, taking care not to jostle his leg. She was careful, gentle, loving.

"What's up with your sister?" Beauty asked him.

"Didn't she open the door for you?" Bolaji asked her.

"She did. She looked upset."

"You should have said, 'Hey Anita, what's up with the attitude?' She would tell you if she had anything to say," Bolaji joked.

"You got jokes. That was very funny, too. And now you've got me laughing."

In the wake of their conversation Bolaji devised a scheme to make Anita mad; he told Beauty to let them pretend they were having actual sex and he asked her to start screaming loudly as if wrenched with pleasure. He wanted to shock and upset Anita. That'd teach her to not greet his girlfriend with more respect. Still laughing, Beauty agreed. The door had been locked already; they always locked the door from behind, even if they were just talking. After a count of three, they began uttering sexual words, very raw and deliberately unbearable.

Anita could sense the jogging of bed up and down. She was silent for a while, but tip-toed to her brother's bedroom door. She believed they were having sex for real and she hated everything at the moment; the trick worked on her. She sat in the living room afterwards, waiting for Beauty's face to come out of the room, but to no avail. Finally, she fell deeply completely asleep on the couch and by the time she woke up in the morning, Beauty had already dressed up for her first class.

She was happy she enjoyed the whole night with Bolaji and even though the actual sex did not take place, she was looking forward to having it one day soon. Bolaji could not go to school because his foot at the time and he yelled for Anita. She got up and with great trepidation answered Bolaji by rushing to his room which she scrutinized for any trace of Beauty.

"She left for school, early." Bolaji said, noting Anita's zealous search for his dear one.

"Am I looking for anybody in here?" she asked in denial.

"Yes, you were looking for Beauty and she had gone. She beat you, Miss." He laughed.

"I hope you both washed your nasty bodies." She was madly jealous of the sex thing.

"What, were you jealous because you did not have Karl around last night? That was too bad because we had a great time last night. Yummy." Bolaji then mockingly licked his lips with his tongue.

"Shut up, loco. I have got news for you, stupid. No more sleeping here at night for her…" She declared, intending to set an ultimatum.

"That's not going to happen as long as I am still living here. You slept over at Karl's place the other night. Did you think I didn't know? I just acted like I did now, but I knew. She is free to come over to me anytime she wants. That's my future wife and your sister in-law…" Bolaji said to her.

"Well, I am getting late for my class and I'll deal with you later." She left for bathroom.

Bolaji took a shower, then went to bed eager to sleep. Anita said good bye when she got ready to leave, but he could not answer because he was lost in his dreams. Six hours later and surely after the school, his girlfriend called to let him know she'd be spending the weekend with her Mom in Atlanta and that she would definitely be back on Monday. She asked him if it was alright with him to drive his Odyssey to Atlanta and he gladly granted her his permission; she was madly happy to drive the car to her home town of "Hotlanta."

On Saturday afternoon, Beauty was giving her mom a ride around downtown Atlanta, and although Rebecca was confused about her daughter for her rapid changes, though she loved the fact that she was clearly happy, even her already magnificent skin glowed more beautifully than ever; she was both toned and tan. At the same time, she discerned a change in her daughter. To make it worse, Beauty then innocently started the CD player in the car and the music was from one of the Southern rappers that had newly come out with his hit single 'Is going down,' she was happy to dance to the music and every move she was doing was both strange and marvelous to her mother.

"What in the world had gotten into you, young lady?" Rebecca asked confusedly.

"What did you mean, mom?" she asked in return.

"You know exactly what I mean, young lady. Are you trying to be smart with me here? Stop that stupid music now! Take it out…" she commanded her.

"The dance is cool, mom. Don't be hateful. You know everybody is doing it; even Tom Cruise did it on TV. And the guy is from Atlanta too. Let's be supportive, mom," she said.

"Are you crazy? I did not send you out there to be going out with drug dealers and thugs. I sent you to pursue your future career, not to undertake a dangerous pursuit, Beauty."

Beauty rolled her eyes and said, ""I have no idea of what you are talking about. What drug dealers?" she asked innocently.

"I am talking about the one who gave you this car and all the money. I am warning you now be careful out there. You need to go back and give this car back to him, do you hear me?" Rebecca was now searching through her daughter's purse.

"Bolaji is not a drug dealer. He is just lucky to be born rich. And leave my purse alone. I know you hate him, but that's my future husband…"

"I know you are joking around. Would you mind taking me home, now?"

"Sure, why would I mind?"

Rebecca was so scared and concerned about Beauty's safety around the campus and she thought Bolaji might be a drug dealer, which was the only way she could imagine that he could afford so many big cars and other things that Beauty said he had. She even considered enrolling her at the Georgia Institute of Technology in Atlanta. She discussed her thoughts later with Beauty, who refused the offer and promised that she would be safe out there. She knew the number reason was just trying to avoid the relationship between her and Bolaji. The fact that Bolaji was a black guy scared Rebecca and she did not know what exactly she should do because Beauty was clearly deeply in love with him and she remained stubborn about being with him. The whole situation confused Rebecca tremendously and she decided to seek advice from her friends and of course her boy friend, Hudson.

Twelve – Weeks later

Seven weeks later, Bolaji had recovered from his wounds and the broken foot; he'd resumed his classes and was talking with Adam outside the Lupton Library. They both wore blue jeans and casual shirts. Adam was trying to give him advice about the whole situation.

"Are you okay, man?" Adam asked.

"I'm good; I heard you went to Texas," Bolajo replied.

"Yeah, I went up there for the freaking finger prints. How is your face anyway?"

"My face?"

"Yes, your face. How is it?"

"It's fine." He was drinking a Coke from the bottle.

"So what's next now?" Adam was curious to ask his next step about the whole thing.

"I don't understand you. What did you mean?" He asked him to explain more.

"I mean what are you going to do now?" Adam replied.

"I still don't get it. What am I going to do about what, Adam?"

"I mean about her, Beauty or whatever her name is…"

"What about Beauty…?"

"Brother, I am your friend. I mean that sincerely. I'm really worried about you, man. I don't want anything to happen to you again. Somebody is getting hurt here and that person is you…" Adam was genuinely concerned about him.

"All right, dear friend I appreciate that you are looking after me and everything, but I am fine. So just drop it and find something else to say or shut up!" Bolaji said, raising his voice.

"I'm worried about you. We never know what might happen next time. It could be worse than that beating and broken foot. Trust me, I pray nothing else happens, my friend. Listen now before it is too late."

"Can't you find something else better to say?" Bolaji asked him.

"All that I am saying…"

"Drop it Adam! I don't want any misunderstandings between me and you. Please drop it for God's sake. Have you ever been in love with someone?"

"Nope…! I don't like love and I don't believe in it."

"Oh, it's worse than I thought, so do me a huge favor…"

"What kind of favor…?"

"Drop the subject."

"You are crazy, Bolaji."

"We both are."

"After today I am not going to say anything about it anymore. I promise."

"Thanks a lot. I appreciate it."

"Come on, let's go for a walk." Adam said to him.

They both agreed to go for a walk; there were girls, beautiful ones of course, running around with knickerbockers to get prepared for their next coming championship matches that they couldn't afford to lose. Adam's eyes were scoping out their buttocks and their breasts, but he tried to make it covert to Bolaji since he claimed not to like any girl. After a thirty minute walk, they went separately to their respective classes.

A poetry event was to be held at the University Center and it had been advertised on the school website and on posters around campus. Bolaji hadn't noticed, but Beauty wanted to attend. She invited Bolaji to attend the reading with her, and he agreed. The place admitted a variety of students from different countries and backgrounds and all were given the same opportunity as it was claimed even though some were indirectly deprived of their rights. The host talked and joked with welcoming words to make students feel calm and welcome and later he called upon the dance group followed by the mimes. Then it later came to a poetry reading from some selected and famous school poets. The first reader represented black people and he dedicated his poem to the black community and the poem as well talked about nothing but black people and black culture; it talked about how beautiful they were, how creative and intelligent they were and so on. Then the second reader was called upon and he stepped up there for the white community and he read his work to beautify the white people as well and those black attendees were jealous and did not like his verses, but the host calmed everybody down at last. Then Beauty, having known her man to be a creative writer even though he loved to be anonymous, walked up to the host secretly and told him someone else would like to share his poem and the name was Bolaji. The host made the announcement and it was accompanied with round of applause, but it was totally a shock to him; he wished he could find a miraculous thing to aid his disappearance. He stepped up to the stage and let it known to all that the poem he was going to read would be dedicated to his lovely girl, Beauty. He pointed at her and the all of the students looked to see who exactly Beauty was and every student, even the white ones hated to see that the so-called Beauty was a white girl. He did not feel discouraged to announce the title of his poem and he called it "God Sees No Color." The poem was written to fight against racism, discrimination and to promote love amongst all of them. His words were magnificent and made every girl at the reading uncomfortable and ready to lose their undergarments. He focused nonetheless on Beauty's inner beauty and solicited jealousy from the women who envied her.

Beauty flushed with joy, her skin supple and soft like a fresh blooming magnolia. She was so proud of Bolaji. Many already knew his name as the student beaten recently. This was their first glimpse of the man behind the name. She swelled with pride. He earned and received a standing ovation for his work even though in some hearts he was a racial sell-out. He managed to escape those girls that would probably want to get him into trouble by asking him to autograph their body parts.

Later, he kissed Beauty good bye and they went home separately. Adam was there at his house waiting; he had gotten out of class early and decided to spend the rest of the day with him. He was not that surprised to see him waiting and led him in after when he had finished parking his car in the garage. He offered him a Coke, but when Adam said he was in the mood for some hot tea, Bolaji fixed two cups of green tea and then they headed into the game room to play pool. Adam was much more better at playing pool; he beat Bolaji several times even making some shots with his eyes closed. They played the first round and Bolaji cheated to earn the victory. Adam won the last five rounds. They called the game off and then headed to the living room to watch television.

The first station was not very satisfactory to Bolaji and he had to change it to something else and Adam then changed the station finally to MTV. Bolaji knew Adam belonged to the world of black and white because he was a Brazilian guy and Bolaji did not even care about whoever came along to him as friend as long as the person was a human being. He and Adam were very cool and respectful of each other. After four hours of MTV, Adam was ready to go home; Bolaji followed him to his car and waved good bye as Adam drove off in his car. Anita entered by 10:00 p.m. He guessed that she'd spent few time with her boyfriend and she walked straight to the kitchen after dropping her bag down on the couch. She met Bolaji in the living room where he was watching a program on We TV; it was a life time story of mysterious murder that took place a decade previously. Anita, because she did not like Beauty, always found something to say about her and she decided to talk bad behind her back.

"Beauty came here today?" She asked Bolaji while peeling potatoes.

"…you mean after school. No, she didn't. Why did you ask?" Bolaji was eager to know the reason.

"I am telling you, that girl is so nasty. Did you see your car she was driving? That car had turned grey. She needs to wash the damn car."

"Thanks, Anita. I'll wash it." Bolaji said.

"You are such a damn fool. She used it. She should clean it."

"And it's my car and I don't mind washing it, got it?" He stood up and walked up to her.

"Well, if a woman is that special let her realize that…" Anita said.

"Is that true? And you are not special too? You never saw that one coming, do you? I'll tell you what sister, I know you hate her and everything, but you have to let her enjoy her man, which is me, of course, and she is special to me," he said while wrapping his hands around her shoulders.

She then continued her cooking. She was fuming. She cut the potatoes into pieces; she added salt to the water and set them to boil. She fried up some eggs as the potatoes boiled.

Bolaji's mind had being occupied with the program he was watching and he did not know when she finished cooking. All he knew was when everything was later set on the dining table. They said their prayers, ate and left for their individual rooms after the good night hugs.

The following day at around three o'clock, the temperature was not friendly at all and it was so cloyingly hot both indoors and outdoors. Looking up at the sky you would see the day brightly smiling with its white clouds spreading out across the sky. Anita had gone to school and Bolaji did not have any class that day; he felt lucky to be at home. He sported blue running shorts and wore white shocks. It was too hot to be wearing a shirt. Thus, he was in living room half-naked and exposing his chest and abs. He knew he looked good and was proud to be in shape. He didn't feel like watching television so he decided to listen to music and he was listening to one of the newest arrivals on the rap scene. He heard a knock at the door. He was happy and surprised to see Beauty when the door was opened. He was trying to stop the music, but she told him that was not necessary. All she was into at the moment was admiring his sexy body. Bolaji sat on the couch and she jumped impatiently into his lap, turning quickly around to face him as she sat on atop his thighs. She had to remove her top, leaving her bra and jeans alone and she eagerly wanted to kiss him to get the foreplay going. Her heart was pumping faster than ever and she developed uncontrolled tension all over her body, which made both of her legs tingle like they had been charged with an electrical sensation from his body. Bolaji was expected to make the move and ignite the flame of love, but he was distracted mentally. Beauty waited a bit, then won his attention back and all his senses were focused on her.

"Are you really here with me, Bolaji?" she asked.

"I am sorry, say that again," he said, patronizing her.

"Stop patronizing me. You always want to be smart with me. What's wrong with you? I can't understand you sometimes, do you know that?" she explained.

"What was it with the attitude, girl?" He pretended to ask the question like he didn't know what he did wrong.

"What were you thinking about? You are ruining this moment again for me…" She let it out.

"Oh, I was busy looking for your breasts…" He said to her confidently.

"What…? They are right here in front of you. Put your hands on them, come on…" She was totally confused and upset.

"Kiss me, come on." She demanded.

He kissed her passionately.

A few moments later he stopped and asked her how her math class had been.

She responded, "God, is this good time to ask? It was fine and the professor was very good as well." She answered reluctantly and yet expecting the play to move on.

"I know we have good professors at UTC. Most of them even better than world renowned professors, but a lot of people don't know that," he said.

"I know. But it is very hard to believe unless you are attending the university," she added.

"We have talent, too; I am talking about in Tennessee generally. We have stars and super stars like Usher, Justin Timberlake, Samuel L. Jackson, JR, "The King," Lawler in the Hall of Fame and many more who are still unknown," Bolaji said proudly.

"Is Usher from Tennessee? I thought he is from Atlanta, my town. And Timberlake is he from Tennessee for real or you are just kidding?" Beauty asked.

"You people from ATL are trying to steal our son; he is from here in Chattanooga, and I'll take you to his grandmother's street one day. I am not kidding about Timberlake either," he explained.

"You forgot to mention one very super star that I know. You did not mention yourself." She leaned her head against his while rubbing her palms against his cheeks.

"What about me? I don't have any talent," he said pathetically though deliberately as well.

"Yes, you do, poor guy. I have confidence in you and I believe in you. Just follow your heart with your dreams and you will see that everything is possible," she gushed, encouraging him.

"Well, this is the kind of girl I need. Would you still be in love with me if I decided to be an artist? Or you would that scare you off…?" Bolaji asked to know what was on her mind.

"You know I will always love you. I might be scared of those girls who would come around you though, but I trust you and I know you are a trustworthy guy." Beauty answered the question perfectly with confidence.

"What if I wanted to be a rapper, you know how hardcore and raw I would be?" Bolaji asked further.

"…actor, rapper, singer, boxer, and writer, it does not matter to me. The only thing that matters is love and we have that. I love you and you love me back, can't anything change that. As long as you are not going to fail me or chase me off, I'll be happy to be with you forever," she said to him as if she was going to burst into tears.

"Women of earth…! You know what is has always been funny in my mind? If I happened to be a star, my fans would want to have these tattoos on their faces to match my own marks, don't you think?" Bolaji asked.

"I actually love those marks. Can I have them on my face too? I can get it done tomorrow." She fixed him with a soul-deep stare.

"I'll fight you madly not to do it. Don't you dare change your face. Tell me you are kidding. Good thing I was little when I had them done, otherwise it would not have been easy for them," he said.

"Okay. Would you teach me some black things?" She asked.

"What did you mean black things? Don't be saying that around people of my color; they might be offended," he warned her lovingly.

"I meant to say Hip-hop languages such as rhymes, slang and so on. I actually love it; I mean the sound and the pronunciation. You don't even know I feel right talking about."

"Seriously, how do you feel?" He was curious.

"I feel great. I wanted to learn those words- love me, don't hurt me. You know those rhymes are great. I love black conversation. You all don't even know we love you all," she confessed.

"I'll tell you what, smart mouth. I don't mean to disrespect you, but when I first met you, I saw an innocent beautiful young girl who was smart, motivated, full of dreams, for real and down to earth. She did not talk like I talk and also she did not wear the same color of skin that I wore, but I accepted her just like she was. Why would you wanted to change? You don't have to change anything about yourself; I love you the way you are. That's how God made you and I love it. Don't try to be black or a ghetto girl or rock and roll girl; just be yourself and I'll love you forever. I mean you can talk rhyme jokingly with me if you want to, but don't change an inch about yourself," he said.

"Wow. That's what I love about you. You're not afraid to express your feelings. I love you so much." She gave him a loving kiss.

"Do you want something to drink, my lady?" he asked.

"What do you have to offer, my lord?" she asked him as well.

"Do you want fruity juice? Let me get up to give you some." He asked her again.

"No, I don't want anything but you. My stomach is killing me for real," she expressed.

"What happened? Do you have stomach pains, tummy aches, an ulcer?" He asked fearfully.

"Nelly, because my belly is hurting..." She deliberately rhymed those words thinking that the word 'ulcer' sounded like Usher.

"Oh, that was a good one though. Why are you trying to be funny every time?" he said like he was curious about it.

"Because you taught me how and you were always funny to me. Have you studied for your test? I know you don't have to if you don't want to." She complimented him on his ability.

"That was not an academic compliment. You are supposed to blame me for being lazy and not to compliment me on it," he argued.

"I thought about blaming you first, but on second thought, I knew you were smart and a genius and I had the belief that you would pass it," she said to him.

"If I were you, I would not say that, young lady," he said to her.

"I said it anyway, young man." She laughed hard.

The lovely conversation hindered their ability to notice the arrival of Anita's car and as Beauty made an attempt to kiss Bolaji, Anita disturbed them by opening the door and entering with Karl.

Beauty bounced back from kissing Bolaji and she felt like the whole time she had been spending with him had just been sabotaged completely. She wanted to greet them at first, but the unfriendly face of Anita overwhelmed her ability to talk and chased her off. Bolaji noticed the changes and he tried to erase the hurtful feelings out of her mind. She decided to go for it anyway and asked Anita with her boyfriend if they were doing okay. Karl answered her, but Anita, her supposed to be sister in-law, refused to say even hello to her the only thing that came out of her mouth was an ugly hiss, which hurt Beauty terribly. Karl whispered into her ears to say something nice to her; she refused like she did not care at all. Bolaji then asked Beauty to come and play pool with him. She agreed and followed him to the game room. Anita then walked into the game room with Karl asking Bolaji and Beauty to excuse them, because she and Karl needed to play pool. Bolaji was seriously mad, but he did not reveal it. Beauty did not feel comfortable anymore and she decided to get going by saying goodbyes to Karl and Anita.

"You need to be nice to her at least. She said hi to you, but you hissed instead. I get the part that she is white, but she is a human being too," Karl said in the absence of Bolaji and Beauty.

"I don't have anything nice to say to her. I know it's good to shut my mouth when I don't have anything good to say.

You know you are about to ruin my day with you now, Karl," she claimed.

"I'm sorry; come on, let's start playing." Karl apologized. Beauty walked angrily to the car and she demanded that Bolaji should take her home. She had been hurt badly by Anita's attitude and she did not want to drive the car again. She refused to talk while Bolaji was talking to her to make her feel better. This irritated Bolaji as well and he got angry.

"What's wrong with you, Beauty? I keep talking to you and you refuse to answer me –
making me sound like a lunatic guy talking to himself," he said angrily.

"Stop talking at me, Bolaji..." She was mad as well.

"I am not talking at you. I am talking to you," he explained.

"Your sister's attitude is annoying. It's unbearable for me... If she wanted us to break up that would be fine. What did I do wrong to her anyway?" She shed tears as she was expressing herself.

"Now you are going to talk about my sister, huh? Let's us talk about your brother too. You knew he attacked me personally and later sent thugs against me. I had a broken foot because of you. I had a fight with my own sister because of you. I knew your Mom even detested me, but I acted like it didn't bother me. What else do you want me to do, Beauty?" He did not mean to get mad at her, and then he calmed down.

"How dare you yell at me like that! I knew you went through something, but hell, I was facing mine too…" She madly criticized his points.

"I am so sorry. I shouldn't have talked to you like that. I apologize, do you forgive me?" He smiled and he was then playing with her cheek to make her laugh.

"Apology accepted. I am sorry too. I did not mean anything I said earlier and I do not want to break up with you…" She laughed.

"Me either. Did you say you wanted to break up with me? I didn't listen to catch that part."

"No, I did not. I said I would love you forever." She then moved towards him and rested her head against him. The dispute was finally settled and they kept laughing till they reached Beauty's apartment. She got out of the car, kissed him as usual and then headed upstairs with a satisfactory face that every man would love to welcome at his place. Frank had peeped to see who dropped her off and he was mad to see that it was Bolaji again, and he wanted to break his promises. He oddly wanted to have another odd plan, a very stupid one indeed; he then kept the plan secretly in his shallow mind. He welcomed Beauty like a friend with pretence and acted like he did not have right to question her movement. She, on the other hand, kept enjoying her freedom of overstaying outdoors whenever she wanted to. She left happily for her room to have some rest before she could finally die temporarily with sleep. On her bed, she lay on her back facing the bedroom sky and placed Bolaji's pictures on her chest; she was looking at them one after the other. She always thought of Bolaji as oddity for his unique personality, and she was happy every time she found out she was yet his girl. She did not stop looking at him from the pictures with nondescript captivation until she was finally overwhelmed with sleep.

By the time Bolaji got back home, Anita and her boyfriend had left the game house for the living room to take the whole thing to the next level, but why the living room? Bolaji entered with shock to see how ergonomically Anita positioned herself on Karl's thighs, just like when Beauty was playing with him without actually having sex. His arrival was like that of an evil maniac and it stopped everything for them. Anita decided to frustrate him by talking trash about Beauty again, which Bolaji could not tolerate any further.

"Have you taken that trash home?" She said while putting her top on.

"What trash, Stupid? Don't you ever in your life call her trash." His eyes rapidly turned red and he was hurtfully mad at her at the moment.

"Oh, you gonna beat me for her? Go ahead beat me up, psycho." She moved towards him like she was ready to take the beat down.

"I am not going to put my hands on you, not ever. I will only talk to you."

"Come on guys, let it go," Karl said, trying to settle the matter.

"I thought you would." Anita said again to Bolaji.

Karl told Anita to leave with him and she finally agreed to go with him. Bolaji was left alone inside, the hurtful feelings yet bulging his mind and he decided to drive around for a while to dissipate the feelings. Amidst the driving, Adam's call arrived to let him know they would study early tomorrow morning for the test before going to class; Bolaji agreed. He finally felt great with the conversation he had with Adam on the phone and he turned around heading back home to have a good night's sleep.

The following morning and at the students' resting area, Adam and Bolaji and some other students were studying for their mathematics test.

Adam had respect for Bolaji and Bolaji also knew that Adam was very a smart guy. They started going through each question and all seemed very easy to them except one question that Adam considered to be a little bit tougher.

"This question though was very difficult to me. I spent hours on it yesterday, yet I could not understand it." He showed it to Bolaji.

"That's simple. I've known how to do that since I was in Africa. I can't even believe you are having difficulty with this one. You are smarter than me. You always answer questions in the class too," he said simply.

"I don't know about that one, but you are smart too. Why don't you like answering questions in the class?" Adam asked curiously.

"That's my nature, brother. I'd rather be anonymous. I am bolajical, remember?" he said with a very simple smile on his face.

"Excuse me, did you just say bolajical?" He was curious to ask if he heard the word clearly.

"Oh, you heard me, didn't you?" Yes, I said bolajical," he answered.

"What the heck does that mean, anyway? Do you think your name is going to make it to the dictionary?" he asked further.

"It could make it into it. Bolajical means to live life simply, which is my philosophy of thinking. You know I am simple guy," he said to him.

"The other time, you said Bolaji meant to be born wealthy or be born with a silver spoon or some like that. Now you have changed it," Adam criticized him.

"You are right, but the term is complicated and has different meanings," he explained meaningfully.

"Okay, bolajical child. Who am I then, an Adamical child?" he jokingly asked him.

"Ain't no such thing, brother. You are the first creature though, if you know what I mean." He then smiled at him.

They then left the place for class to tackle their test. When Bolaji finished with his test, he was going to walk to his next class.

He was walking past the designed students' passage while Tasha was walking from his behind and grabbed him unexpectedly from his shoulders; he was shocked at first and then mad to find out it was Tasha. He immediately withdrew from her and asked her to leave him alone. He proceeded angrily towards the exit and she kept following him.

"Wait Bolaji, I just want to talk to you. Wait…" She kept calling him.

"I don't want to talk to you; leave me alone," he said while he was still walking away from her.

"Would you just wait for a damn second?" she said angrily. "All right, what is it?" he asked her, but he never stopped walking away.

"I have been trying to talk to you all these days, but you don't want to listen. What the heck is your problem?" she said out of frustration.

"Do you have anything important to say? I don' think so…" he claimed arguably.

"I am in love with you and you know that. I came to you personally; I sent your sister and yet you acted like I did not matter to you. Anyway, what are you doing on Saturday?" She thought the question was very laughable and she was laughing.

"Why would you wanna know what I would be doing on Saturday? I would be home watching television for a while…" he explained to her.

"I was just wondering if we could go out together, as a date," she said trying to be friendly.

"A date…? Why would you think I would go on a date with you? I have a girlfriend; she came into my life first. Just because you are black or something does not mean I am going to leave her for you, not ever. First come, first served, and you should remember that. If you happened to be the first one I knew I would not deceive you either. She is a woman like you and you have to respect that. Plus you have someone you are dating, be thankful and grateful with him. If I had to go on a date with someone other than my sister it would definitely be my Beauty. I am sorry if I hurt your feelings." He was then walking away again.

"You know the guy was a jerk and I had to break up with him. I did it for you anyway…" she said while pushing him with her body.

"Do you hear yourself? You left him for me. What would guarantee me that you wouldn't leave me for another guy? I appreciate it anyway, but you need to go back to your man and apologize to him," he advised her.

"You know I've always been crazy about you. I would be happy to have you in my life, you know that for sure. Why are you doing this to me, Bolaji?" she said sympathetically.

"What did I do? Have I done something wrong now? Hey, stop that. I said stop it…" He was stopping her from kissing him.

"You are very stupid and blind as well. Get lost, mother lover…" She slapped his face and walked away with anger.

"Thank you very much for the slap," he said to her from a distance while rubbing his cheek with his own hands. Later that day and when the night was gently approaching Bolaji then left outdoors for indoors and he lovingly accepted the dinner his sister had made for him minutes before his arrival. Anita was on the phone by the time Bolaji was eating and she asked him what the matter between him and Tasha was when she got off of the phone. He explained everything that happened and he was curious to know why she was trying to be stubborn. Anita asked Bolaji to give him a chance; she claimed she knew Tasha was madly in love with him. Bolaji then furthered his explanation by telling his sister that once he had made up of his mind with a woman he would never change it. To avoid an argument or fight, Anita did not say anything further, but she decided to leave for her room after when she had said good night to him. He waited around for a while watching television before he finally left for his bedroom as well. He called Beauty's phone number, but she did not answer the phone on purpose; Bolaji did not know that he thought she might have deeply gone to sleep. She was mad at him for the rumor she heard that Tasha was kissing Bolaji; her friends told her the news.

Friday morning, Bolaji had been waiting outside for Beauty to come out of the class when she got done with her test. She walked out of the door and kept walking away like she did not notice his presence. He ran after her and grabbed her from behind. He thought she was trying to ignore him jokingly, but he did not know she was mad at him about Tasha. Bolaji asked her why she frowned at him and she did not answer.

"Why did you act like you didn't see me? Are you okay, pretty girl?" he asked jokingly.

"Bolaji, we need to talk," she said frankly.

"I am listening…" he said holding her hands lovingly.

"You know I trust you, but now you are trying to betray me. Why, why Bolaji…?" she said angrily.

"What, I am betraying you…? What were you talking about…?" He was totally confused.

"You know exactly damn well what I am talking about. Don't patronize me trying to act like you are innocent here. What's up with you and Tasha? Now what do you have to say…?" She wept.

"Is that the reason why you're angry? No wonder you did not even pick up the phone when I called last night. Poor thing, baby…" He said without having qualms about it.

"What's going on Bolaji? Are you trying to leave me? What have I done wrong?" she said further.

"I cannot believe you are actually saying this. I swear to God ain't nothing is between me and Tasha. The woman is crazy and I have told her I don't want her. I can't do that to you; you know that, don't you?" he explained while wiping tears off her face.

"But what about the kisses, Bolaji…?"

"Oh, please, what kisses again?" He kicked the pole, his mind disturbed.

"My friends told me they saw you, both of you, kissing at a corner of Mathematics department."

"Oh, stupid broadcasters. Your friends told you they saw us and you believed them? I'll tell you what, you need to learn how trust me and second if you want a perfect relationship you do not listen to any informant because if you do and you get screwed, they would come to fill in your position and you would be the loser. That is the truth, baby. I swear to God, I don't kiss anybody. Oh, I forget I did…" He said jokingly to refer to Beauty.

"I knew you were lying, Bolaji. You did kiss somebody, who…?" she asked horridly.

"You of course, you are the only one I love to kiss and matter fact I won't mind kissing you right now." He was drawing her towards himself to have some kisses.

"You are very silly, do you know that?" She erased the angry face and brought forth the smiling one.

"You love me for my silliness, remember? Where would you like to go right now, baby?"

"Wherever you'd love to take me, you know I don't care," she replied lovingly.

"This is my girl, everybody." He lifted her up.

They then held hands heading to the cafeteria to have some food and drinks. They came across Frank and he greeted both in pretence, and he finally realized that he almost forgot about the next plan he had in mind. He wasted no time to go to the gang again and this time he paid them some amount of dollars to get Beauty kidnapped; he thought the idea could help stopping their relationship if Bolaji did not see her for some time. Despite the fact that prison was meant to correct and scare people, it was the opposite for gang members. It always made them worse and they were happy to get the job done again. They promised Frank they would get his sister kidnapped and hold her in a safe place for some weeks; he loved the idea and kept it to himself. The gang was then planning how and when they would kidnap the innocent girl.

"Are we going to cover her face or just grab her or carry her? But I have to tell you all, no stupid game with the girl. Do you all understand me? She has a late class on Monday evening according to her brother," Cobra said demandingly.

"I do not know what the heck is wrong with the guy anyway. We kicked his ass and yet he is addicted to the girl. He was just a wayward guy," Samuel said.

"I know why, white chick is so sweet," Cobra told him.

"Perhaps I should try one myself," Jug said but jokingly.

"You try it and you die, do you hear me?" Cobra warned him.

“Chill, I was just kidding man,” he let him realize immediately.

Saturday morning around eleven o’clock, Anita, Karl and Bolaji were all in the living room watching a blockbuster movie they rented Friday night when the doorbell rang twice and Bolaji nominated himself to see who was there at the door. It was Beauty who had taken a cab to his place. She was always being beautiful, but the jeans and her entire outfit that she had on that very day even beautified her magnificence more than ever before. She rarely wore earrings but she wanted to please Bolaji by wearing those diamond earrings he had given her as a gift for her 18th birthday. He was temporarily turned dump and was completely out of words all he could do at the time was stand there watching her feet walking down to him like a super model. Those rings were definitely going to be the talk of any place she attended and the hill shoes, she definitely deserved and earned them. Even the hateful Anita admired her beauty and she felt lessened internally; she for the first time willy-nilly said hello to Beauty, and as for her, she was totally alarmed and she replied warmly. Karl was happy that Anita finally realized that it was not okay to hurt someone’s feelings and Bolaji appreciated her sister’s friendship to his girlfriend even if it was all pretence. He led her to his room leaving Karl and Anita alone and he immediately told Beauty that he had a surprise for her by taking her to a very special place. He relished the taste of her kisses. They walked into the living room again and waved temporary adieu to Anita and her boyfriend. He drove his Mercedes Benz for he considered the whole thing to be special and he refused to tell her where exactly he was taking her to. She had no fear at all because she knew he was not going to hurt her.

“I am so much happy that your sister finally talks to me.” She smiled.

“I was happy too; Frank shook my hand the other time,” he said.

“It was just like they both called each other that ‘hey, dude let’s be nice to these kids, alright’ that’s what it looks like to me,” Beauty suggested.

“Nah, it just happened to be the right time.” Bolaji said while playing with her hair.

“Well, I am thankful. Where exactly are we going?” she asked curiously.

“I am not allowed to tell, ma’am so I am not telling…” he replied, smiling.

“Why can’t you tell, sir? I will keep it secret…” she said, imitating him.

“Nothing, I just can’t tell, ma’am. Man doesn’t tell everything to woman, because woman doesn’t have enough space to keep words,” he laughed as he said it.

“Okay, suit yourself then, sir.” She thought he would change his mind.

“Sure, ma’am I will.” He was then trying to recover from hitting the car against the side pole on the street.

“You need to focus on the road. Why are you driving like a drunken man? Stop playing Bolaji, we are on the road…” She slapped at him jokingly and with love.

“You do not realize that your beauty not your booty was enough to hypnotize somebody into drunken behavior, don’t you? I deserve some credit for even driving safely every time I am with you, because it is very hard for me to concentrate on the road. You are too beautiful for a man and I am glad I have you.” He intentionally upgraded her with his words.

"You actually beautify me with your words. Thanks anyway, but you did not act like you noticed the beauty in the first place. I was talking about the first time you saw me when we collided together," she said.

"My mind was not for something like that at the moment and besides I noticed the beauty and I appreciated it, but I did not want trouble. I knew you hit me on purpose not by the accident..." he claimed.

"No, I did not. That was an accident. I told you that was an accident, didn't I? She denied it.

"I am not going to argue with you. Man will never win anyway." He then made a right turn into Rock City.

"Which way is this place? I have never been into this area before," she said to him.

"Were you scared at all?" he asked.

"Why would I be scared? I mean I get scared around black people sometimes, but not you. You are unique and very different; you have some sort of uniqueness that I cannot explain…" she said before she was interrupted.

"Excuse me; did you just say black people? I keep telling you..." he was then interrupted as well.

"Isn't it okay to say black people? How about African American…?" she asked innocently.

"You know what…? You all keep making mistakes about saying white, black, Caucasian, African American and so on. Some of you even call us people of color. I have to ask you this, if I happened to be man of color what are you, girl without color? It doesn't make any damn sense to me at all. I wish I could be on nationally broadcast television one day…" he explained to her.

"On TV, trying to do what exactly?" Beauty asked interruptedly. "Let them know I have got a better idea. I could make the announcement about the names I came up with," he said.

"What kind of names, exactly…?" she asked again.

"We would be using beautiful and gorgeous to name ourselves. We would be calling us black people beautiful people and we would be calling you white people gorgeous people. I am very sure both mean the same thing and they would be very much appropriate," he replied, smiling.

"Fantastic! You are very smart. Perhaps they would listen to you." She doubted it.

"Look up, Beauty. Read what's on the sign board," he said to her.

"What's it. Rock-City… why didn't you tell me we were coming to Rock-City?" she said like she was angry.

"What, you didn't like it here? We can go to somewhere else," he suggested to please her mind.

"Are you kidding? I love the place. My friends told me about it and I had been willing to come since. They are living around Lookout Mountain. I love you. We are going to have a lot fun. We are going to play hide and seek…" she said with excitement.

"What do you know about hide and seek?" He asked her while paying for their tickets.

"Everything Bolaji…I know all about it. Try me and find out," she replied.

"Okay we will find out," he said while they were walking in through the gate.

They followed a very narrowly thin passage that led gradually into an uphill and inside the hill were different places one could go to. Bolaji ran quickly to hide from Beauty and she was given the assignment to find him. She sought every nook and cranny of the first place they entered and for almost ten minutes she could not find him; she got scared and started screaming his name and she was begging him to come out of his hidden place. She spanked him with her wet eyes and she said she would try to hide from him too, and it only took him seconds to grab her out of the place she thought would be best for hiding.

She kept climbing onto his back like a lessened baby and he actually loved it, and hence he could not complain about it and to make it lovely he then carried her to tour around some other places. They went up there to see the thirteen flags donated by the first thirteen of the United States of America and later went down to see some animals that were kept underground. The next place was very empty and dry. The only things they met up there were three benches with sculptures that were decorating the place just like an African Palace for kings. Bolaji stood up there for a while looking around without sharing his thought with Beauty and later he decided to ask Beauty a very romantic question. He had bought engagement and wedding rings three days previously and he was willing to ask Beauty to marry him secretly before they would later re-marry openly after their graduation.

He was filled with different thoughts and he did not know what exactly would come out of her mouth though it might hurt his feelings if she said no but he was not going to get mad at her. She clung unto him from behind and she was willing to know what he was thinking about. Meanwhile some other people at the Rock-City had come to check the place where the couple stopped before proceeding to the next place. Bolaji revealed that he had something to ask Beauty and nosily those people having heard that he was going to ask her something they refused to vacate and they were eager to witness whatever it was he wanted to ask. He smiled and at the same time he was shy for the presence of those people but he fought the shyness and kneeled down with his right knee first, followed by the left one. She was totally confused and thought maybe Bolaji thought he had offended her in some way. She felt like running away at the moment and later she decided to stay and hear him out. They were only eighteen and twenty years old respectively. He asked her to marry him and she was emotionally upgraded and did not waste a second to say yes; he put the engagement ring onto her finger and asked her to do the same and lovingly she did. The attendees thought the whole thing was joke because they seemed too young to get engaged. They left the place for another and inside it was a very hidden and romantic home that would be perfect for a couple. The house was small and it was brightly left opened with colorful lights ranging from yellow, blue, red to green, wired all over the wall. They were enraptured by the room by the force of and were willing to enjoy a romantic moment with each other. Being newly engaged, Beauty thought the room was the most perfect place to share the newly ignited love between them and to perfect it all; he had something else in his mind. He took out the piece of cloth they used at the beach the other time and they both sat on it enjoying apples. Then Bolaji looked at her face and smiled with a very pleasing face; she gave him the same look as well. She lay on her back using his legs as the ergonomic pillows and rested her head on them to enjoy the rest of their stay in the lovely room they found.

"How long have we been engaged, Beauty?" He asked while playing with her face.

"…while ago, why did you ask?" She asked him looking at his face.

"Do you like it, or are you embarrassed?" He asked again by kissing her this time.

"I didn't like it, but I loved it and I was not embarrassed at all."

"I meant it for real. I was not playing and we had just become engaged, okay?" he declared further.

"I knew it was for real; why would you be kidding with such thing? And when are we going to get married anyway?" She asked meaningfully.

"When would you like to get married to me?" he asked by playing with her hair this time.

"You know I am always with your wishes. It doesn't matter if it's going to be tomorrow, next week, next year..." She smiled.

"I have wanted to call you my wife longtime; let's get married secretly between you and me and later when we graduate then we will re-marry. How is that?" He asked happily and was waiting for her reply.

"You mean right now? How about wedding rings?" she asked him.

"I have got them right here with me," he said by showing them to her.

"What, oh my God…You bought wedding rings too? Why didn't you…" She was then interrupted.

"I wanted it to be secretive, just between me, you and God of course. Shall we…?" he asked with gentle voice.

They agreed to get married and then shared their vows with the promise to remain husband and wife till death would do them apart. Once the marriage had taken place Beauty was so happy that she could finally get a chance to have sex with her husband now, but she did not say anything about it at the moment. All she did was smile and laugh happily and she was madly all over him with kisses. They finally decided to step out of the room, and to some noisy people who caught them coming out of the very small house they were thinking of something else about them instead, sex. They did not care a whit and then headed to visit the last place before saying good bye to the place. The whole place was full of memories and histories and Beauty did not hesitate to ask Bolaji when they would visit again, he kept laughing instead. Beauty had it in her mind that she would be using the place as an eternal story for even her grand-children if she knew them before she died. He carried her like a newlywed princess, letting neither of her feet touch the ground, and he opened the car door with his right hand to set her inside. She warmly appreciated the love and the respect even though there were girls outside strongly jealous of her fortune and she could not help herself but crying happily like a little princess. Bolaji started the car and drove off with the car CD playing Celine Dion's track, "Because you loved me."

The day was getting growing long but there were still many hours to play outdoors. Bolaji took Beauty to the Tennessee aquarium, which was acclaimed to be the largest aquarium ever. She refused to separate herself from him the whole time they were touring the aquarium. They did not spend much time inside and they left for Burger Kings to have some fast food for dinner before he would finally take her home. He warned her to keep their secret. She agreed not to tell anyone, not even her close friends. She got home by six-thirty pm and Frank could not complain because that was not too late for anybody to return home.

Bolaji came home to an empty house and thought that perhaps Karl and Anita had gone somewhere to enjoy themselves as well. He found dinner in the microwave, but had no appetite, still full from the burger he'd eaten early. He called Beauty again to talk to her before they could finally go to bed.

From then on they started using the words "husband" and "wife" in their conversation. They talked from seven-fifteen to ten o'clock and they kissed the phone as if they were actually kissing each other's lips and they hung up to meet again through their dreams, if possible.

Inside Bolaji's bedroom were photos of Beauty at each one of the four corners of the room and every morning they were the first things his eyes saw. Sunday morning after he brushed his teeth, he refused to step out of his bedroom. He kept looking at each picture one after the other while deep in thought; he had so much buried in these thought that he hardly knew it was raining outdoors. He had been feeling some sort of weird and strange things in his mind and he tried to be strong and decided to fight them aside. Then by 9:00 am, after three steady hours of rainfall, Beauty knocked and entered his bedroom. He was shocked at first to notice someone was opening his bedroom because he knew Anita had not been returned home yet since the previous night. He was calmed to discover that it was his wife at the door. She was shivering and her clothes were soaking wet trek from bus stop. She had felt compelled to see him at any cost. Bolaji jumped up off the bed like a good husband and he immediately took off her wet clothes including her blue jeans. She confessed that his love kept growing in her heart with every passing second. She felt she could not afford to be away from him for even a minute, which he appreciated. His eyes rolled up and down covertly to scan her body and he noticed she was now grown and developed more than she was six months ago; she was now going on her nineteenth birthday.

He invited her to join him in bed. He wanted to be with his womanly woman. Her body felt magnificent, silky and he was thrilled to have her in bed. They remained silent, doing nothing significant in particular but facing each other for a five minute staring contest, which he deliberately let her win. He was a gentleman, after all. This game invited more jokes with laughter and then the game of love, basically foreplay with the absence of sex as usual. She did not complain about not having the chance to experience sexual intercourse with Bolaji yet; she knew she did not have to be sad or rushed as long as she knew she would always be his wife. Their kisses were totally changed this time. They shut their eyes with excitement and either of them could feel the air coming out of the other's noses through heavy and instinctive breathing, and their lips were stuck together to make it very difficult for even an atom to pass between them.

They played for almost six hours without interruption except when each one of them needed visit the bathroom. By five o'clock they had fully satisfied their urges. Beauty then took a shower and prepared to leave, although she was reluctant to go. Bolaji assured her that they would see each other at school the following day, and she agreed with kisses. Bolaji gave her the keys to take one of his cars home since he did not feel like driving. He entered back inside after he had waved good bye to his girl. He quickly micro-waved himself something to eat and ate in voraciously.

At 10:30 p.m. Anita then entered, feeling shameful. She should not have been feeling shame or qualms because she was the eldest in the home. Bolaji kept laughing after he had welcomed her back home and she could not say anything momentarily; she felt embarrassed and she sat there on the couch looking at the television without really paying any attention to it.

"What's matter, my big sizzle Anizle?"

"Nothing, I just needed a moment," she replied while playing with the remote and then stood up walking to get a drink from the refrigerator.

"How is your man, Karl? He must be good, I mean very good to keep you all day and night yesterday and almost today too. He is strong…" He laughed.

"I was not with him. I went to Atlanta with my girls. We just came back today, about an hour ago." She lied to him to save her from the embarrassment.

"I ain't going to argue with you, woman. I have to believe you somehow. I will tell you what; I will be leaving for my room. We have school to attend tomorrow, sleep tight, homie." He told her.

"You need to stop speaking slang, Bolaji. You ain't from the street. See you tomorrow. Good night." She waved at him. His phone had been ringing on the bed and he had seen the name of the caller through caller ID. He did not feel reluctant to say hello to his lovely but also secret wife as well; she missed him already and he told her that he was one step closer to calling her before she would be going to bed. He further said Anita delayed him. She could not understand herself anymore; perhaps something about marriage had changed her. Bolaji noticed a difference, too. His body felt weak and took some aspirin. They both confided their strange symptoms to each other and then agreed to talk more about them the next morning, which was Monday.

He later pardoned her to go to sleep by throwing her a goodnight kiss through his cell phone, and he had the same from her.

He had barely shut his eyes when Adam's call came through; he thought about turning off his cell phone already, but he forgot and he picked it up by giving a lazy hello to his friend;

he was very sleepy at the time. Adam made fun of him for his weak voice; he told him he had gone to collect their mathematics exams and that each of them had earned an A. Afterwards they exchanged goodbyes with the hopes to meet again the following day at school.

FINAL – The reality of Judgement

Monday morning, Beauty and her friends were there at the university center for breakfast; the place itself led to book store which was narrowly linked to many other academic places for the student's easy access. After ten minutes of their presence at the UC Center, a beautiful female student led a group of new students on a tour of the facilities as part of their first orientation. The place, the so-called University Center, as it was revealed, never suffered an absence of people unless the school was closed. It was a hive of activity when school was in session. Each of these girls, Tracy, Mickey, Faith, Trish and Beauty, seemed tired and were not ready to come back to school, but seeing each other at school always ignited the spirit they needed for attending school regularly and they could not complain any further. Tracy told the other that she was thinking of trying out for the Mrs. Teen pageant of the year and she needed her friends' advice. Alas, out of jealousy and envy, Trish and Mickey mocked the idea and they tried to discourage her courageous ambition so that she could finally forget about the thought. Beauty knew Tracy could be anything if she wanted to and she was the only one who backed the thought up and advised her not to waste her time if she really wanted to enter the contest.

Tracy promised she would never forget her support and the belief she had in her. Beauty then looked up facing the narrow path that led to students' advisor-rooms; she could see Dr. Thomas coming towards their way. She had been planning to see him later that day, but decided to seize the opportunity to approach him now. He asked her to come by to his office. Her friends asked her why she went up to him and she told them the deal, then Faith remembered that Beauty hadn't answered any of her phone calls during the weekend on both Saturday and Sunday.

"Where were you all day Saturday and yesterday, Beauty? I called several times and I talked to Frank, and he told me you were not home. I called back and you had not come back yet, what's the deal friend?" Faith asked her while opening pages from her book.

"I went out with my… man. It was totally romantic for me, both days. I will never ever forget Saturday and yesterday, I swear." She almost leaked the word husband out before remembering that it was done to be secretive.

"Okay, tell me about it. Where did you go?" Mickey asked demandingly before she started giggling.

“Yes, share the romance…” Trish asked adding her support. “I went to his crib; I took a cab there on Saturday morning. He told me he had to take me to somewhere…” Then she was interrupted. “Where exactly….?” Tracy asked interrupting her.

“I asked him, but he refused to tell. We kept listening to music in his car and we were talking and laughing until we got to the place.”

“What place…?” Tracy eagerly demanded to know.

“The place was Rock -City; I had never been up there until Saturday. We had a lot of fun. We played different kind of games – hide and seek, dancing…” She then paused, smiling.

“I loved Rock City. I was there once with my now ex-boyfriend. The place was very romantic,” Trish said.

“What happened between you and your ex? I meant to ask why you two broke up,” Beauty asked her friend.

“It was too much to say. I was at fault. I did not know what was good for me at the time and he caught me sleeping with his friend. I was totally embarrassed and I later let him go, too.” Ashamed and wanting to change the subject she perused her book without really seeing any of the words she was pretending to read so that she could nip the subject in the bud.

“We are all human beings and we cannot avoid making mistakes sometimes. Have you tried to work it out?” Beauty asked further.

“What, are you kidding? If I was a man I would not work that kind of shit out. That was too bad, my girl fucking my best friend…” Mickey said angrily.

“Well, aren’t you the perfect lady? You ain’t no man. I am very sure; you could make the same mistake that I made. Nobody is perfect around here.” Trish argued her case frankly and she was emotionally hurt.

"I agree with you, Trish. Well, pray for another better relationship, God will answer because he always listens," Beauty encouraged her.

"Did you feel comfortable around him, Beauty?" Tracy asked her. "About God? Nobody ever sees God with naked eyes…" Beauty didn't have a clue about how to answer Tracy's question. "I was not talking about God, I meant with your boyfriend," she declared.

"Oh yeah, I am always comfortable with him. He is kind of different and very sweet…" she was interrupted again.

"Did you mean he was sweet down there? Have you guys been having…you know, sex…?" Mickey asked nosily.

"You are stupid, Mickey. I was not talking about down there or up there. And if I had sex with him, that is none of your business. If I told you I had sex I knew you would be asking stupid questions like how big he is and what we did exactly. She was trying to shut the subject down.

"Damn woman, slow down. My bad and I am sorry," Mickey apologized.

"Wow, love can be so strange and scary. I might want to find me a black lover, too. Maybe I would madly fall in love with him just like you. Black lovers must be very good in bed, I guess." Tracy was just playing. She would never go out with black guy; that was what she believed and had been told at home.

"Well, black, white, yellow are all words of racism. They are not black."

"Yeah, what are they, green?" Tracy asked jokingly.

"They are beautiful because they come from a beautiful land, Africa. And we are gorgeous," she replied.

"Who told you all that? Who are you, young lady?" Trish asked. "Nobody told me anything, but that was what I know and I believe," she answered.

"If you all don't mind, I have got a class to attend." Tracy stood up before packing her books. They all decided to leave the place after several more minutes of chatting and arguing. They went their separate paths calling out promises to call one another later on. Beauty did not have class to attend at the time so she decided to go to Dr. Thomas' office. When she finally stepped out of his office, who should she see but her husband, Bolaji. Beauty quickly up to surprise and catch him unaware. She reached and tickled him from behind; he was shocked and dropped his calculus text book on the floor.

She laughed harder than necessary at his shock and then took his arm while they walked downstairs to the lower level. He told her they would be going under a friendly shaded tree that would shield them from the sun. She knew they had nothing new to talk about other than usual romantic or erotic words. They finally found a quite friendly tree with the qualities they had in mind, which was located about two miles away from Mathematics department but facing directly across from the English and Writing department. The only things that always satisfied their thirst were kisses and they would never deny each other any kisses before doing anything else they needed to do. She relaxed herself on his legs like she was lying on a bed and she felt more comfortable than ever before; her body was strangely trying to tell her something, but she was too young to understand or notice. Amidst their conversation they innocently agreed to play a game of no-call-no-show for a good week and whoever called or showed up first would lose to the other with penalties, some sort of love related fines and the game was to be started the following day. She suggested going to his place Monday night provided she was not too tired after her last class that would be ended by 7:30 p.m. and he loved the idea.

They thought about having sex for real for the first time and they were very excited about it. She decided that even if she was tired she would go for the sake of nothing but the opportunity of experiencing what her friends had experienced for God knew how long ago. She also wanted him to teach her some topics she was struggling with in her Algebra class. They had been there under tree for almost four hours and it was five o'clock; they needed to vacate the place because the air had grown chilly. Bolaji even sacrificed his last class just to make his wife happy; they departed with the ultimate aim of seeing each other later that night. But before they actually did depart, they walked happily and lovingly together to the parking lot and later Beauty left for the library to do some reading prior to her last class.

She spent only five minutes at the library due to her lack of concentration that might ascribe to anxiety, and later decided to be an early bird for the class by arriving thirty minutes early. She was so early that she had to wait for the class prior to hers to be dismissed. The first person in the room for her class, she waited for everyone else to arrive. Her mind was totally with Bolaji all the time the class was yet in progress; she had lost her patience with the class and fidgeted in her seat uncomfortably waiting for it to end.

Having told one another about her schedule, the gangs members were there, lying in wait to kidnap her as they had planned. Upon leaving class she walked in a clumsy pattern to get away from the congested foot traffic of all the students rushing to get home. Well, it might be excited for all to get home sooner to have time to rest or have fun outdoors, but for her she thought different she was going to be deflowered for the first time ever; she was both happy and anxious at the same time.

The gang was having difficulty grabbing her in public. They had no choice but exercise their patience and follow her to the parking lot. She would have escaped the kidnappers if she had taken public transportation, but she had one of her husband's cars. She had no clue that she had been followed and the last thing she knew she had her hands pinned behind her back, they slept duct tape over her mouth before she could make more than only the slightest noise. Next her legs were duct-taped together and chained at the ankle. It was now 8:00 p.m.

Bolaji was there in his room getting ready for the big thing, his thighs were happily quaking with joyful expectation. He had to do some pushups and sit ups then do some weight lifting for about thirty solid minutes and then rushed into shower bath to cool his overheated body. Afterwards he could not do a meaningful thing, but he was patiently waited for his love to arrive. For her no-call-no-show result, he later concluded she might have got tired with her last class. Ergo, he didn't worry overly, thinking she'd already decided to start the game. He used her pictures wisely to lure away the awkward thoughts and to serve as another way of keeping his own company. He was then contemplating giving her a call, but he did not at last, because he could not afford to be the loser of their game. He went to sleep at long last at about two in the morning. He slept fitfully and each time he woke up, he fought his stubborn eyes to go back to sleep, but he failed and he just sat cross-legged at the end of his bed feeling defeated somehow. He sat there rigidly for two and a half hours before he could go back to sleep and the time was six-thirty in the morning; his class started at seven. He did not really care much about the class, so he was long gone into sleep. Anita would have been a better help if she had woke him up when she got up for her own early class, but thinking he could manage his own time and classes, she didn't bother her brother.

Beauty was being held in a warehouse remote from the school's premises; the place reminded her of a prison and she struggled furiously – feeling both hopeless and helpless at the same time. She felt heartbroken. They tried to feed her, as part of their deal, but she refused to eat; she was intelligently paranoid. She only wished she would get a chance to call the police and bust the gang in action.

Frank came by secretly to check on her and he was informed that she was doing fine in the lockup and that he needed not to worry about her safety for the whole week. Beauty had no idea why she was held in the closet. If I could say it out loud, I would. They were trying to get money out of her husband's pocket kidnapping her. Bolaji's wealth was no secret on campus and the gang was hoping to make a huge score off the ransom they stipulated. She was bloody, hurt and mad because she missed her moment of joy with her man and she could not even get a bit chance to see him the next morning. How about classes she was missing? Terror was creeping up on her and she began to panic.

Bolaji was a worrier by nature and not seeing his newly ringed wife, he felt some concern, but then convinced himself it was simply his wife playing along with the innocent game that they'd innocently agreed upon. He initially had second thoughts about not even seeing her at school, but logic won out and he concluded that she was deliberately avoiding him because of their game.

Beauty's friends were seriously worried and they went to notify school authorities. They reported that the only guy they knew who might have something to do with her disappearance would be her boyfriend, Bolaji. Having told the authorities that the guy is black, Beauty's friends easily convinced the authorities that something was amiss with Beauty's mysterious absence from school. Posters were made up and included photographs of both Beauty and Bolaji. Anita and Karl had traveled to Kentucky for a week, and Adam had gone to Texas again for an immigration interview.

Bolaji decided to spend the rest of the week at home; he was not feeling well, not that he was severely sick, but he was paranoid and depressed perhaps from not having anybody around, especially his girlfriend. His absence at school made it believable to many students that he may have found a way to elude the charge that he was involved in Beauty's disappearance. Although some knew Bolaji as an outstanding and ideal young African-American, others were quick to believe that he was guilty.

The Chattanooga PD was out in force, searching for Beauty. Trisha hoped that the FBI would be called in on the case, but her friends laughed at her, knowing that the FBI would only become involved if a federal crime across state lines had occurred and it was still too early to know whether or not that was the case. Trisha fumed, but also hoped they'd find evidence soon to exonerate Bolaji and at the same time, she wished desperately that Beauty was gone forever.

The city's detectives gathered as much information as they could about the missing girl and covertly watched Beauty's friends and acquaintances. They did not initially question Bolaji at home, maybe it was an order from above.

***

The gang was totally confused as well when they learned things had turned upside down and they did not know how exactly to release Beauty; they did not want to get arrested as well. Cobra told them all to chill while he took pains to develop a perfect plan. They all agreed that not one of them would speak and that they'd have to avoid the police following them to the warehouse.

Thursday afternoon, Cobra decided to change the story by having his own posters made and they were displaying a photograph of Beauty bound, gagged and deceased. The school broke into pandemonium. Time crawled and some of her friends were utterly hysterical. The school authorities exercised patience any more, but then ordered that Bolaji be taken in for questioning.

"Frank, I know you know where my girl at. You should either tell me right now or I'll call the police and get you arrested," Bolaji said seriously while his legs were dancing impatiently.

"You need to get out my face before I shoot in the head," he said, pointing the gun towards his face.

"Calm down, Frank. We don't have to kill him now…" Cobra said taking charge.

Then Bolaji could hear Beauty's urgent but fruitless efforts to scream audibly from inside of the ugly looking warehouse; he rushed into it and found her tied down, her mouth duct taped shut. In the process of untying her, the crew came in with guns and they pointed them at him.

"What the heck do you have to say now, punk?"

"Why are you doing this?" Beauty asked innocently.

"Shut up, stupido! You think it's a big secret how much money your boyfriend has? You're here because we want that money and we want it now."

'How many times I had told you not to hang around with this stupid bastard? Answer me!" He yelled at her madly.

"I love him, Frank. And I will forever."

"This needs to end right now. Frank pulled the trigger and nicked Bolaji's arm, drawing blood.

"Hey man, what are you doing? Cut that out, Frankie." Samuel Edie said advisedly.

"Stay out of this, brother. Stay the fuck out of this. I am fucking mad right now." He then pulled the trigger again and fired at him. Beauty dodged in front of the bullet to defend her lover. The bullet tore into her abdomen and she began to bleed profusely. Bolaji screamed 'no' many times before he woke finally from the nightmare. The first thing he did immediately when he woke up was taking up the album and looking at his lovely girl's pictures one by one.

He was in his bedroom, trying to recover from the dream, when he heard the bell ring, he only had his blue jeans on, and he walked up to the door with happy face thinking he had won the contest if it was his girl friend. The police were at the door where they arrested him and put him in the back of a squad car. He was being charged with Beauty's murder.

He wondered if it was because he was black. Everything that Bolaji said, even swearing that Beauty was his wife was scoffed at because nobody believed it. His sister's friends all spoke against him – each one of them taking a turn to tell the detectives everything they could think of about their deceased friend.

Saturday passed and then Sunday followed. Monday morning Beauty woke and was terrified. Where was she? What a nightmare she dreamt about both she and Bolaji dying – dying for the sake of their sacred love.

LOVE SEES NO COLOR. THE END!

THE AUTHOR

4Kit is Nigerian-American Rapper/Singer/Songwriter, and a poet- five-time Editor Choice Award winner for his poems – Az-Salat, USA, Women-Sugar of life – presented by International Library of poets, Baltimore (Maryland).
His works have been featured in collection of poetry books published by international library of poets; by Noble House publisher, which has branches in Paris (France), London (UK) and New York (USA); and by America Society of Poets.

He's been honored as poetry Ambassador of the year 2006, 2007, 2008 and 2009, and also awarded one of the best poets of 2007 by the same International Society of Poets, MD. He won a Directors Award of Merit presented to him by Paramount Group, Nashville, TN for excellence in songwriting for his lyric titled “Valentine”.

He's an Actor, a Model; film Director, Playwright, and Screen writer/Producer and of course, Writer/Author/Novelist. He was a high school teacher - Mathematics, Economics, Biology, Geography, and English Language. He earned two nominations by "Tennessee Knock down Independent Awards" for "Bout to Blow Artist of the year" and "Song of the year – Tennessee" in 2009 for his music. He is a member of ASCAP as a Songwriter. His music and books are available on iTunes, Amazon, Rhapsody, Best Buy, Target, Wal-Mart, Barnes and Noble, etc.

Follow 4Kit – Instagram at @i4Kit; Twitter @i4Kit ; Facebook @l4Kit ; SoundCloud @i4Kit

www.ingramcontent.com/pod-product-compliance
Lightning Source LLC
Chambersburg PA
CBHW061025120726
47910CB00006B/2098